Demon Amulet

by

Margo Carey

Watcher Clan

Demon Amulet

Cover Art by *Lisa Dawn MacDonald*

The Wild Rose Press, Inc.
PO Box 708
Adams Basin, NY 14410-0708
Visit us at www.thewildrosepress.com

Publishing History
First Edition, 2025
Trade Paperback ISBN 978-1-5092-6154-3
Digital ISBN 978-1-5092-6155-0

Watcher Clan
Published in the United States of America

Dedication

To my mother, Theresa Gallagher Colbert, who taught me there is nothing more healing than losing oneself in a book.

I want to thank my wonderful writing group who inspired me to keep writing and my awesome editor, Kaycee John.

Chapter One

When Lia Ferguson strode through the crowded wedding reception in her wispy sapphire dress, every man present turned to check her out. The women looked too, but not with the same interest. More like envy. No matter, Lia decided. She was only here to placate her mother who couldn't attend and had insisted on Lia substituting for her. Then Lia's plus one, her cousin, Alexandra Ryan, had ditched her to spend the weekend with her fiancé.

To top everything off, the new sandals she'd purchased on a whim were killing her feet.

Still miffed that Alex had refused to play 'date', Lia checked out the contingent of males present. No one was worth a second glance, not that she was in any mood to hook up. Rich Austin, the only man who might have cured her commitment phobia, died last year. Temporary encounters had sufficed in the time since she'd lost him, but she'd given up the idea of looking for a soulmate.

For her mother's sake, she played the wedding-guest role, smiling and nodding to keep up appearances, but when the DJ called for all the single women to come to the dance floor, Lia abandoned all pretense of social niceties and headed to the bar. She knew a third glass of champagne was unwise, but she needed to chase away painful memories and escape the cutesy wedding games. The thought of being jammed into a group of unattached females fighting to catch the bride's bouquet made her cringe.

Just before the champagne flute reached her lips, a familiar psychic ripple seared the atmosphere. For a second, she tensed, then relaxed and shook her head. Too much of the bubbly.

But moments later, the air trembled again, this time with a heavy pulse. She staggered from the sheer force.

Magic.

There was no doubt in her mind. Only those with psychic powers had the ability to sense it—and that was rare. The only magic she'd experienced in her twenty-eight years, other than what her Clan practiced, had happened during a sorcerer's assault last July.

When she heard a shriek from another room, she responded immediately, even though her feet cried out in pain from the uncomfortable sandals. As she wound her way through a jumble of tables, other guests reacted to the sounds of distress and managed to block her way. Lia spread her hands and sent pulses of air ahead of her to make a path, then squeezed into a small room jammed with panicky guests.

A woman, eyes wide and gasping for breath, pointed a shaking finger at the floor. "It just flew at him. All on its own."

The body of a young man lay on his back on the parquet tiles. Blood flowed from the knife wound in his neck and started to pool beneath him. A broken vase and fragments of red carnations spread across the floor beside the victim.

"Dear God. What happened?" Lia asked as she used her healer's gift to sense any warmth or tingle of life in the body. Only the cold finality of death reached back.

A white-haired man, positioned at the boy's other side, looked up at her. "It nicked the jugular. He's gone."

The intense smell of dark magic clogged Lia's throat as she used telepathy to contact Duncan Stuart, the only one of the Watcher Clan who lived nearby in Narragansett, Rhode Island.

When the next psychic pulse reverberated, she rose to her feet, kicked off the damn shoes and took off at a run toward the burst, praying no one else was dead.

The minute she ripped open the outside door, a third powerful blast tore through the air, followed by the crack of a gunshot. Muscles tensed, she scanned the area. There. At the end of the parking lot, someone was running away. She squinted, disoriented from the alcohol and half-blinded by the afternoon sun that ricocheted off the chrome-enhanced sea of cars. As she raised her hands to bring the runner down, she spied someone lying on the ground a few feet away. She'd been unable to save the young man inside; maybe she could help this person.

When she sprinted over, the sight of the victim's uniform sent pain crashing into her. Rich had been a cop. She made herself slam a lid on those memories. This man was still alive.

Dropping to her knees on the hot pavement, she placed her hands over the wound on his stomach. As she touched him, trying to shake off the liquor haze, an image of the bullet's trail formed in her mind. Eyes closed, she sent a healing pulse along the course of the injury through tissues and muscles in his abdominal region. Sensing the shot had missed major vessels, she concentrated on stemming the blood flow and healing the torn tissue. Unfortunately, the champagne she'd consumed diminished her powers.

At the welcome sound of sirens, she relaxed. If she could keep this officer stable until the EMTs arrived, he might have a chance. She sent Duncan another message, *Hurry*, and thanked God for the gifts her Clan had inherited from their Templar ancestors.

The injured man groaned. She leaned down. “Stay with me. Help is coming. Just hold on.”

When the EMTs arrived, she moved back from the scene. One of the responding police officers followed his colleague to the ambulance, a second insisted on taking her statement. Under the best conditions, healing depleted her strength. She needed to rest. The officer, however, wanted answers and led her to a nearby bench.

She closed her eyes and leaned against the ribbed wooden back. “When I heard screams, then gunshots. I ran outside to help.”

“Did you see who did it?”

She shook her head. “Just some guy running away. Long darkish hair. When I saw the wounded man, I hurried to him.” She pointed to the area where a large bloodstain glistened in the bright sunlight.

“Did you catch any details on the vehicle?”

“Sorry. I was too busy trying to help the officer.” As her hands clenched the bloody wreckage of her lovely dress, she noticed the small mark on her wrist, the sign of her Templar ancestry. The tiny cross, enhanced by psychic use, had turned a bright red, resembling one more splash of blood from the wound.

“Yeah. Well, you did a good job. Thanks.”

A few minutes later, Duncan arrived. Sun glistened off the silver streaks peppering his dark hair; concern etched the corners of his blue eyes. “I told my friend, Ted, the detective in charge, you were my niece. He said

I could bring you home as long as you stay handy if he needs to speak to you later."

Duncan wrapped one arm around Lia's shoulders to support her. She still felt shaky, and her head ached. Although he wasn't technically her uncle by blood or marriage, he'd always acted like one. Their families shared ownership of a crumbling mansion that sat between their Newport estates, one that held supernatural secrets. Last year, a bloody battle between the Watcher Clan and a dream walker had cost the lives of Rich and her cousin Tony.

As they headed toward Duncan's car, he paused and looked over at his detective friend, who was currently chewing out a young, uniformed officer. Most of the Watcher Clan had excellent hearing, and Ted's voice carried. "How the hell could he have shot himself with his own gun?" His words shocked Lia.

The deputy shuffled his feet, ran one hand over his mouth, and looked around as if help might fall from the sky. "I'm just tellin' ya what he said. The gun turned in his hand and shot him."

"Geez, kid," the detective barked in clear, unmistakable tones. "Don't you dare say that to anyone else. Understand?"

When Ted swiveled his head, checking for eavesdroppers, Duncan spun Lia on her heel and hurried her to his waiting car. Anger and confusion colored his voice. "Did you hear that? If what the trooper said is true…"

Lia grimaced. "There's a killer loose, and no police force on earth can stop him."

Chapter Two

Once inside Duncan's car, Lia leaned back against the seat, stretched her neck, and exhaled. "The strength of that magic pulse almost knocked me off my feet. Whoever did this has extraordinary power. The woman said the knife that killed that boy flew on its own."

"Lots of people can throw a knife with pinpoint accuracy," Duncan said.

"Except I felt the explosion," she replied, remembering the force of it. "I tasted the corruption of the spell as the aroma reached my nose. It smelled like an electrical fire. Really vile."

She slumped in her seat. Psychic powers had always surrounded her, but this was different—almost demonic. What dug into her gut, though, was the fear that the killer's strengths exceeded those of her Clan.

When she saw the red sports car in Duncan's driveway, the one that belonged to his son, Nick, her mood lightened. The Newport contingent had arrived. That meant her cousin Alex, Nick's fiancée, would be with him.

Inside the house, Alex rushed over to Lia, "Are you hurt? Is that your blood?"

Lia looked down at the rust-colored stains on her dress, now seriously rumpled from her attempts to clean her hands on it. She glanced at a nearby mirror and saw that some of the officer's blood had transferred to her long, blonde hair. "I'm fine. This is from the injured guard."

Nick scrutinized her appearance. "Must have been some wedding."

Alex punched his shoulder. "Not funny. If I'd gone with her instead of you, we might have gotten the killer." She tucked her arm through Lia's. "Sorry you had to go through that alone. Let's find you something else to wear."

Duncan rubbed the side of his face and pointed toward the stairs. "Syd's room. She leaves stuff here for when she visits. It's upstairs…"

"I know where it is," Lia said. She'd grown up with Nick and Sydney Stuart and had grieved with them at their mother's death almost twelve years ago.

After a quick shower, Lia felt better. She surveyed herself in the mirror and grinned at the transformation. With her hair tied back into a ponytail, and wearing a black University of Rhode Island T-shirt over her long-legged friend's jeans rolled up at the ankles, the chic seductress of the morning had morphed into what looked like a carefree, slightly older, teenager.

When she joined the others in the living room, Nick chuckled at her appearance. "Cute. Love the pants." He ducked away from her intended smack and headed off to fill drink orders, non-alcoholic. With a dangerous psychic threat, everyone needed their powers to stay crisp.

Lia sipped her water and watched Duncan pace before he sat next to her. "Okay. I briefed the rest of the Clan about what happened. Is there anything else you can remember?"

She put her glass down, the hellish morning still

fresh in her mind. "The horrible smell. Good thing the normals couldn't sense it." She paused and concentrated on the floor.

"What?" Nick said.

She looked at him and sighed. "I spied the killer running away, but when I saw the second victim, I let him go."

Alex hugged her. "Of course you went to the injured. You're a healer."

Lia pulled away from Alex and tossed her head back and forth. "I could have struck him—the runner—with a blast of air, but my mind was fuzzy. I'd been drinking. Otherwise, I would have been able to take him down *and* help the guard."

Duncan's voice held authority. "Stop it, Lia. You helped the man survive until they got him to the hospital. I called Ted to see how the officer was doing. They've taken him into surgery so there's hope."

She sighed, grateful to have done something right, but refused to let her guilt go. "And the killer?"

Nick piped up. "Are you kidding? Everyone drinks at weddings. It's a good thing it wasn't me. I'd have had trouble finding the door, let alone stopping some killer." He shot her a grin. "Since when did you become Miss Perfect?"

Lia's glare turned into a grudging smile. "Jerk!"

Duncan clapped his hands. "Okay, kids. Play nice. Let's figure this out before anything else happens. We should go back to the crime scene. One of us may pick up residual clues."

Lia agreed. "We'll try to determine what kind of magic he used and figure out how to keep him from killing anyone else. I'm concerned about the officer's statement to the rookie cop. If someone forced that guard to shoot himself, we're in big trouble."

****

A freshening breeze stole some warmth from the afternoon sun. Lia rubbed her arms as she joined everyone in Duncan's car to return to the site of the murder. As he maneuvered out of his driveway, he filled them in on what he'd learned from his conversation with Ted.

"Right now, the cops think the woman who saw the murder was hysterical, and the guard was in shock. Ted can't do anything about the witness's account, but I'm sure he'll keep control over what his men—the injured officer as well as those at the scene—have to say."

"Everyone heard the woman's story," Lia said, concern in her voice. "And it's bound to get out about the gun turning in the guard's hand. What do we do if people think the killer used magic?"

Nick's voice boomed from the back seat. "Don't worry. People fear the supernatural. They're afraid to think someone is that powerful. I'm sure they'd all enjoyed a few cocktails and will chalk it up to hysteria."

Lia hoped he was right. As they approached the wedding venue, she tensed. The parking lot, now jammed with official vehicles, was closed to the public, but they found a spot on the street close by the entrance.

During the bygone era known as the Gay Nineties, The Towers was part of the Narragansett Pier Casino, a renowned resort for the elite. The well-loved landmark, with its distinctive twin granite towers connected by an arch over the road, would now forever remind her of dark magic and death.

As spectators gathered outside the cordoned-off

area, cool ocean air swirled around them. Inside the building, a slight scent of magic still hung in the air. An officer stood by the sealed-off crime scene. The presence of yellow tape around pieces of distinguished furnishings caused a jarring intrusion that only intensified Lia's bitter regret at being unable to stop a killer.

Beside her, Alex cleared her throat. "Is this where it happened?"

She nodded.

Nick kept his voice down as he spoke. "How long ago?"

"Around one."

He checked his watch as he inhaled, then wrinkled his nose. "Almost two hours? Then, we've got trouble. Only strong magic would linger like this. I can still smell it."

Duncan squeezed his son's shoulder. "I know."

People filled the lobby. Time to leave. As Lia turned, she bumped into someone with a well-muscled torso. "Oh, excuse me." She tipped her head back to see him. Tall, curly black hair and blue… She blinked. He had one blue eye and one green eye.

As she contemplated this oddity in his appearance, she realized he had his hands on her shoulders and was staring at her. When an intrusion of magic swept over her like a psychic ultrasound, she shook her head and twisted out of his grip.

Nick came up behind her, menace in his voice. "Is something wrong?"

Lia took one more look at the hard planes of the man's closed face and shook her head. "No. No problem." She sent Nick a telepathic message. *Let's get out of here.*

He nodded, gave a warning glare to the cold-eyed man, and escorted her and Alex outside.

Intent on revealing her discovery of another with psychic abilities, Lia hurried past the curious onlookers to reach Duncan. As she spoke, he stopped her, then checked their surroundings. "It's better if we talk in the car."

"No. Listen." She shook her head so hard, the tips of her ponytail slapped her face. "There's a guy in there with tremendous power. And he knows what I am."

Nick moved in beside Lia. "You mean the one who had his hands on you?"

Duncan put his arm around her, steering her toward the car. "Did he threaten you?"

"He didn't like me." She gave a snort. "That doesn't happen very often."

Alex came up behind them. "I saw him. He wasn't alone. He had three others with him."

Sitting in the car, Lia explained how she'd bumped into him. "He was angry, although not at me personally. His probe was more curious than threatening."

As they sat there in the idling car, Lia's antagonist and his friends emerged from the building. Their interest in Duncan's vehicle showed loud and clear in their body language.

"I can feel their power from here," Alex said.

Nick pulled her closer. "So can I."

Duncan slapped the car into gear. "I don't like it." He took his time before driving off. "Let's see if they follow us."

While he cruised along the coast road, Nick kept watch out the rear window. "They're behind us, three cars back. It's a black high-end SUV. I couldn't get the plate number."

"Maybe we can get that information when we stop at the store." Duncan took a right into the parking lot of a small plaza. "Nick, go buy some soda and snacks, then try to sneak behind them and get the plate number."

Lia chewed her lip. "You think our pursuers have something to do with this morning's magic?"

"I don't like coincidences," Duncan said.

Alex, who'd only recently discovered her family and her powers, could follow psychic trails. "I'm sending out a vibe to locate them. They're close."

Lia looked in the rear-view mirror. "Where?"

"Behind and to the left."

"Good," Duncan said. "Let Nick know."

"Uh, oh," Alex said. "Someone's trying to get into my mind. They must have followed my connection. I hate that tell-tale squiggle in my head. I blocked them.

Lia gave Nick the information, then said, *Tell me when you're close. I'll whip up a little wind to obscure their vision.* In addition to her healing powers, she also possessed the ability to tweak elements of the weather.

"You'd better start now," Duncan said. "They'll be able to feel Nick approach."

Lia stirred up the air around the black car. When Nick arrived with the groceries, she poked through the bags. Chips, cookies, beef jerky, and something called Crick-ettes.

"What's this?" she said as she looked closer, then squealed and threw it back at Nick. "Are those bugs?"

Nick tore open the bag and took a bite. The loud crunch made Lia's stomach twist. "Salt and vinegar crickets. I can't believe they have them here."

"Never mind the food," Duncan said, "Did you get

the license number."

"Yeah."

"Good. We should soon know who we're dealing with." Duncan, who worked at the Naval War College in Newport, had sources. "We might as well go home. They can find out where I live from my license plate. I've contacted Rosemary. She's put the rest of the Clan on alert." Rosemary Stuart, Duncan's mother, was the head of the Watcher Clan.

Duncan slammed his hand on the steering wheel. "I can't understand it. The guy from this morning blatantly displayed his magic abilities. We've been keeping our gifts hidden for decades, and the crew following us seems to do the same." He referred to the powers he and his Clan had inherited from their ancestors, the Knights Templar, to protect the Templar treasure.

"Something isn't right," Lia said. "The murderer has unbelievable skill. Why kill someone in plain view of a witness and cameras?"

She thought back to the man who'd tried to read her. He wasn't the person she'd glimpsed running away from the wounded cop, but she feared the odds of his magic having nothing to do with the murder were slim.

****

Kane Fahey, in a pair of custom fit slacks and expensive loafers, monitored the curiosity seekers at the wedding venue turned crime scene. The moment he sensed psychic vibes, he came to attention and watched the interplay between the curvy blonde and the well-built man who'd collided in the lobby. More concerning, the two weren't alone. Each ran with their own posse and though their powers felt the same, mutual distrust separated the two groups. Good. He could handle potential enemies, a few at a time.

Police had started to clear out the sensation seekers milling around. Kane didn't care. He was ready to leave. He'd only come here to track his stolen amulet, but as it had happened so often since the theft, it was gone. Every time the thief used the amulet's power, Kane's connection to the silver disk grew. This afternoon's blast had guided him to this building. His insides burned whenever he thought about the theft. Now, he seethed as he watched these powerful strangers sniff the air, recognizing his property's essence.

Who are they?

A sticky warmth seeped through his fingers as he dug his nails into his palms. He glared at the interlopers, memorizing their features. A growl formed in his throat. If they got in the way of him recovering his amulet, he'd kill them.

****

As members of the Watcher Clan gathered in Duncan's living room, Lia paced. "I don't understand why someone would commit murder in such a public place. Why risk being seen, and why use magic?"

"Nothing about this killing makes sense," Duncan said. We need more information. Who was the victim and why would someone want him dead?"

"Yeah," Nick said. "Motive is important, but I want to know how the killer forced the cop to shoot himself."

Duncan gave a helpless shake of his head. "None of us have seen anything like it."

"Are you sure?" Lia asked.

"I've contacted the entire Clan. No one could duplicate the killer's actions."

"Not even Rosemary?" Lia asked. "She's the most

powerful."

"No, but she had hope for Alex."

Alex, who'd inherited some impressive gifts on her twenty-fifth birthday last year, said, "Okay. I'll try."

Duncan nodded. "We all will." He left the room and returned with a gun. "We can use this. I took out the bullets."

Nick checked for himself, then placed it on the table. He flicked his right hand, and the gun floated in the air. He twisted the fingers on his left hand, trying to turn it around and move the trigger, but he couldn't do it. The weapon fell to the table.

Alex picked it up like it was a snake. Turning to Lia, she said, "The guard was holding the weapon in his hand?"

Lia nodded.

"And it turned on him and fired all on its own?"

"That's what he apparently told the responding officer."

"Okay." Alex handed the gun to Lia. "Point that thing at me."

A smile moved from Lia's eyes to her lips. "Yes, Ma'am." She remembered Alex as she'd been just last year, uncomfortable with her new family and all their psychic powers. She admired her cousin's new confidence.

Alex concentrated, lips pressed tight, moving one hand and then the other. "Damn! I can't even budge the gun, never mind pull the trigger."

Lia, who'd had to keep a tight grip on the weapon, feigned innocence. "If it helps, a few vibrations came through."

Alex narrowed her eyes. "Oh, thanks, Cuz. That

makes it much better."

Duncan had no more success than the others, and Lia threw her hands in the air in defeat. "I think we've come across a unique power."

"I agree," Duncan said. "It took us too long to try. This creep had no trouble forcing the cop's hand. I shudder to think what else he might be capable of."

Lia straightened her shoulders. "Let's figure out how we can find this guy and shut him down."

"Right," Duncan said. "What do we know about him?"

"He doesn't care about human life," Alex said.

Nick pulled Alex close. "Maybe he isn't human."

Lia cringed. When a demon stalked Alex last year, two of their own had died. "Maybe Nick's right. The residue I smelled reminded me of our fight with the demon."

"God, I hope we're not facing another monster," Duncan said. He lifted his hands in a gesture of hopelessness and walked away.

Lia followed him into his office. "You look like you're carrying the world on your shoulders."

He raised his eyebrows. "I may be."

"You've got that wrong. *We* may be. This is a team effort. Remember?"

He nodded. "I'm going to call Ted. He may have new information. I'll put him on speaker."

Duncan's orderly desk mirrored his military background. Leather accessories flanked a laptop set in a precise line across the clean workspace. Behind him, beyond the window, the blue waters of Point Judith Pond sparkled. While he placed the call, Lia slipped into a comfortable chair to take advantage of the view.

Worry filled the detective's voice as his report on his wounded officer poured out through the phone. "Still alive, thank God. They've got him in the ICU."

Duncan's question about information on the killer brought out a cynical laugh. "Oh yeah. We've got a *great* witness, but how reliable is someone who sees knives fly on their own? The camera showed the perp stealing wedding gifts, for crying out loud. Then the victim caught him and got a knife in his neck. Can you believe it?"

Duncan agreed that murder was a drastic solution for the crime, then added with a chuckle, "And the knife didn't fly through the air by itself?"

"Of course not, Duncan. The camera angle didn't catch the blade's arc, but I'm not stupid. Knives don't move on their own."

Duncan frowned as he ended the call. He groaned, scrubbed his hands down his face, and looked out across the pond. "Where would a petty thief get that kind of power?"

Chapter Three

As Lia leaned back in the office chair, thinking about murder and dark magic, a slight breeze from the window brushed her face. She closed her eyes and drew it in, then blinked at the sound of a soft chuckle.

Duncan favored her with a knowing smile. “Go outside. Indulge your cravings. You need to restore your balance.”

Whenever life became uncomfortable, Lia escaped to immerse herself in nature. “Great idea. I could use an energy boost.”

Like a child released from school, she hurried outside, drifting across the smooth, green lawn toward the water’s rhythmic, slapping cadence. Sparks of sunlight glittered across the choppy waves. As Lia inhaled the salty tang on the wind, her spirit soared.

The power thrumming beneath the water’s surface called to her. It only needed a push to explode. Closing her eyes, she held out her hands to freshen the breeze. Bits of foam spattered against her legs, and cool tendrils of air swirled around her. She hugged herself, ready for more, until a silent call from Duncan brought her to her senses—and to the situation at hand.

In the living room, Duncan waved a piece of paper in her direction. “I’ve got new information.” He grinned at Lia. “About the dangerous guy with the green and blue eyes.”

Her breathing quickened. Everything about that man had intrigued her from the first look. His strength, determined chin, and angry mouth. Most of all, his immunity to her charm. She wondered what his lips would look like when he smiled.

"You with me, Lia?"

Her musings caused her to miss Duncan's words. "What?"

"I said the guy's name is Aiden O'Connor."

Lia rolled the name around in her mind. Mmm, it fit him, strong and independent.

"He lives in North Kingstown, Rhode Island, and owns a business called AOC Security that specializes in corporate protection."

Nick tossed down the magazine he'd been reading. "Damn. You can bet he has sheets on all of us by now."

Duncan agreed. "I've got my people digging, but so far, everything about O'Connor is straightforward. He's got a reputation as someone who gets things done. I couldn't find anything negative about him or his business. He has some important friends."

"It makes no sense," Lia said. "What does a guy like that have to do with the attack today?"

"That's what we have to find out," Duncan said. When his phone rang, he walked into the kitchen to talk.

Nick kept worrying about the *why* angle. "There's a lot of power running through the upper echelon of corporate America." His face brightened. "Not our kind, but the international scene is rife with schemers. O'Connor might have his fingers in some of those pies."

With an innocent smile, Lia said, "Oh yeah, I can see how important those wedding gifts might be to international security."

Nick held his hands up in surrender. "Point taken."

"Or, one of Aiden's clients wanted to eliminate a guest at the wedding." Lia enjoyed using his first name.

"No. That's not it," Duncan said from the doorway. He dropped into his chair with a sigh. "My detective friend called. The guard's out of surgery and the prognosis is good."

"That's great news. Why so glum?" Lia said, relieved she'd done something right today.

"He also told me why Aiden O'Connor was there. His brother-in-law, Wyatt Smith, was the victim."

"Oh hell." Nick's somber face regarded his father. "O'Connor and his crew think we had something to do with it."

"Bingo," Duncan confirmed. "Ted said O'Connor was asking about me."

"How did your friend respond to that?" Lia asked.

One eyebrow lifted as Duncan said, "He told O'Connor I was an upstanding citizen and demanded to know why he asked."

Nick chuckled. "I can picture the scene. The detective, hands on his hips, giving O'Connor his Dirty Harry impression." As Nick said it, he tried for an Eastwood glare and mimed holding a gun.

No one looked impressed except Alex, who wore an infatuated smile on her face.

Lia spoke up. "So, what did Aiden say?"

"That I'd been nosing around the crime scene, and he was concerned. Of course, my friend brushed that off, telling O'Connor I always had my snout in crime scenes to bring to my law students."

"You know O'Connor wasn't buying that," Lia said. "He knows about our gifts."

Everyone agreed.

"What about them, the O'Connors, I mean?" Alex asked. "Where did they get their powers?" She leaned against Nick when she posed the idea that Aiden might have had a reason to want his brother-in-law dead.

"Yeah," Nick said. "Maybe the sister wanted to eliminate her husband and asked her brother to take care of it."

Lia frowned and rolled her eyes.

Nick snaked his arm around Alex's waist. "I'm hungry. I think we should all go out for dinner and discuss our options." He turned to his father. "What's going on at Chet's hotel?"

"That's not a bad idea," Duncan said. "I can say hi to Chet. I missed our usual Friday night get-together. He was too busy overseeing the meal for the regatta participants. Those sailors are usually ravenous after a day on the water. Besides, we can't do anything else here tonight."

Lia raised her arms in a long stretch. "You go. I want to relax for a while. I'll find something to munch on here."

"The fridge is full," Duncan said. "Help yourself, but are you certain you don't want to join us?"

"Positive. It's been a long day."

"Do you want me to stay with you?" Alex asked.

"Don't be silly. I'd rather be alone. Besides," she said, feigning fear, "I don't want your boyfriend mad at me."

Nick grinned, trying to tuck Alex under his arm. As she squiggled away, she said, "All right. If you're sure. I'll see you later."

On the way out, Duncan cautioned, "Everyone, keep

alert for any sign of magic."

No one noticed the *normal* person in a car down the street.

****

The computer results from his search on Duncan Stuart, that he was a former Navy Seal who worked as an instructor in the Navy's Judge Advocate General's Corps, came as a surprise to Aiden O'Connor. "Son of a bitch!"

"What's your problem?" his cousin asked from his position on the hotel bed.

"This Stuart guy doesn't fit the profile of a killer, let alone some petty crook. He's a JAG lawyer."

"That doesn't mean he isn't a thief." Jaime Cassidy's lop-sided smile gave his face a comic twist. "He's a lawyer, isn't he?" At thirty-two, Jaime had three years on Aiden, but his smooth face, clear blue eyes, and unassuming manner made him look younger.

Aiden ignored the corny joke. Stuart and his crew confused him. He could usually read people, but this was the first time he'd come across anyone other than his Clan who had psychic gifts. He knew Smitty's killer was powerful. That fit in with what he knew about Stuart's group, and he didn't think it was a coincidence that Stuart showed up after magic was used to kill his brother-in-law. He shook his head. The nature of the crime didn't fit, and the leggy blonde with Stuart carried no malevolence in her, nothing like the darkness he'd sensed at The Towers. His attempted mind probe had shocked her. She'd felt like an innocent.

One side of Aiden's mouth turned up in a half grin at her reaction to his eyes. Her own feisty green gaze had been exciting, reminiscent of a wary cat. In any other circumstance, he'd want to get to know her better. He shook himself. It didn't matter how intriguing the beauty was. She was part of a psychic group. Though she might only be a pawn, he couldn't trust her.

One of Stuart's crew had superior mental abilities. When he'd tried to track their psychic trail to discover more, not only had he been unable to get anything, but he'd come up against an impregnable stone wall. Before he confronted these people, he'd need to know more about their talents. Although certain that his Clan would prevail, he didn't want to come up against an unknown threat. Smitty's death made him cautious.

He wished his sister had never dragged her husband to her friend's wedding. Since Smitty hadn't known any of the invited guests, he'd tried to wiggle out of it, but Meg prevailed. Thoughts of Smitty caused a grinding pain deep in his chest. Who would want to hurt him? Aiden hated that none of his Clan had been there to help him.

A call from the lookout he'd posted at Stuart's house shook him out of his painful memories. "They just took off. You want me to check the place out?"

"No. Stay where you are. I'm coming over. Watch for their return."

Aiden congratulated himself for calling in his "non-magical" operative to do the surveillance. Although excellent at his job, he had no psychic talents, a fact that made him the perfect choice for tonight. No magic—nothing to alert his quarry. Stuart seemed to be an upstanding citizen, but he'd been at the crime scene and power emanated from him and his group. Even if he had nothing to do with Smitty's murder, he still might know something.

It took Aiden less than five minutes to get to Duncan Stuart's house. He hurried around to the back and put his hand against the door edges to test for electrical vibrations. Surprised that he found no active alarm, he used his lock-picking skills to open the door. He hoped Stuart didn't have a dog. He listened. Hearing nothing, he moved inside and closed the door.

Power emanated from the walls. It made sense. A group with psychic powers had been in here fifteen minutes ago. Aiden gave an appreciative nod to the setup. The place was neat and welcoming for a guy who lived alone. He'd read that Stuart's wife passed away, and there was no mention of anyone else in his life other than his mother and his kids, none of whom lived with him.

Aiden's movements, though stealthy, were quick and thorough. He found Duncan's office and was rifling through his oak desk when a sound alerted him. He looked up.

Damn! The blonde stood there.

And she had a gun.

Chapter Four

Kane Fahey burned the faces of the interlopers sniffing after his talisman into his memory, then left The Towers to track his property. A few miles away, he felt the familiar tug. Someone was using the magic again. He'd have to hurry. He knew that the thief who used the amulet and therefore tasted Agamorth's strength would crave more. That was the curse. The thirst for power would become so great, it would ultimately destroy the user.

He drove along the road with the ocean on his left for a few minutes until a slight whiff of something scorched drifted through his window. At the next right, he turned but lost the scent. "This damn wind."

As he passed The Towers once more, he picked up the trail again. Slamming his hands on the steering wheel, he drove inland. Away from the breeze, a faint psychic mist filtered through the car window.

"There you are," he said and sped up. The surroundings shifted from scruffy fields to streets peppered with neat, two-story homes and large ranches.

After about ten minutes, the scent strengthened, and the neighborhood changed—small cottages, neglected yards, and a boarded-up storefront. By the time he reached his destination, he was ready to commit murder.

He parked in front of a large brick building and locked his car, using a protection spell to keep it safe.

The old sign in front advertised, SeaView Aims—the top of the letter "r" in the word Arms having disappeared.

The tiny entryway contained mailboxes attached in a line against one wall and an old glass door leading to the lobby. He tried the grungy handle. Locked. Closing his eyes, he chanted. When he reached for the door this time, it opened.

The pungent aroma of fried foods and garlic assaulted his senses. It was dinnertime, but Kane wasn't hungry. Not for food, anyway. He needed his talisman. Ignoring the small elevator on the left, he hurried up the stairs, trying to cull out his property's scent from the other strong odors.

On the third floor, the trail led him to apartment 3B. He leaned toward the door, listening for any sign of movement. Hearing none, he chanted, opened the door, then wrinkled his nose. Papers and food containers covered every available space. A quick peek into the adjacent cell-sized room made him cringe. Bed unmade and clothes all over the floor. Finding no sign of his amulet but reluctant to miss his prey, he returned to the living area to wait for the thief's return. After a quick look at the mess, he tossed a gossip magazine on a grimy chair to protect his slacks as he sat down. "This guy is a pig."

While he waited, he sorted through the mail to see if there was any information he might need. The correspondence, addressed to Benjie Peters, held nothing of interest. Kane growled in anger and whipped the mail across the room. Forty-five minutes went by as he checked his phone, sent a few texts, and paced. His fingers flexed, itching to destroy something when magic exploded nearby.

A blast that strong meant the amulet was getting hot. “Damn!”

Kane leaped up and sped down the stairs. Outside, he smelled the mix of sweet and burnt hanging in the air. The change in the magical scent alerted him to the danger. His pulse raced as the smell wrapped around him. The thief had no idea what he was doing. The magic of the amulet came with a price. If he continued using it, he would cause a psychic overload. Kane shuddered. He had to stop him before that happened. The consequences would be catastrophic.

****

The minute Lia turned on the lights in Duncan’s office, her chest tingled. Aiden O’Connor, with his dark, wavy hair, strong jaw, and full lips, looked as good as she remembered. Though she stared into his eyes—this time, she didn’t flinch. She held the gun with confidence. “Enjoying yourself?”

He grinned as his gaze roamed over her body. “I am now.”

Unclouded by anger, his face came alive. The sensual smile transformed him into a different kind of dangerous, and Lia wanted more. Too bad he’d broken into Duncan’s house, and she was holding a gun on him.

She tried to ignore the lure of the sexy bad boy in front of her and take control. “What do you want?”

He paused, raking his stare over her again. “I’m thinking a kiss might be nice.”

“Not going to happen, Romeo.”

Her gaze traveled to his lips, imagining how they’d feel. Either her stare lingered there too long, or he saw the hitch in her breathing, because his grin widened. From this distance, it was difficult to see the difference in eye color, but the way he held himself, like a jungle cat, sent heat through Lia's body. She reined in her libido with difficulty.

"What are you looking for in Duncan's desk?"

He lifted his shoulders and tightened his lips.

Ooh, too bad. She missed that smile.

"Anything to tell me how he's involved in my brother-in-law's death."

Lia changed position, softened her voice, and inclined her head. "I'm very sorry for your loss, but we had nothing to do with it. We're trying to find out who did it and how."

"I see those pretty lips move, but I can't believe what they're saying." Aiden's voice hardened. "Where did you get your powers?"

She wished she'd met him under different circumstances. Even though he'd broken into Duncan's house, she sensed no evil.

"I'll notify Duncan you're here. It will only take him a few minutes to return. Why don't we sit down and wait?"

A predator's smile appeared. "Oh, no, sweetheart. I'm afraid that won't suit me. Time for me to leave."

Lia straightened and pointed the gun. "I don't want to shoot you, but I will." She prayed he couldn't maneuver her gun the way the killer had at the wedding.

"I believe you, sweetheart. I'm sorry to have to do this."

Lia blinked. When she looked around, she was alone. Her prisoner had escaped. Rubbing her forehead, she checked the whole room.

Her gun sat on Duncan's desk. She ran over, picked it up, and sped toward the back door. Throwing it open, she raced around to the front of the house. The street was empty.

"Oh, my God, what happened? Where did he go?"

****

No longer feeling like eating alone, Lia left Duncan's house to join everyone at the hotel.

The Tavern, part of the Bayside Inn, owned by Duncan's friend, served good food and provided decent entertainment. Lia paused at the entrance, squinting in the low light in search of her friends. She spotted Nick's unruly head of hair in a booth along the side of the room and wove her way through the tables to join them.

"Miss me?" she asked as she flopped down and snagged a couple of Alex's fries. "I had an unexpected visitor."

When Lia finished her story, Alex's eyes had widened in concern and Nick swore under his breath. Duncan slammed his hand on the table. "Did he hurt you?"

Still a little unnerved, Lia calmed her breathing and assumed a flip attitude. "No." She shrugged her shoulders. "He was there, and then he wasn't." She grinned and snatched a bite of fish from her cousin, who grumbled and suggested that Lia order her own food.

"Mm. Good idea." As she waved for the server, a shock of magic knocked her off balance. She held on to the table. "That was strong."

"Damn," Duncan said. "He must be after the money from the regatta."

As they all followed the acrid scent toward the stairs at the back of the room, Duncan took the lead. "Chet's office is up there."

Lia called after him to be careful. "That blast was

stronger than the other two I experienced."

Duncan plowed ahead up the stairs and shoved open the door to his friend's office. Behind him, Lia saw Chet's body on the floor. A young man leaned over him, looked up, and flipped a sharp object at them. She shoved Duncan out of the way, but not in time. The point of the missile hit his left arm. He went down, and Lia, focusing on his wounds, failed to see the paperweight screaming toward her head until the last minute. Too late.

The crack assaulted her ears, but she felt no pain. Behind her, Alex had covered them with a psychic shield. Lia saw the thief scoop up his spoils and head toward the back exit. *Oh no, my friend. You're not getting away again.* She made a fist and puffed out her fingers, sending a shock of wind to knock him down. While Nick ran over to secure him, she bent down to help Duncan.

The long barb of a spiked paper-holder with papers still attached had torn through the muscle of his upper arm. Lia's hands trembled as she removed it. She wrapped her fingers around the wound, and unwanted images swirled in her head—those loved ones she'd been unable to save. If she hadn't pushed Duncan aside, the spike would have pierced his heart.

From the back of the room, Nick crowed in triumph, "Got it," then dropped whatever it was with a yelp. "It's red hot."

Lia stared in surprise. "That's it?" A disk lay on the carpet. It looked like a gimmick from some souvenir store. A silver orb with strange writing on it, some sort of amulet and small enough to fit in her palm.

With a groan, Duncan tried to sit up. "What about Chet? Is he…"

"He's breathing okay," Nick said.

Lia checked Chet before hurrying back to Duncan. "He's out cold, but he'll be fine."

Nick wrapped the amulet in a couple of napkins and handed it to his father. "Watch it. The thing is still hot."

Duncan took it with his good hand. "This must be it, the origin of his magic. God, I can feel the power. It's unbelievable."

Lia, whose insides pulsed with the emanations from the metal, agreed. "I can't sense any magic other than the evil oozing from that thing."

Duncan tried to steady himself as he called Ted at the police station to explain what had happened. "We've got the culprit here in the office. An ambulance is on its way. I'm going to turn him over to security."

Before the guards arrived, Nick found the kid's ID. "His name's Benjie Peters."

After Lia helped Duncan over to his attacker, he gave the thief a couple of slaps to bring him around and received a glazed stare in response.

"Hurry," Lia said. "Hotel security will be here in a minute."

Duncan got into the young man's face. "Where'd you get the amulet?"

Benjie's eyes went to slits of suspicion. "It's mine." As he said the words, he looked around.

"Searching for a weapon? Forget it. I have your trinket now."

Anger, then fear flashed in his eyes. "What'd you do to me?" He slumped back. "I don't feel good."

Between clamped teeth, Duncan repeated his question. "Where?"

When he dug his fingers into Benjie's shoulder, the

kid ducked his head. "I stole it."

"From whom?"

"I don't know. There was a car crash. Some broad was lying there. It was on the ground."

"Picture her in your mind."

"What?"

"Do it."

Minutes later, hotel security arrived. Chet was coming around. He'd be fine until the EMTs got there.

Lia kept her hand around Duncan's arm as they left. Dull pain bloomed behind her eyes, and her energy dimmed. Healing deep wounds was exhausting.

On the ride back, she described, again, Aiden's disappearance, punctuating her words with sharp movements of her head. "He apologized and then…" She threw her available hand in the air. "I don't know what happened."

****

Back at Duncan's house, Lia followed him into the office. "I was here with the gun, and he was behind your desk. That's all I remember until I snapped out of it and found myself alone."

Duncan turned on his computer. "Calm down. Let's find out what's going on." He tilted his head and concentrated as the fingers of his right hand played on the keyboard. "I monitor this room."

Lia stood next to him, taking care of his left arm. She peered at the computer screen and caught her breath. They were looking at Aiden sitting behind the desk. Duncan pressed another key, and the sound came on.

They listened to the conversation and then watched as Aiden walked over to Lia, took the gun out of her hand, and placed it on the desk. Lia gasped when Aiden walked back to her and kissed her mouth, whispering, "I'll be seeing you."

"How dare he?"

Duncan chuckled. "He seems quite interested in you."

"I don't remember any of it." *Damn!* An exciting warmth spread through her. She wished she could remember the kiss.

Nick strolled into the office with Alex behind him. "What are you looking at?"

Duncan beckoned with his hand until they could all watch the computer. He played the scene again. When Aiden kissed Lia, Alex exclaimed, "Wow! He's into you."

"Yes, there is that," Duncan said, "but what else did you see?"

Nick's voice carried a trace of shock as he said, "It looks like he stopped time. No. Wait a minute. I saw something glinting in his fingers."

Lia piped up. "I didn't even see his hand move." She'd been too busy concentrating on his lips. "Since you mention it, though, I think I remember a flash."

Duncan replayed the scene.

"You're right," Lia said. "I see it now. There was something in his hand."

"Hypnosis?" Duncan said.

Lia shook her head. "He never had time to put me under."

Duncan sighed. "We're not dealing with an ordinary human being. I'm grateful O'Connor did nothing to hurt you or, I might add, my home."

He patted the artifact in his pocket. "Let's go to Newport. This damn thing is calling to me."

****

Aiden's police scanner alerted him to trouble at a place called the Bayside Inn. When he and his friends arrived there, the stench of strong magic caught in his throat.

He shouldered his way to the detective in charge, the same one from The Towers, and asked if the incident had anything to do with the murder of his brother-in-law.

"We think this one is the same guy who killed him. He fits the description. I'll let you know when we learn more."

Aiden scanned the crowded hotel lobby. The seating area, a couple of couches and chairs arranged on an aqua and orange geometric patterned rug, was empty, but groups of people stood around, staring at the police presence. All conversation quieted the minute he spoke to the officer.

Aiden lowered his voice, "Where is he?" He didn't see anyone under police guard.

"Right now, he's on his way to the hospital. A couple of people who walked in on the robbery injured him during the altercation."

"Did he hurt anyone?"

Ted rubbed his face with both hands. "Yeah. He attacked a friend of mine. Thankfully, he'll recover."

Aiden looked away. His throat muscles constricted. "You're lucky."

"Yeah, I know, Mr. O'Connor. Sorry."

Shaking off the pain, Aiden said, "So, someone caught him, huh?"

"Yeah." The cop uttered a half snort, half laugh. "Another friend of mine. Geez, I was just playing poker with Chet and Duncan last week."

Aiden shook his head. "You never know." He nodded to his men and walked out to the car. "What do you want to bet this Duncan's last name is Stuart?"

They headed to the hospital. Flashing blue lights served as a beacon when they arrived. Emergency rooms everywhere had the same smell, the same feeling of fear and pain. When they walked into the packed waiting area, Aiden had to strain to discover the killer's faint magical essence.

He turned to his cousin, Jaime, the peacemaker in the group. Though Jaime's muscular physique made him seem dangerous, he enjoyed the power of persuasion and could talk down an angry man or charm an unwitting female.

"See what you can find out. I didn't get the impression that the guy was in bad shape."

Aiden asked the other two to poke around for information, then watched Jaime stroll over to the nurse's station and lean down to the lone woman sitting behind the desk. Aiden moved in closer to listen.

"Excuse me," Jaime said, "Why are all the police here?"

The woman frowned, concentrating on the computer, and said, "I'm sorry. You'll have to take that up with the officers."

Aiden chuckled, knowing his cousin would prevail.

Jaime's tone radiated sympathy. "I can understand how busy you must be. Miss?"

Her head snapped up, eyes flashing. She opened her mouth to say something and stopped as she stared into Jaime's blue eyes. Aiden watched the slow smile transform her face. "I am very busy. It was bad enough before, but then the police invaded the place with some guy who's supposed to be a murder suspect."

Sandy hair dipped over his forehead as Jaime leaned his elbow on the desk. He must have checked out the name badge hanging around the nurse's neck, because he said, "What happened, Alice? Did someone shoot the guy?"

She peeked around before she, too, leaned on the counter. "That's not what I hear. I hear he came in with a concussion. Other than that, he was fine."

When she checked for eavesdroppers once again, Aiden pretended to study his phone. She dropped her voice, but Aiden could still hear her. "But something weird happened."

Aiden suppressed a chuckle as she motioned Jaime to lean in further. "His vitals dropped, and he had trouble breathing. Now, I hear, they're losing him."

She finished with a flirtatious smile.

Jaime covered her hand with his enormous paw. "Thank you, Alice, you've been wonderful."

Aiden moved toward the door, sending a silent message to his men, *Time to go.*

In the car, he said, "Something strange is going on. If that's the guy who killed Smitty, what happened to his powers? He's dying in there, but not from being subdued at the hotel." Aiden shook his head. "Unless Stuart did something to him. It doesn't make sense, but I'll bet he had a hand in it. He's the only thing consistent between the two crimes."

Too bad. I didn't want the feisty blonde to be involved.

Chapter Five

Kane rolled down his window and followed Agamorth's noxious scent to a hotel where he mingled with the onlookers. His prize was no longer there, but the heavy residual odor, as well as distinct tingle in the air, revealed the demon's heightened power. Anyone invoking its energy would soon be dead. He intended to find the thief before that happened. He wanted his talisman back.

Ignoring the eager curiosity of the stupid humans around him, he concentrated on the plain-clothes cop speaking to a man he'd seen earlier at The Towers. Kane couldn't tell what the cop said, but the satisfaction in the other guy's face gave him a reason to stay on his tail.

He followed the car to the hospital and soon learned the fate of the kid who had been using his amulet. Kane struggled to contain the rage building inside him. The stupid shit was here dying, but the amulet was gone. It had never been inside this hospital.

For the second time in two days, he found himself surrounded by whining people and the disgusting scent of sweat, blood, and worse. He touched the healing gash on his head, still furious at Gianna. The stupid bitch had picked up the amulet before he could stop her.

"Ooh, I'm hungry," she said as she pointed. "Let's go in there."

Agamorth obeyed the person who held the amulet.

Seconds later, the steering wheel spun to the left, almost wrenching Kane's wrist in the process. His struggle to gain control of the steering wheel was useless. The car swerved into the oncoming traffic. He could still hear the heart-stopping explosion of the collision—feel the painful jolt of the airbag crashing into his head.

The wail of an arriving ambulance snapped him out of his reverie. He had to get the amulet back. His mind spun as he considered the possibilities. It hadn't been in the hotel. It wasn't here, and the people he tailed didn't have it. Where did it go? He stood to the side, watching the group he'd followed. After one of them spoke to a nurse, the leader spun around to leave.

Kane, with no other options, stalked after them, blending into the busy parking lot. When the black SUV pulled out onto the road, he stayed behind, using his sensory skills to follow their faint psychic trail. He slowed down when they stopped in an upscale neighborhood and parked over to the side. The leader slipped out of the car and crept around the house. Not long after, the guy came running back to the car. The engine revved up, and they sped away. They must have found something. He pulled up to the house and gasped. Agamorth!

The essence came from a large house on the water. Not caring about the people in the car anymore, he hurried up for a closer look. The place felt empty, but the vestiges of his amulet remained. Whose house? Where had they taken the demon's medallion? He sneaked around to the back and opened the door.

He'd found a new trail.

****

That night, Rosemary Stuart called a meeting at her

home in Newport. Lia suppressed a grin as she watched the head of her Clan change from unflappable leader to worried mom fussing over her son's healing wound.

The French doors opened onto a lighted patio, but, at ten p.m. the rest of the estate was dark. Cocooned in a comfortable chair, Lia's spirits lifted. With family and friends around her on her own turf, all things were possible. Together, the Watcher Clan was unbeatable.

Her mother, Francesca Ferguson, Franki to her family, and her aunt, Bree Brendani, arrived a few minutes later.

Rosemary clapped her hands. "Sit. Have some refreshments and we'll talk." She'd provided cheese and crackers, soft drinks, and homemade cookies. "I shouldn't have to remind you to avoid stimulants from now on. Our gifts must remain sharp."

Duncan cleared his throat, and all conversation stopped. He took the amulet, which he'd wrapped in a small towel, out of his pocket as if it were a fragile piece of glass. "This is the artifact that gave a young man the ability to manipulate objects more thoroughly than any of us could. It has incredible power. I can feel it now playing with my head, urging me to use it."

He handed the cloth-wrapped amulet around so everyone could see it, but cautioned, "Don't touch the metal. It's dangerous."

Warmth leeched through the material as Lia gazed at the symbols carved into the amulet. It looked old. Her fingers twitched with a yearning to stroke it. She blinked and passed it on.

When Rosemary received it, she insisted on taking it from the covering.

"Be careful, Mother," Duncan said. "The magic tries

to ensnare you."

As Rosemary turned the amulet over in her hands, she said, "It feels warm. What do you know about it?"

Lia piped up, "We know its magic is beyond our skills."

Duncan dipped his head in agreement. "When used, it sends out a strong flash of energy and the metal heats. I pulled an image of the owner from the mind of the young man who stole it. I'm sending it to you all now."

Lia grimaced at the scene. The woman, covered in blood, lay at an angle in a wrecked car with her seatbelt holding her in. Dark hair obscured her face, but she looked no older than Lia herself. *What was she doing with such a dangerous artifact?* Aloud, she said, "You forgot to mention the thief died in the hospital after using the amulet at the hotel."

"How?" Rosemary asked.

"We think it has something to do with using the magic," Lia said, a sense of urgency burning in her chest. "It's powerful. I'm worried the owner might track this thing to us. We've got to get a handle on it before that happens." She turned to Alex. "Would you try to read it?"

Alex's head snapped up. Since her gift included seeing past events, she was the obvious choice, but Lia sensed her fear. Alex rubbed her arms. "Me?"

"Yes. Your visions should be stronger since you got your gifts last year."

"No way," Nick said. "It's too dangerous." He pulled Alex to his side. "This thing has already killed two people."

Alex raised her palm to caress his cheek. "I won't be using the amulet's magic, just my own. If I sense trouble, I'll end the vision."

Rosemary interrupted, "We know nothing about this kind of magic. It's ancient."

"That's why we have to find out more—its origin, strengths, flaws," Lia said.

"That may be true," Rosemary said, "But it's late. We're all tired. Attempting this now is asking for trouble. Let's get some rest and revisit it in the morning. We don't want to make a serious mistake."

Something in Lia said to hurry. "We know it's stronger than we are. Once the owners track it, we'll be vulnerable, and we don't know what other talents they have. I think we're running out of time."

Concerned for her cousin, Lia put her arm around Alex's shoulder. "I'm right here. I'll stay with you."

Alex gave her a grateful smile.

Rosemary sighed. "All right. We'll all be here. Don't take any chances. If you feel at all threatened, drop the damned thing."

Lia watched Alex reach for the amulet and gave her a reassuring squeeze. Moments later, she felt a shock. A tingle in her cousin's fingers became her own. She heard Alex's thoughts inside her head. Irrational images pushed into her conscious, mean and childish ideas, like flinging objects around the room. Heat leaked into her palm and the pictures darkened, centered more on pain and humiliation. She watched in disgust at suggestions of soda burning eyes and books smashing into people's heads. The insanity stopped when Alex regained control, sending out mental probes.

Where did you come from? Nothing. *Show me who you are,* she commanded.

Lia felt woozy as she blinked into flickering light.

Murmuring stirred her senses. They weren't alone. She saw through her cousin's eyes. Markings on the floor—a pentagram. Black candles. A nearby voice startled her. It sounded like a mantra. Incense invaded her nose. The strange words ended with a shout. Candles burst into flames, and a red glow flared from the amulet inside the circle.

Lia's senses whirled. *How could they see this? Where were they?*

Chanting grew in volume as a young woman entered the circle. A furry bundle squirmed in her arms. Then a knife flashed, and blood dripped to the floor.

Lia jerked back, and one of the participants turned toward her. Black eyes hollowed out of—a face? Flashes of light against—bronze-tipped scales? He reached for them.

Alex screamed.

****

The sharp sound of her cousin's voice snapped Lia out of the vision.

Alex wasn't so lucky.

Lia watched in horror as Alex tried to shake off the amulet. "Get her out of there," she screamed as she reached out to her cousin.

Nick slapped the amulet out of Alex's palm. She opened her eyes and leaned into him, holding her hand away from her. Lia looked at the bright red skin and recognized a nasty burn. As she leaned in to help Alex, fear spilled out. "That horrible mask. What happened? Did he get you?"

Alex jerked her head toward Lia. "That was a mask? Thank God. Wait a minute. How do you know what I saw?"

"I was there."

"What?"

Lia ignored the sounds of shock behind her. "You brought me into your vision."

Alex shook her head, her eyes still wild. "You weren't with me."

Rosemary interrupted, her voice sharp with concern, "What do you mean, Lia? You saw what happened?"

Lia, who by this time had calmed a bit, snorted. "Not only did I see—I experienced. And they caught us." She swiveled to Alex. "I thought he'd get you."

"I-I felt his fingers on my arm."

Lia found a long scratch on her cousin's wrist. "Oh, God." She shivered. "We were there." She'd never get the picture of that bloody knife out of her head.

The room erupted with questions for Lia. "How did you become part of Alex's vision?" "Were you actually there?"

Before Lia could answer, Alex held up a hand. "Wait! My mom's here." Her mother, who'd been murdered almost two years ago, was one of the Brendani ghosts. Only two Clan members had the gift of clairvoyance, the ability to see spirits: Alex and Rosemary.

"She saw the ceremony, heard the incantations, and said the amulet was more dangerous than we thought." Alex paused and swallowed. "The blood ceremony was a rite of protection. It's a curse. Any outsider who uses the artifact will die."

Lia's nerves pinged. "That's what happened to that kid." Worried about her Clan's interaction with the unholy medallion, she asked Duncan if he'd had any communication with the amulet.

He shook his head. "No."

"Thank God. Alex, let me see if the vision caused any changes in you. I'll check everyone who's handled it—make sure nothing strange is going on. In the meantime, put it away." After a thorough inspection, Lia found nothing more than traces of its presence. "The amulet must know when its powers are safe. I guess if we don't use it, we're not a threat. At least, not to the spirit." She grimaced. "The owners, though, will be another story. And they've seen two of us."

Franki and Nick hovered over Alex as Lia said, "So, how did I end up along for the ride? Has anyone heard of a vision hitchhiker?"

All eyes turned to Rosemary. She shook her head. "Never."

"I've always been alone in my visions," Alex said. "I wasn't even aware Lia was with me in this one."

She cleared her throat. "Wait a minute. My mother says she has." Alex paused for a minute, as if listening to someone or something only she could hear. "Stories from tribal leaders when we lived in Arizona—shamans who traveled through time, and spirits who transported others."

Lia tried to stave off a chill. "Your mother believes you time-traveled?"

Alex bit her lip and breathed out. "Although I'm sometimes part of my visions, I think, this time, the amulet brought us in deliberately trying to trap us."

Lia shuddered at the thought of Alex at the mercy of those demons. "We've got to do something about that damned disk—I think it's watching us. We need to destroy it."

"How?" Alex said.

"Research." Lia turned to Duncan. "Any ideas?"

Duncan scratched his head. "I've come across various cults in my Templar research. Some were dangerous fanatics. I'll check again."

Lia feared they had little time.

Duncan huffed out a breath. "I have a friend I can ask to help us search for some way to bind the amulet's magic so it can't be used. Maybe someone at the college might know something."

Lia paced. "We need to hurry. Those men could turn up any minute."

"I'll call my contacts tomorrow." He looked at his watch. "I mean today."

When she checked the antique clock on the wall, it read well after midnight. Lia hadn't realized how late it was. Feeling as though she'd done all she could, she smoothed the hair off her forehead and felt a flush creep up her face. "What about Aiden O'Connor?"

Duncan frowned. "He's going to be a problem."

Lia had already filled the rest of the Clan in on her brush with Aiden, including his vanishing trick.

"We need more information on him," Duncan said, "what powers he has, and how he got them."

"He's as curious about us," Lia said. "He demanded I tell him about our gifts."

Duncan nodded. "He suspects we had something to do with his brother-in-law's death. When he finds we have the artifact that caused the murder, he'll come looking for us. I'd like to unload it before then. I don't think it'll take long for him to track us."

Lia noticed her mother as she glanced up at her daughter and then looked down at her lap. She was much too quiet.

Something was up.

****

After the meeting, Nick who lived with his grandmother Rosemary, insisted on walking Alex and Lia home along the back path. They passed the Convent House, a decaying mansion where they'd fought the demon last year, then on to the Brendani estate which Alex and Lia shared with their aunt and Lia's parents.

Lia knew she should be tired, but her mind wouldn't quiet. She squeezed Alex's arm. "I'm so sorry I insisted you read that thing."

"No. You were right," her cousin said. "We need to know what we're dealing with. If I hadn't used my gift, we wouldn't know about the curse."

Alex's words instilled a sense of dread, but Lia shook it off. As she lifted her face to the wind, she breathed in the tangy essence of the night and wondered how long it would be before the inevitable invasion of their peaceful existence. Aiden O'Connor and those men in Alex's vision would show up soon.

She banished her mounting fear and concentrated on the distant wash of the Sakonnet River against the shore. "It's a beautiful evening. I think I'll stay out for a while. Tell Mom and Bree I'll be in the garden."

Alex clutched at Lia. "Do you think that's wise?"

"I'll be fine. If I sense anything, I'll call you."

Nick tried to dissuade her, but Lia laughed. "I'm always up late, and I know every inch of this property. I'm good."

As Lia drifted along the leafy path with its sweet and pungent scents, the quiet night enhanced the evening sounds. She heard Nick and Alex as they stood on the back porch—whispers, then Nick's deep voice and Alex giggling. Lia watched them kiss before she turned away. She was happy for them. She was. They were a great couple. But she felt like crying. Seeing them together heightened her loneliness.

Lia didn't expect to find what Alex and Nick had. Love wasn't for her. She fell into lust easily enough, but her heart had never threatened to quit over any guy. Though the *normals* she'd dated were nice enough, she'd never consider anything permanent.

She envied Alex. No matter how hard her cousin had tried to deny it, her feelings for Nick bubbled out of her. Now they were engaged.

With a sigh, she put everything but the comforting evening air out of her thoughts and embraced the nighttime song: leaves whispering in the wind, crickets trilling their love, and an occasional solitary hoot. She reached out to rub a small leaf, brought her fingers to her nose, and inhaled the soothing scent of lavender.

Her thoughts veered to the incredible events of the day—the death of Aiden's brother-in-law and the guard bleeding in her lap. How could a person kill so easily? She blamed the shiny piece of silver whose siren call begged for release. Then she remembered the vision.

Damn! No more battles. Last July, Rosemary reactivated the Watcher Clan to protect not only the Templar treasure but their own existence. They'd had less than a week to recondition rusty skills and learn to work together as a unit. It was a deadly and hard-fought victory.

An owl's screech pulled her back to the present. Some poor little critter was doomed.

****

With the hospital a dead-end, Aiden returned to

Duncan's empty house. It told him nothing, so he searched his database for the man's connections. To his surprise, he found that Duncan's mother and son lived at the same address in Newport. That's where he'd start.

He explained his plan to the others. "I've secured rooms there. I think that's Stuart's destination. Buckle up."

They settled in at a Newport hotel, and Aiden set his alarm for six a.m. He'd run a couple of miles, eat breakfast, and then cruise around. No sense starting too early. Sunday morning traffic would be light, and he didn't want his car causing undue notice while he familiarized himself with Stuart's neighborhood.

As he lay down, he thought about Meg, his newly widowed sister whom their mother had brought to her home. She was a mess: in shock, and under sedation. He rubbed the lump in his chest as he thought of Smitty and Meghan, so in love. If he'd been there, he might have done something. Damn! He punched the pillow, wanting to kill someone. Time to confront Stuart.

Using a trick he'd learned in the service, he cleared his head. The heavy snores from the next bed made him grin. He'd been too busy to call dibs on his room partner and ended up with Jaime. *Mr. Chick Magnet. I wonder what his women think about this racket.*

****

During breakfast, Aiden and his men sketched out what amounted to a covert op to discover more about Stuart. The heavy rain would limit the usual Sunday tourist traffic around Newport, so their car would be more noticeable in a residential neighborhood. Also, they'd need rain gear. Surveillance equipment posed no problem. Aiden always kept it in the trunk of his car.

With a plan in mind, they headed out for a quick reconnaissance of Stuart's locale before getting the extra accessories they'd need. Their exploration uncovered problems. The Stuarts lived in a high-rent district on a dead-end street. No tourist traffic. Like a country road, this stretch had long driveway entrances. A car parked anywhere would raise questions. The size of the estates and their landscaping might provide his only leverage. People here embraced their privacy by keeping a wide buffer of trees and bushes between their properties. Aiden would use the woods surrounding the Stuart home to his advantage. With his military-grade equipment, he could eavesdrop from a suitable distance. Then an Internet map gave him the ideal solution—water. The house had river access.

They'd have to be careful. With Duncan's Navy SEAL training, he might have an early-warning system in place. Aiden hoped not. Psychic skills might preclude the necessity of monitoring equipment. Thinking about their powers, Aiden frowned. They'd be able to detect his men if they got too close.

At the sports store, Aiden purchased four sets of rain gear and a four-man inflatable raft. They'd leave their rented truck at a nearby beach and approach the property from the river. Darkness and the rain, projected to last a few days, should give them enough cover to implement their plan.

****

In Kane's search of the house that still held his amulet's scent, he discovered Duncan Stuart's address book. More digging revealed a Newport address for two people with the same last name. If Kane failed to find Stuart there, he'd use one of his relatives as a bargaining chip. As he headed to their location, he wished he had Gianna with him for backup. Her spell casting had advanced nicely, but she had one more day in the hospital.

It took six rings before Jago answered. "*What's up?*"

Kane hadn't told his associates about the loss of the amulet. "We have a job in Newport tonight." He gave him the address he'd found. "After I scout the place, I'll call. Then, you and Tapper get there, lie low, and be ready."

By the time Kane reached his destination, it was close to midnight. The neighborhood increased his aggravation—exclusive, with no safe place to park, so he left the car a couple of miles up a side road. A twenty-minute jog didn't improve his disposition.

When he reached the stately home, he paused, held out his hands, and scanned for life forces. What he found spoiled his hope of recovering the amulet. Not only did he sense the presence of his property, but also that of seven others with heavy psychic powers. Neither witches nor wizards, yet dangerous. Terrible odds. Although he himself possessed a warlock's strength, Gianna was only a fledgling witch, and his other two allies were normal. He had to investigate the grounds himself before summoning his minions.

When the gathering inside the house broke up, he sensed two people leave by the front door and watched three exit the back. He ducked into the trees. The trio, one man and two women, walked toward him, forcing him to retreat farther. They didn't have the amulet. He waited until they passed, and their voices faded into the night before moving toward the house.

Lights went out downstairs then reappeared on the

second story. Kane closed in to search for the amulet's scent. Although its odor lingered on the lower floor, the amulet called out from above. He detected two people in the house, a number he should have been able to handle, but their combined power was strong. Unused to any resistance or barricade to his schemes, he took out his frustrations by ripping off the blooms from a nearby bush.

With nothing more he could do now, he left to work out a plan. Half-way to his vehicle, the rain began. By the time he reached the car, water oozed through his clothes. He shook himself and cursed. It was as if the goddess had deserted him. His rumbling stomach reminded him he hadn't eaten, so he took off to find some food.

Once he returned to the side road, he wished he had a change of clothes. Pushing the car seat back, he stretched his legs and sipped a hot coffee before calling Jago. They could cover the house while he got some rest. Then he'd watch for his chance—when the house was empty or relatively empty. Too bad if one of them remained. He wouldn't worry about a lone disposable person.

Chapter Six

Lia slept late, but not well after her dreams were hijacked by visions of bloodied fur and the endless drone of chanting. Sitting at the familiar round table in her family's kitchen restored her needed sense of security. Things were happening too fast. Leaning back, she experienced a wave of gratitude for her own earthbound powers. She couldn't imagine having to endure visions like Alex had last night which defied time and space.

Pondering the mystery of the deadly amulet, her reverie ended with the telltale jingle of her mother's gold bracelets as she entered the room. "Hi, Mom. Everything okay?"

Franki blinked as she rubbed her hands together. "Yes, dear. It's just the weather. I don't know what to do with myself in this rain."

Since rainy mornings hadn't seemed to bother her mother before, and Franki had unaccountably shadowed her all morning, Lia was concerned. Franki, although somewhat flighty, had never been prone to anxiety. Her actions today were off.

Tamping down her own unease, Lia smiled. "Why don't you sit down? We'll have a cup of tea. I could use one."

Franki sighed and pulled out a chair.

Lia patted her mother's hand. "If you're worried about me, I'm fine."

"Your exact words before you fell into that pond when you were six years old. You're twenty-eight now. When will it stop?" She rubbed her hands together, setting up a golden symphony of sounds from her wrists. "Don't touch that horrid piece of metal again. It could have killed you."

"It didn't." She kissed her mother's forehead but noticed Franki was still upset. "Out with it. Something else is bothering you."

Her mother twitched her shoulders and looked away.

"What's going on?"

"It's Kitty. She's driving me crazy."

Lia chuckled. Her grandmother, safely in her ghostly resting place inside the family's labyrinth, continued to wield a heavy measure of control over her daughters. "Nothing new there. What's she done now?"

Franki turned her attention to the table, worrying an invisible speck.

"Mom?"

With a rebellious glare, she said, "She wants me to paint."

Lia tried to hide her grin. Franki, a successful artist, spent most of her time in her studio over the garage. "How dare she?"

"It's not funny," she complained with a toss of her blonde curls. "She wants me to do one of my *special compositions*." She dropped her gaze to her hands and continued in a mumbling rant. "It's not as if I can control it. I don't even know what I'm creating until it's finished."

Lia's grin disappeared. Her mother, besides being an important artist, also had the gift of spectral painting. Her prophetic rendering last year had alerted the Clan when a dream walker stalked Alex. “I don’t understand. How could Kitty know you needed to get to work? I thought only you knew when you were ready.”

Instead of answering, Franki glanced away from Lia.

“Oh. I see. You do know. Why pretend?”

“She expects me to paint the amulet.”

Lia ignored the chill that slithered up her spine and softened her voice. “It’s frightening, but you know she’s right. I can see the amulet is already calling you.”

Franki bit her lip. “I knew the minute I held it. I hate that thing. It’s malevolent.”

“All the more reason to unlock its secrets. You know you’re unable to resist your gift. Ignoring your destiny won’t change anything. Tell Duncan you need to paint the *sphere of evil* before he has it bound.”

Franki rolled her lovely eyes and gave an exaggerated sigh as she looked out the windows overlooking the luscious gardens. “All right, but I won’t walk in this rain. Oh, wait. Your father took the car. Give me a ride on your way to work?”

A friend of Duncan’s had returned Lia’s car that morning. “I’m not due in until later this afternoon.” Lia curled her lips in a soft grin as she recognized the mother-daughter role reversal. “And I’m sure Duncan would bring the amulet here if you asked.”

Her mother, unhappy, answered like an undisciplined child. “All right.”

“Good. You let him know, and I’ll take a short walk in this glorious summer shower.” Unlike her mother, Lia loved nature’s cleansing liquid.

She gave Franki a supportive hug and walked

outside. Earthy smells of rain-soaked soil filled her nostrils, and a cool mist teased her face. She opened her mouth to catch a taste of the sweet nectar as she ambled through the garden. Recent events captured her thoughts. Her mother's looming session with the amulet worried her. It meant that her family had some kind of connection to it. Franki's special work always involved family or Clan. Lia intended to remain with her mother until she finished the painting. Too bad if she missed work. She didn't trust the amulet.

Thoughts of the sphere's owners made her cringe. They'd proven their ruthlessness with the curse. Murder would pose no problem for them. Then there was Aiden O'Connor. What kind of power did he possess, and would he unleash it against her Clan?

She received a message from her mother—Duncan was on his way.

As Lia climbed the porch steps, she felt the pressure from an invisible stopwatch as it ticked away the seconds.

****

The sound of the cell alarm woke Kane. He groaned and jabbed at the phone, cutting off the music from the California hotel song. With a wry grin, he wondered if a witch had ever locked the writer of that annoying tune in a punishment spell.

He sat up, twisting his neck in several directions trying to work out the kinks. Parts of his body he'd never considered ached. He hated sleeping in the car, and he hadn't seen six a.m. in years. The rain beating against the windows soured his already lousy mood. He was grateful that Jago had thought to bring him a rain poncho.

The thin plastic stuck to him as Kane pushed out of

the car. At least the deluge provided privacy for his run back to the house.

Jago and Tapper, hidden in the tree line between the ruined mansion and the Stuarts' home, reported no activity during their watch. The downpour, though aggravating, gave them excellent cover.

Kane slipped behind the bushes. Rain dripped off the plastic hood onto his face and leaked down his neck. He shivered when a cold trickle worked its way down his chest. As he squished his toes inside the now ruined, expensive Italian leather shoes, his chest burned with anger. Those who stole the amulet would pay.

He briefed his men on the plan. "I'll go in after the amulet when they least expect it; you can back me up." He gave them earbuds so he could keep them apprised.

A couple of hours later, he heard someone leave the house. He scurried through the trees in time to see a man get into a car. Before the guy closed the door, the scorched scent of Kane's property wafted out. *He's got it!*

Shoving away the wet bushes that had been his hiding place, he made it to the street. He told his men to get to their car. Kane prepared for a hard run, but his quarry, instead of speeding up, only turned into the next driveway. *With thanks to the goddess Diana,* he brushed rain from his face and ran toward the vehicle.

He found the car parked in front of a large house, steam still rising from the hood. The driver had disappeared. Staying low in the underbrush, Kane circled, sniffing to find his property. Poor visibility allowed him to sneak through the open area in the back, where he finally caught the scent. He crossed a stone patio, crept up onto the porch, avoided the light spilling from the double doors, and chanced a quick glance into what looked like a breakfast room. His target sat at a large antique table with three women. Magic clung to them. He ached to use an eavesdropping spell, but feared they might detect it. If he could get his hands on the amulet, their strength would diminish to nothing, but he didn't dare challenge them now. He needed help.

He'd use his men as a distraction. Before calling them, he took another peek through the window and froze. The man was gone, and two of the women had donned raincoats. The younger one slid something into her pocket. His prize! They picked up an umbrella and headed directly toward him.

Shit! He tripped and almost fell down the steps in his rush to get away. As the door opened, the odor of cinnamon and sugar floated through the air. Panting, he shoved himself behind a set of tall shrubs and bit back grunts when sharp twigs jabbed him. He held his breath until the women turned in the other direction. One of them laughed as they huddled under the umbrella.

Where were they going? He gave a frantic glance around. Nothing but land. Straightening his shoulders, he growled. *Now's my chance. I can handle two women.*

****

In the kitchen, Lia gathered a few snacks while she waited for her mother to change clothes. Franki always needed sustenance after one of her sessions.

"I'm ready." Her mother's unsmiling face made Lia feel like a brute for insisting she paint the amulet. But one look at Franki's outfit dragged her lips into a half-grin. Her mother wore one of her father's old cotton shirts with the sleeves rolled up, jeans, and a colorful scarf to hold back her blonde locks. Quite different from her mother's usual fashion statement.

When Duncan arrived, his face lit up. "Franki, you look like that tomboy who taught me to climb trees."

Aunt Bree walked in behind him. Dark hair swished across her cheeks as she shook her head. "And sometimes she acts like that little girl." Lines creased her forehead as she regarded her sister. "I'll accompany you while you paint that devilish trinket."

Franki frowned and shook her head. "I'm fine."

"Don't worry, Aunty," Lia said, "I'm going with her. You can help Duncan find someone to bind the amulet's power so we can get rid of it."

Bree threw the envelope she had in her hand onto the table. "If you want my opinion…" She wrinkled her forehead and pursed her lips. "Even if you don't, I think it's too soon after the horror of last summer. I vote we get rid of the amulet immediately. Let someone else worry about it."

Lia, understanding her aunt's concern, softened her voice. "But who, Aunty? We vowed to keep people safe. With two men dead and a gravely injured police officer, we're the only ones who can end the destruction this medallion can cause."

Bree answered with a sigh, "I know. You're right. I only hope we don't have to fight the renegade group and O'Connor's men as well."

Cold sliced through Lia's body. "Let's pray they aren't in this together."

The former misting rain had turned into a full-blown soaker. Lia shared her mother's umbrella as they hurried to Franki's studio over the garage. Though she laughed as they snuggled together and skirted puddles, her efforts to cheer her mother failed. Franki had already embraced her gift.

Danger flashed across her mind seconds before something slammed into her.

She went flying into her mother. Someone was on top of her, digging at her coat pocket. The amulet! Just as she scrambled to get away, she felt a shock of magic, then the weight on top of her disappeared. She looked up to see her mother kneeling in the mud, preparing to throw another energy bolt. A cloaked figure retreated.

With a flick of her hand, Lia created a small twisting wind to hold him, but when she turned to check on her mother, he escaped. Lia, worried about Franki, let him go. Her mother brushed at the mud on her jeans. "I'm fine. Let's go after him."

"Too late." Heat rushed through her, and her hands still tingled. She straightened her shoulders. He'd taken her by surprise, but now she'd be ready. After sending out a telepathic message to the others to search the grounds, she wrapped her arm around her mother. "It's begun."

****

Lia hurried her mother up the steps to her art studio above the garage, locked the door, and dropped her head into her hands. After she'd telegraphed news of the attack to the Clan, everyone answered at once, some rushing out to catch the assailant, others wanting to come and safeguard them. She squashed a spike of anger at the implication she couldn't protect her mother. *We're fine. I'm on alert now. And Franki needs no more distractions.*

While she dealt with the problem, her mother swirled her hand above her head, changing the lighting to mimic a sunny day. The studio always responded to

Franki's wishes. Alive with scents of paint and turpentine, the cheery atmosphere displayed bright-colored canvases scattered around the room.

Instead of welcoming the illumination, Lia's attention turned to the wet, gray reality beyond the windows. With unknown danger waiting to pounce, gloom felt like the more appropriate setting. She knew the minute her mother unwrapped the damnable piece of metal. A clawing sensation scratched at her mind. Her fingers itched to throw the devil's bauble into the storm.

As she watched her mother succumb to the imperious urge to paint, her throat tightened. Franki's usual soft expression transformed into pinched lines of strain across her forehead and a haunted stare.

The room's atmosphere had changed as the brush darted from palette to canvas. An eerie sense of inevitability spread through the studio. Her mother's twisting lips and flaring nostrils personified the impression.

Lia's heart cried out, wishing her mother wasn't their prophetess. She tried to ignore the frenzied movements and concentrate on finding a solution before things worsened. Her assailant had gone for the amulet, so unless others were involved, he must be part of the ritual group she'd seen in the vision.

A message from Duncan startled her. *Everything all right? Nick is still out there looking, but I think whoever attacked you has gone.*

Although she reassured him, she sent a worried glance to her mother who appeared lost in the task at hand. Franki, engrossed in her work, wouldn't even know if she was in danger.

All good, she told him.

Great, Duncan said, *I've got a lead on someone to help us. I'm trying to get in touch with him now.*

Good luck.

She stared out at the storm and dropped her chin to her chest wondering how soon before another assault.

A knock on the door sent her leaping off the sofa to a protective stance in front of Franki.

It's me, Duncan.

Lia sucked in her breath before blowing it out of her mouth. "That idiot." She checked on her mother. Still absorbed in her work.

Lia stayed where she was, flicking her fingers to unlock the door. Duncan walked in, took in Franki's absorption and Lia's defensive posture, and held his hands up in a gesture of surrender. "Sorry. I wasn't thinking."

Lia swallowed an angry retort and led him to the sofa. "I told you we were fine."

"I thought you'd like to know about my research."

"To bind the amulet's powers and keep anyone else from using it?"

He nodded. "While I reached out to friends at the War College, my mother dug through our Templar library. She recognized the partial symbol on the artifact. I should have seen it myself. The Rooster's head, part of the Abraxas or 'Snake-foot' symbol. That triggered a memory for her—some paperwork about dire circumstances." He paused, pushing his hand through his hair.

"And?" Lia said as she held her breath.

"She found a phone number for emergencies." He looked sick as he said, "Someone will be here soon."

"Who?"

He shook his head. "He hung up before I could find out."

Goosebumps peppered her skin. Except for her Clan, the Templars were a shadowy, unknown entity whose ancient brethren had materialized in the Convent House last year to help them defeat the demon. She hugged herself. Too much was happening too fast.

While she and Duncan worried over the escalating danger, Franki's brush strokes noticeably slowed. When she dropped her arm, Duncan rushed over to help her. Lia contemplated the glassy stare in her mother's eyes and shuddered.

Duncan supported Franki as he surveyed the painting. "According to this portrayal, they've found us, and we're in for trouble."

A feeling of dread rippled through Lia as an irresistible impulse pulled her toward the easel. The look on Duncan's face gave her pause. Was it pity she saw?

As Lia moved forward, Franki came out of her trance, blinked at the easel, and said, "Oh, God." She snapped her arm out toward her daughter. "Don't look."

Despite her mother's warning, Lia peered at the painting and gasped.

****

In the Brendani living room a few hours later, the easel stood out like a mouse in a group of hawks. The painting, though it remained hooded, continued to pull at Lia. Her heart danced in her chest. Annie, her cat, jumped up on her lap. She slid her hands into the yellow fur, eliciting deep-throated purrs that eased her anxiety. She barely noticed when the rest of the Clan entered.

Rosemary immediately walked to the canvas. "Yesterday, a little over twenty-four hours ago, the amulet appeared. Since then, it's brought death, a vision that could have been fatal, and a physical attack. We hoped that by sealing its powers, we could prevent a confrontation. It seems, however, that Franki's inner guardian disagrees."

With an apprehensive look toward Lia, she continued. "Franki's gift reveals a warning only, not the future." She flipped back the covering.

Lia tried to ignore the painting and failed. She tightened her lips and inspected the canvas again. Her mother was an excellent artist—the detail, superb and the figures lifelike. She'd captured the beauty of the amulet as it hung in the air—as well as the taut muscles of the two men straining to reach it. One had dark wavy hair, powerful shoulders, cargo pants and a black jersey. The other, slim, with a shaved head and tattoos circling his neck, wore jeans and a T-shirt.

Somber colors dominated the scene except for two bright spots. Though a vivid slash of orange highlighted a fire in the background devouring Lia's sanctuary, it was the foreground that caused Lia's breath to catch. Bright honey-gold strands of hair smeared with red trailed along the grass where her body lay.

Her hands clenched and a knot of fear squeezed her chest. Unable to examine it any longer, she blinked and looked down. Her lap was empty. Annie had fled and Lia's hands now gripped her arms in a self-protective hug.

Her mother's work was representative, but a voice in her head whispered, *You're the only healer. Who can save you?*

Her cousin Alex, the focus of Franki's terrifying prophecy last summer, broke the silence. "It could mean anything."

"Yeah," Nick said. "You've probably got your nose in the grass studying some rare species to add to your herb collection."

Nick's fresh mouth pulled her out of her funk. A corner of her lip turned up as she swung toward him. "Jerk!"

"We have a lot to discuss," Rosemary said. "Obviously, after today's attack and Franki's painting, the amulet's owners know we have it. We must act. This atrocity can't get into the wrong hands. It's too powerful. We think we've found someone to help us. A Templar representative." She spread her hands in a helpless gesture. "Hopefully, he'll be here soon."

"You've heard nothing more about the rep?" Bree asked.

"No. We don't know who he is or when he'll arrive. In the meantime, watch your back." She turned to Lia. "I think you should stay home until we get this settled."

Franki concurred.

"That's ridiculous," Lia said. "I know the enemy, and I can take care of myself. Besides, it's the amulet they want. I'm going to work tonight."

Franki protested, but Nick broke in, "You won't change her mind. She's too stubborn. I can drive her to the hotel and do some work at the Pub." He grinned. "An unexpected visit from the boss never hurts. If Lia has any trouble, I'm five minutes away."

After a brief argument, Lia prevailed. The discussion then turned to the Templar emissary who didn't bother to give Duncan his name. What and how much should they reveal to him? Rosemary suggested they wait until meeting him. "We'll use telepathy as we evaluate him, and Nicky can tell if he's lying." She covered the painting and shook her head. "Okay. That's it for now."

Ready to leave for work, Lia stood. Rosemary stopped her. "These people are desperate. Promise me you'll contact Nick if anything seems off at the hotel."

Lia snapped out, "I'm not exactly helpless."

Rosemary gave her a pitying smile and turned to the painting.

Lia followed Rosemary's gaze and sucked in her breath. "Of course. I'll reach out."

****

On this quiet Sunday evening, an after-dinner calm descended on the hotel. Lia sat behind her desk in her office, printing out flyers about the mansions and art museums popular in Newport. She'd have them out in the lobby in a few minutes.

As she tackled the problems in her inbox, she felt better. The hotel was a world she understood and loved. Complaints? She welcomed the challenge. Her excellent record with unhappy customers made her the darling of management. Her superiors couldn't understand how angry and litigious customers became reasonable, practically docile, after Lia spoke to them. She knew her periodic bonuses reflected the hotel's appreciation.

Lia's success had less to do with her negotiation skills and more to do with her healing powers. During the conversations, she'd make it a point to touch the irate customer or employee and use her special gift. It worked most of the time. Of course, Lia always added incentives: money off the bill, free tickets to Newport events, and a future night's lodging on the house. One of the premier hotels in Newport, The Chandler Regency Arms, took care of its guests.

She was on her way back to her office from the third floor, where a young tyrant had broken the hair dryer during a tantrum. This was what she needed to clear her mind and escape from her family's overbearing concerns. Work helped her put things into perspective. The thought that those men had tracked the amulet so quickly sent a slight quiver along the back of her neck.

Voices in the lobby disturbed the evening silence. In some Newport clubs, the action didn't start until ten o'clock. Likely a few guests headed out for a late night's entertainment. Lia sighed and turned toward the kitchen for a much-deserved cup of coffee.

Another flutter invaded her neck. Something wrong here. A detour to the front desk placed a barrier between herself and whatever she felt. She pretended to check paperwork as she perused the remaining guests. When she met his eyes, a tiny gasp escaped. Aiden O'Connor leaned against one of the decorative pillars with a cup in his hand.

As adrenalin kicked in, her fingers twitched in anticipation. What the hell was he doing here? Like a warm breeze, his power reached out, and hers hummed in response. She shook her head to clear it and slammed down her protective shields. Until she knew better, he was the enemy. She wanted to retaliate for what he'd done to her at Duncan's. The memory of the kiss she'd seen on the tape had her face heating. Damn, the man had her addled.

While she debated whether to call Duncan, Aiden put down his cup and walked in her direction. Unconsciously, she looked behind her for an escape and then straightened her shoulders. She wasn't afraid of this man. She'd meet him stare for stare and stand her ground.

While he sauntered to the desk, she noticed drops of water glistening on his dark curls. His strange blue and green eyes never left hers. They held mischief. The corners of his mouth lifted. Oh Lord, she thought, he's enjoying this.

When he stood in front of her, she had to tip her head back to keep eye contact. He said nothing, and Lia waited him out until she realized where she was. Swallowing her aggravation, she said, "Can I help you?"

Again, he said nothing but looked at her breast where the tag held her name. Heat swelled inside her. He smiled. Devastating, she thought.

"Lia, is it?"

She forced the words from her mouth. "Yes. Did you want something?"

That brought a slow grin to his face as his gaze traveled over her body.

Fighting to maintain control, she stood straight. She didn't have to endure his insolence. About to give him a firm, but polite put-down, he spoke. His tone, low and intimate, heated her insides. "I'd like to speak with you in private if I could."

She leaned toward him, her body craving closer contact, before she remembered Duncan's warning. She knew nothing about this man except that he had extraordinary powers, and he didn't trust her or her Clan. "I'm very busy right now. Could you tell me your concerns here?"

The junior clerk standing beside Lia poked her. "I'll man the desk if you want to talk in your office."

Lia wanted to wring her little neck. It wasn't smart

to be anywhere alone with this guy. Triumph shone in Aiden's expression. "Your office would be perfect, Lia."

The slow, soft pronunciation of her name was like a slap. She couldn't resist playing his game. "Fine, Mr. O'Connor. Please follow me."

Chapter Seven

Lia sensed Aiden's scrutiny of her body as he followed her to her office. Scenarios raced through her head on the short walk. Would he try something? She rubbed the tips of her fingers against the tiny runic symbol on her wrist, a birthmark inherited by all blessed with Templar gifts. The brief act worked to clear her head and help her gather her magic to her inner self. She would not, could not, let him incapacitate her again. Then, she remembered to send a message to Nick. With him as her back-up, she'd be fine.

Seconds away from her office, she inhaled, releasing some of her tension. She paused, about to tell him to go away, when his whisper tickled the back of her neck. "Having second thoughts?"

Pride surged. She wasn't afraid of anyone. She turned the knob, strode to her desk, and sat down. He continued to stand, towering over her. "Please," she said as she gestured for him to take a chair. He gave her a slow smile before complying. His obvious enjoyment angered her. The hell with small talk. "What do you want?"

"I want to know who killed my brother-in-law."

"I'm told the man's name is Benjie Peters."

"I know the puppet's name. I'm looking for the puppeteer."

Lia decided meeting Aiden in her office had been a

poor idea. She had trouble meeting his eyes. "I don't know who that is."

Aiden's features hardened and his posture threatened as he sat forward in his chair. "I think you do."

Furious that she had to lie, she stood. "Look, I don't know who you are, and I don't have the answers you seek. I'd like you to leave now."

"I'm sure you would, but I'm not finished."

As Lia contemplated whipping up a whirlwind, the office door opened. "Hi, Lia, am I interrupting anything?"

Relief softened her tone. "Nick. I believe Mr. O'Connor was just leaving."

Aiden stood up and glared at them. "This isn't over. When I find out the truth about my brother-in-law's death, you'd better have had nothing to do with it."

Nick stood facing Aiden. The air vibrated with thinly controlled power. Lia intervened before their posturing morphed into something more serious. "Would you please show Mr. O'Connor the door?"

Keeping his composure, he complied, but the smile he flashed at Aiden had nothing to do with civility.

Aiden turned to Lia, his face a mask of controlled fury. "I will find out."

After the door slammed, Lia said, "Thank you."

"You're welcome. Are you okay?"

"Yes, but he rattled me. He's a very angry man."

"I noticed." He frowned at Lia and sat down. "Now, tell me why you were alone with him."

She lifted both shoulders in a brief shrug. "I thought I'd be safe on my own turf."

"Wrong. Anything could have happened. And why didn't you call me right away? The Pub is just minutes from here."

"Sorry. He had me confused."

"How did he find out where you worked?"

"No idea. I almost died when I saw him in the lobby." She fiddled with a pencil on the desk. "We should tell him about the amulet and the secret ritual." Before he could object, she said, "I'd rather have him as an ally than an enemy."

"Are you crazy? We know nothing about this guy. How did he get his powers? Is he allied with the amulet's owners? This whole thing could be some kind of fallout between them. Or, he knows we have it and wants it back."

Lia's hair slapped the sides of her face as she gave her head a vigorous shake. "I don't believe that. If he harbored any malice or cunning, I'd have felt it."

Nick's eyes blazed, and he sounded like an angry parent. "I can't believe what I'm hearing. Until we know better, he's the enemy. Don't start imagining a victim, Lia. He's just a slick and creative liar."

Because one of his gifts was an ability to ferret out deceit, she asked, "Did you detect any lies?"

With a smirk, he said, "I'd have to hear him say something first." He then suggested she leave work early. "It's been a tough night."

She was about to disagree, when an image from her mother's painting flashed in her head—men fighting beside her body. One had looked a lot like Aiden. Wishing she didn't have these doubts, she checked her desk: in-box cleared, no other burning problems. "Okay with me. Sounds like a plan."

"I'll go secure things at the Pub, then meet you back here in twenty." On his way out, he spun around. "Be careful. We don't know where, when, or from whom the next attack is coming."

Lia hated the fact that the word *attack* felt almost normal. "Okay. I'll try to stay safe."

She followed him out on her way to alert the staff that she was leaving. With the dispersal of the evening crowd, the soothing quiet of the hotel lobby wrapped around her. Muted gray and maroon carpet cushioned Lia's steps as she moved through the wood-grained lobby ever alert for potential concerns. The seating area to the left of the front desk always calmed her. She enjoyed the scent of fresh flowers in the ornate vases and the large painted screens that insulated guests from the daily hubbub.

An older woman relaxed by the fireplace, engrossed in her tablet. Beyond, seated by the bar, a man flipped through a newspaper. He didn't look right. Lia's nerves pinged as he finished his drink and checked his watch. When his stare met hers, he paused, then tossed the newspaper down and stood. She flinched.

"It's about time," he said.

"What?" Lia choked out.

Behind her, a strident female voice answered, "You're so impatient. It's only been fifteen minutes."

Lia turned, heat bathing her face. *Damn, now I'm paranoid.* Angry with herself, she vowed to ignore Aiden's intrusion and concentrate on her work. She moved off toward the elevators and almost bumped into him. Her temporary sense of security vanished, and she took a step backward.

He smiled at her. "You don't have to be afraid of me."

As if he cared. She knew better. It took her a second

to get her voice working. "From the man who just threatened me."

"I'm sorry about that, but my brother-in-law and best friend, Smitty, is dead, and I think you know something about it."

She felt a stab of guilt and hoped it didn't show on her face. He had good reason for his anger. She understood, but what was he doing here? "So, you tracked me to the hotel?"

"Don't be ridiculous. I didn't know you worked here."

"Why do I find that hard to believe?" Lia tried to sense the vibes coming from him: confusion, pain—but no real threat. When she looked into those strange eyes, though, she couldn't trust her emotions.

The side of his lip curled. "You know how difficult it is to find decent lodging in this town."

"Look, Aiden."

At the sound of his name, his eyebrows rose.

She swallowed before speaking again. "You're wrong about my family. We would never hurt anyone. We try to help when we can."

His tone became a plea. "Then tell me what you know about Smitty's death."

She bit her lip as the urge to explain almost overwhelmed her. "I—" She couldn't finish.

He leaned toward her. "You may not be involved, but what about your boyfriend."

"My boyfriend? Nick?" She stood taller and smoothed down her dress. She didn't think he was involved, but Nick was right. You can't take chances with strong magic. "He isn't my boyfriend."

As she waited for his reaction, his head snapped up,

and he scowled. "And yet, here he is."

Lia checked behind her and saw her protector striding toward them. When she turned back to Aiden, he'd closed down. "Later." He spun around and stabbed the elevator button.

The desire to explain her relationship with Nick was so sharp it surprised her. She'd never worried about the impression she made on any man. She'd always enjoyed her role as the mysterious woman to be pursued. Before Nick could express his exasperation, Lia took his arm. "Don't worry, I'm fine. Let's take the stairs."

The sporadic lighting in the hotel parking garage left eerie dark patches, making her grateful to be with a friend. He was right. She needed to stay focused. They were dealing with serious threats, and she knew nothing about Aiden O'Connor. "Thanks for babysitting. The place has a negative vibe tonight."

"Until we know what we're up against, none of us should be alone."

Although she knew he was right, the thought angered her. Her inner guardian and psychic gifts had always been enough. A brief flashback of the attack on Alex last year sobered her. But this was different. She could take care of herself. Pasting on a smile, she said, "How does Alex like her journalism internship? I think it's so cute that she works for a bridal magazine. She must be getting all kinds of helpful tips for your wedding."

Nick went with her lead. "When the fiend attacked you, she almost chucked the job to join in the hunt. I told her we had it under control without her, then got a frosty message saying if I was trying to protect her, she didn't need it, and I'd better get over my hero fantasies."

Lia laughed. He and Alex would make a perfect couple if he would just stop teasing her. Their powers complemented each other. Nick's gifts centered on offense while Alex's shielding abilities took care of the defense.

As they drove out of the garage, Lia opened the car window to inhale the rain's sweet smell.

Nick's voice intruded, "You're too quiet. What are you thinking?"

"Noth…" then she realized it was Nick, the human lie detector.

"You still thinking about O'Connor."

Nick's gift could be such a pain. "Yes. Your father should show him the amulet."

"I told you—"

"I think he deserves to hear what killed his brother-in-law."

"Unless he already knows."

****

After his meeting with Lia, Aiden reported to his men that one of their quarry worked at the hotel, and another one was located nearby. "I believe they also use telepathy. From the time she saw me until her cohort interrupted us, she had no chance to alert him, yet he showed up minutes after we began talking."

His bunk mate snorted. "If she spies on us, she'll screw up the whole op."

"The truck and the boat all set?"

"Yeah."

"Good. I'll get us another place to stay, but remember, we're in Stuart territory. Be careful. Get those things out of the garage now. If Little Miss Innocent sees them, we're cooked."

An image of Lia marching toward her office, hair curling around her shoulders, and hips swinging with purpose, made him smile. She'd been so sincere when she said her friends wouldn't hurt anyone. Although she believed what she said, he knew she was hiding something. A strong instinct to protect her warred within him. What was wrong with him? Why did he trust her? He'd found before, to his detriment, that a beautiful face could hide treachery.

Slinging his travel bag over one shoulder, he slammed out of the room, then detoured to the lobby where he used his mesmerizing ability to distract the female desk clerk while he discovered Lia's work schedule.

When he checked his extensive office database for Lia Ferguson, he learned her address was only two houses away from Nick Stuart, her backup at the office that evening. Everything about that setup bothered him.

Although he already had information about Duncan Stuart, he also wanted more complete dossiers on the others. By the time he and his crew hit the water tonight, he'd know everything about the mysterious beauty and her pals.

****

Much later, Aiden and his crew arrived at a deserted beach. Rain spattered his face as they launched the rigid-inflatable boat into the Sakonnet River's choppy waters. He squinted at his satellite directional app, trying to steady it against the bouncing craft. They maintained a safe distance from the land to avoid any underwater ledges, but this far away, he found it impossible to compare the dark shoreline with the satellite image of Stuart's property he'd seen earlier. All the outcroppings looked the same.

As a spurt of heavy rain swept in, Aiden pulled the bill of his cap lower and leaned away from the horizontal attack. Jaime spit out an expletive. "How in hell are we supposed to find this place? If the rain doesn't swamp us, the rocks will rip this tinker toy apart."

Aiden hunched over his direction finder. "Stay on this course for another fifteen minutes, and we should be fine." The forecast had promised clearing after midnight. He checked his watch: twelve thirty a.m.

Twenty minutes later, Aiden detected a spit of land that looked familiar. "I think we just passed it."

Jaime turned the boat around and cut the engine. They paddled in. A light drizzle still fell, but visibility had improved.

Once ashore, they stowed the boat under some bushes, and Aiden directed them to a spot behind the abandoned mansion between the Stuart and Brendani estates. From there, they set up monitoring equipment.

"This will work," Aiden said. "I'll check out the Ferguson woman's house." When his cousin raised an eyebrow, Aiden snapped, "She may be up to something."

He ignored Jaime's smile, picked up a handheld scanner, and marched off. Trees lined the property boundary, and he stopped there to turn on his tracker. The rain had let up, but the leaves still scattered their liquid bounty in monotonous drips. He let his senses fan out, looking for trouble. Nothing other than the usual chorus of nighttime creatures. He settled against the trunk, inhaling its piney scent. Minutes later, he noticed a blip moving behind Lia's residence. Someone was outside. He pulled on his night vision goggles and followed the movements.

The figure headed toward the back of the property. He ducked out of sight and prepared to warn Jaime until the dot on the monitor slowed down. Then it began moving in ever-diminishing circles.

"What the…?"

He stood and focused his binoculars. Once again, surprise. Through the lenses, he saw Lia sitting on what looked like a stone bench. He lowered his gaze to the ground around her and made out the small rocks lining a circular path.

Curiouser and curiouser. What was she doing this late inside a stone circle? She laughed. He tore his gaze from her, looking for a second person. No one. He double-checked his scanner. Nothing. Was she crazy?

When she lifted her head, Aiden could see her almond-shaped eyes and remembered their flashing emerald color. Her beautiful golden mane reminded him of a regal lioness. He craved closer contact, much closer.

After about ten minutes, she stood up to leave. Aiden almost choked when she lifted her hands high in the air and stretched. His gaze lingered on her perfect form. She walked the circle as she left, this time widening her path. He didn't understand why she bothered, especially in the middle of the night.

He kept the glasses focused on her shapely figure until she went into the house, then remembered to check the monitor for any other movement. Seeing none, he crouched down and ran in. He was careful as he crossed the path to the center. He noticed writing on the sides of the bench. *What was she doing there? And what had she found so funny?*

****

In the kitchen, Lia received a message from Kitty.

Intruder alert! Someone with strange eye gear has invaded the labyrinth.

Minutes later, Aunt Bree and her mother burst into the room.

Bree slammed her hand on the table. "What were you thinking?"

Then her mother tore into her. "After everything Rosemary said, how could you go outside by yourself?"

Alex joined the party and gave her cousin a look of sympathy.

Lia stood her ground. She'd paid attention to the night sounds. If someone had been there, they would have been far away. "I was careful to check the immediate vicinity. If I met trouble, I could take care of myself."

"Oh, right. Where have I heard that before?" Bree gave Alex a scathing glare. Her cousin's independence during the last trouble had almost cost Alex her life.

Franki rounded on her daughter. "But there was someone out there tonight. He watched you and came into the labyrinth."

Lia's defiance turned into a pretty pout. "Why didn't he come after me?"

Franki cried, "You saw my painting." She held her head and sat down. Bree gave a nervous glance to windows that showed nothing but the black night beyond. She opened her mouth to speak and then laughed. Franki's smile followed.

Lia and Alex shared a look that said, "Have they lost it?"

Bree's grin widened as she spoke to Alex and Lia. "Kitty wants us to know that whoever was out there tonight walked across the labyrinth, *twice*."

The innocuous circular path, like those used for centuries as spiritual sanctuaries, had magical properties. Gremlins lived there, allowing humans to walk along their trails unless they crossed over or disturbed the stones. Alex met Lia's gaze, and they giggled. The gremlins had caused Alex cuts, burns, and what could have been a serious wound when she had stepped over one stone.

"I don't think he'll cause us too much trouble," Lia said. "He'll be too busy trying to stay alive."

****

Aiden couldn't understand what was wrong. He'd tripped on a few rocks as he left the circle, then stepped in a hole and twisted his ankle. By the time he hobbled back to his crew, he'd ripped his pants and scratched his face on thorns he hadn't noticed before.

Jaime jumped up when he saw his cousin. "We've got trouble. They're searching the grounds. I've packed up the equipment. Time to go."

Aiden limped after Jaime. His cousin turned to him. "What happened to you?"

"Damned if I know. I've never been this clumsy."

"Come on. Let's get out of here."

Aiden started forward and fell. His knee hurt and the scrapes on his hands burned. Jaime hauled him up. "Something's wrong with you. Come on, pal, let me help you."

Too late. Aiden's foot slipped on a stone, and he ended up in the water. He spit the salty liquid out of his mouth as his men dragged him into the boat. While they manned the oars, he heard crashing in the bushes. "Hurry, they're coming."

Aiden grunted as his face mashed against the wet

metal. While he tried to stay out of everyone's way, his mind raced. Something serious was wrong with him.

"Shit," Jaime said, "It's too open. They'll see us if we try to go back."

The sounds of pursuers were closing in. Aiden hoped they didn't have a gun. Why had he moved in so close? If his men got hurt because of him, he'd never forgive himself.

"Change direction," Jaime said. "We'll be able to hide if we can get behind that outcropping. We can stay there until they give up."

The rain had started up again. Aiden hoped it would give them some cover. He poked his head above the side. The boat was even with the spit. If they got behind it, they'd be safe.

He saw an arm. Then a head poked out of the bushes as they ducked behind the rocks. He held his breath, listening for an outcry.

****

Duncan and Nick arrived at the Brendani house, breathing hard. Duncan threw himself onto a chair. "He got away. We scoured the property around the Convent House, all locked tight."

Lia grinned. "At least he didn't make a clean getaway."

Duncan exchanged a puzzled look with Nick and said, "You don't seem too upset."

"Oh, we're upset all right," Lia said, "but we can't help laughing."

"Because?"

"Kitty told us the dumb cluck walked right across the labyrinth. Twice!"

Nick looked at Alex, then threw his head back and

laughed. “He’s gotta be in tough shape.”

“Not too bad if he evaded us,” Duncan said.

Nick’s face sobered. “Maybe he had help.”

They all agreed Kitty’s description of the intruder didn’t sound like the man who’d attacked Franki and Lia.

“It sounds more like O’Connor,” Duncan said.

Aiden? In the labyrinth? A pleasurable flash of heat sizzled within Lia as she reacted to the name.

“Yuh?” Nick said. “Good luck to him. It couldn’t happen to a nicer guy.”

Lia remembered Alex’s injuries after crossing the path. “But the gremlins could seriously hurt him. We should let him know.”

“You have his phone number?” Nick said.

Lia ignored the sarcasm. “He’s at the hotel.”

Nick lifted his shoulders. “We don’t owe him anything.”

“I’m sure he’ll be all right,” Bree said with a yawn. “Time for bed.”

“Right,” Duncan said, then pointed at Lia. “And you. No more forays outside by yourself.”

Lia gave him a sour look. “I was fine.” She kissed her mother and headed upstairs, but concern for Aiden nagged at her. She realized how dangerous the next twenty-four hours might be and worried all the way to her bedroom.

As she changed into her nightgown, a foolish idea formed. The more she thought about it, the more it seemed the right thing to do.

Sitting cross-legged in the middle of her bed, she executed her plan. First, she cleared her mind, then she established an image of Aiden. Picturing his blue and green eyes, she sent out a telepathic message. *Aiden.*

You've strayed over the bounds of a magical labyrinth. For the next twenty-four hours, you're in danger. Be careful.

She waited, concentrated, and repeated the message. With a final plea, she said, *Please, Aiden, if you hear this, answer me.*

Chapter Eight

An angry curse reached Aiden's crew over the wind as they floated behind the rocky promontory. Aiden sighed. Safe. They'd escaped in time.

On the boat trip back to the beach where they'd stowed the truck, Jaime kept pestering Aiden. "You need to see a doctor."

Aiden growled in reply. "Not happening."

"Come on, we're worried about you," Jaime said. "At least have your ankle looked at."

Aiden glared at his cousin, stepped out of the boat, and fell flat on his face.

Hands grabbed him, but he shook them off. "What the fuck?"

Aiden had already decided something was wrong with him. A brain tumor, aneurysm, stroke? *Shit, he was only twenty-nine years old. He couldn't be dying.*

Jaime held on to his cousin's arm as Aiden stumbled up the beach. Jaime's face telegraphed his fear, and Aiden saw the same alarm reflected in the others. "I'm bringing you to a doctor if I have to hog-tie you first."

They got the boat in the truck, vetoed Aiden's insistence that he could drive, and headed back to their new digs. "I can't understand how they found out about us," Jaime said. "They came out knowing that someone had infiltrated the property. Did you see anyone, Aiden?"

Aiden managed a negative grunt.

"Damn," Jaime said. "Maybe they had electronic surveillance, but I didn't see any evidence of it."

Aiden knew he'd tripped the alarm. Before he could explain, she entered his mind. "Stop!"

Jaime slammed on the brakes, snapping everyone up against their seat belts. "What is it? What's the matter?"

Aiden opened his mouth, stunned. Then he grinned. "Quiet."

"What the hell are you smiling about? What's going on?"

"I'm fine. Nothing wrong with my brain. Some damn gremlins in a labyrinth cursed me."

He saw the looks his crew exchanged. "No, I'm not crazy." He laughed, then puffed up his chest and looked at his men. "And tough, little Lia is worried about me."

****

Early Monday afternoon, Lia and Alex sat in the Brendani kitchen discussing Aiden O'Connor's surprise appearance at Lia's hotel and last night's intruders. With a worried sigh, Lia said, "You think Aiden is part of this?"

"I hope not. We can't take any chances, though. No matter how hot he is." Alex tilted her head and grinned. "And I've got to admit he is swoon-worthy."

Lia sighed. "He certainly is."

"Cute or not, the stakes are too high." Alex picked at the grapes in front of her. "It is kind of creepy, though, how he followed you to the hotel."

Lia nodded. "He made me so nervous. I was grateful when Nick showed up."

The kitchen door swung open, and Nick walked in.

"Speak of the devil," Lia said. "My hero."

Nick affected a swagger. "That's right, ladies. Your

champion has returned." He ate one of Alex's grapes, leaned over, and pulled her toward him for a very thorough kiss.

Lia watched Alex's green eyes dance as she tried to catch her breath. "What was that for?"

The cleft in his chin deepened. "I missed you."

"Get a room." Lia laughed, but a hollow longing cut into her as she left the kitchen.

Before she'd gone far, a message from Rosemary stopped her. The Clan leader wanted a meeting there in ten minutes. Nick and Alex joined Lia in the hall.

"Something's up," Nick said. "Must be about the amulet."

Franki, Bree, and Duncan were already in the spacious living room when Lia arrived. Nick and her cousin came in a few minutes later, a bright pink flush on Alex's face.

An air of tension charged the room. Duncan stood, gripping the back of a chair, as he spoke. "The Templar representative has arrived. We only have a few minutes before Rosemary brings him over. I want you to use your talents to evaluate him, especially you, Nick. Share observations through telepathy, being specific to our Clan. We'll hope he can't hear us."

Lia wished they had more time. "Is this a good idea? We have a stolen Templar artifact, and we don't know who took it."

Although no one loved the solution, all agreed the immediate danger necessitated action. The sound of voices in the hall ended the discussion. Rosemary and their guest had arrived. An aura of strength surrounded the gray-haired man Rosemary introduced as Josiah Warren. His ice-blue eyes evaluated each person.

Lia estimated his age at around sixty, but his body belied the streaks of time etched on his face, and though his words were polite, his attitude commanded respect. Dressed in a blazer, slacks, and pricey loafers, he exuded confidence. His only adornment, an expensive watch on his wrist and a large ruby ring with a gold fleur-de-lis, a symbol favored by the Templars.

"Mr. Warren is here to help us with the amulet," Rosemary said. "Please cooperate with him." She produced a small box, uncovered it, and showed it to Josiah.

His focus swerved from the Clan to the deadly talisman, but when he reached for it, Rosemary pulled her hand back. "We believe this object poses a serious danger to anyone who touches it."

"You called me. Do you want my help?"

Rosemary sounded confused. "Yes?"

"Then I need to hold it."

Lia spoke up. "This piece of metal has a siren's call to anyone who touches it."

Josiah turned to her. "What do you know about it?"

She blinked and saw Rosemary shake her head. "I can't get into that right now, but please understand it's dangerous."

Although nothing on his face changed, she could feel his underlying power intensify. Meeting his stare was difficult.

In a voice that brooked no opposition, he said, "You used a phone number categorized as secret and urgent to call me here. What did you expect me to do?"

Unnerved, Lia blurted out, "How do we know we can trust you?"

Rosemary opened her mouth, but Josiah silenced her

with a wave of his hand. "As a Templar agent, I'm sent out to diffuse critical situations. My job is to protect our heritage. You called me." He turned to include everyone. "This amulet is old and dangerous." A wintry smile lifted his lips. "As am I."

Lia didn't think his words were a threat, but she felt their force. Nick entered her head. *What he says is the truth.*

Rosemary cleared her throat. "I'm sorry for the distrust Mr. Warren, but as you said the amulet is not safe." With that, she handed it to him. "Could you decipher the markings for us?"

Lia held her breath, waiting for treachery, but he focused on the symbols.

His face seemed resigned when he finished. "As you may have guessed, there's a powerful demon trapped within. I need to do some research, but I believe it may be one of those used to safeguard the Templar treasures. A few of the summoned ones resisted the spells to return them to their duties and had to be imprisoned. Have you tested its power?"

A chorus of "no's" followed before Lia spoke up. "Don't use it. There's a curse."

Josiah glared at Lia. "The complete story, please."

Lia's gaze flew to Rosemary.

"Young lady, I sense the emanations from the artifact and the power of your Clan," he said. "Nothing you say will shock me. The spiritual, supernatural, or magical are part of my life. Now, how did you acquire this?"

"Fine." He made her feel like a recalcitrant teenager. She began with the wedding and the attack at the hotel, then recounted her participation in the vision and the ritual she'd witnessed.

When Alex confirmed the story, Josiah asked to speak to the thief.

"I'm afraid he's dead," Duncan said.

"From his wounds?"

Duncan shook his head.

Josiah frowned and stared at the amulet. He held his hands over the piece of metal and whispered the words of a spell. A flash of black sparked back at him. He growled, "Dark magic."

The moment Lia heard Josiah chant, she froze, remembering others who spit magic incantations—the man in the vision as well as the dream walker who'd attacked them last year. She struggled to shake off her fear. Mr. Warren was different. Nick had vouched for his honesty.

"Can you bind it?" Rosemary asked.

He shook his head. "Any attempt to interfere with it will trigger retaliation." He looked from Lia to Alex. "Did you hear the spell they used?"

Alex answered. "My mother called it a rite of protection."

Josiah looked around the room. "And your mother is…?"

"Oh no," Alex said, ducking her head as her face turned pink. "My mother is a spirit."

As if ghosts were as common as blue-eyed blondes, he said, "I'd appreciate anything she could give me about the ceremony."

He listened to the information Alex relayed from her mother and said he'd get back to them later. Before leaving, however, he turned toward the easel in the corner. "I'd like to see that painting."

Lia's voice sharpened in a wave of self-protection. "That's not part of this."

He turned a knowing smile on her. "I think it is." Then he stepped up to the easel and drew back the cover. He took his time inspecting Franki's work. "These men. Do you recognize them? Anyone from your vision?"

Lia fought for calm as she answered. "They all wore masks."

Josiah turned to Franki. "This is your work?"

"Yes."

"I sense your essence in the creation. This must be your daughter," he said as he gestured toward Lia.

Franki nodded.

"Tell me, have you created paintings like this before?"

"This is the second time I've painted danger for the Clan."

"How closely did the first match the results?"

Franki paused. "It zeroed in on the heart of the danger."

"In other words, a prophecy to be unraveled?"

Franki's bracelets jangled as she touched her neck. "I guess you could say that."

Josiah leaned toward the canvas, holding his open hands inches away. Lia's stomach tightened as she watched him. She hadn't realized she was holding her breath until he spoke.

"Though this portrays a struggle for the amulet, it also foresees a rebirth." He pointed to the fire. "The small animal racing from the inferno?"

Lia hadn't noticed that part of the portrait before he pointed it out.

"That creature represents the release of a malicious

spirit."

When he turned to Lia and touched her shoulder, his ring delivered a startling spark of energy. His voice softened as he pointed to the painting. "The image is deceptive. We cling to the physical, but here is evidence of a spiritual transformation." Then he turned and left.

Lia's shoulders slumped. Had he just pronounced her death?

****

Later, in his hotel room, Josiah reviewed what he'd learned from the Stuarts. The Templar artifact, a demon's prison, had been stolen then transformed into an offensive weapon warded with deadly protections.

The sharp recoil of Josiah's spell from the amulet and the stench of sulfur immediately coloring the air indicated the interference of a high-level witch or warlock. Although Josiah had dealt with members of the occult before, he'd need more help. The Stuart group had the power, but like all the Watcher Clans, they'd become soft. Too much time away from danger. He'd have to work with them.

He opened his computer and consulted the special Templar search engines. A photographic memory proved useful as he entered all the artifact's runic symbols into the site. One reference led to another until he had enough information to transfer to the librarian at headquarters. He clicked the *Send* button and smiled. Someone was always on call. He expected to have the whole story soon.

In the meantime, he wondered at the spark of magic he'd experienced when he touched the Watcher's shoulder. Twisting his hand in the light, he contemplated the flash of red and gold on his finger. Lia Ferguson was only the second person in two decades to trigger the Seeker bloodstone.

Then, there was her mother's painting. It troubled him. The daughter's survival was portrayed as uncertain, yet the ring claimed her, and he sensed her importance in the struggle for the dominance he could feel building.

A Templar soldier for many years, Josiah had honed the few skills he had to a lethal edge. With his knowledge and the Clan's forces, they would prevail.

Last night, before meeting the families, he'd checked out each member on the Internet. When he discovered Lia worked at a hotel in downtown Newport, he'd booked a room there, then sent more thorough background requests to a computer geek he used. In the meantime, he planned to slip into Lia's office and do a little snooping before she arrived for her shift.

The stone had selected her, and Josiah needed to know why.

****

The next afternoon, after Nick dropped her off at the hotel for her four o'clock shift, Lia had trouble concentrating on her work. She tried to make sense of the Templar agent's revelations. A demon? Would the amulet be safer in his hands?

When a lovely young couple asked for directions to Bannister's Wharf, Lia reached for a map of downtown Newport. At the same time, Aiden's voice spoke to her mind. *So, you're worried about me.*

Shocked, she knocked over a pile of brochures.

She tried to ignore him as she straightened out the mess, but he kept at it. *I'd feel a lot better if you'd tell me what you know.*

She wanted to kick herself for opening this conduit.

If anyone in the Clan found out, she'd be in trouble. While she tried to drown out Aiden's voice, she handed her customers the map and gave them brief directions.

Come on, Lia, I need to know what happened. I answered you.

He went on and on for the better part of an hour. Finally, she'd had enough. *Stop. Get out of my mind. I felt sorry for you and wanted to let you know about the gremlins. I did you a favor. Now, do me one and leave me alone.*

She could feel his sigh as he said, *Tell me one thing. How did you know we were there?*

Her psychic voice portrayed her exasperation. *What were you doing on our property in the middle of the night?*

I'll leave you alone if you tell me what happened to my brother-in-law.

Lia didn't answer. Instead, she rearranged her shields to suppress him. Unfortunately, when she did that, she also cut off her family's voices as well. She wouldn't be able to hear her own Clan now.

Around six o'clock, Lia re-opened her communication channels. She knew she hadn't missed anyone because her family would have come here in person if they couldn't contact her through telepathy.

Everything remained quiet. No problems at the hotel, and no more aggravating interruptions from Aiden. She'd noticed that he'd checked out last night.

After work, she contacted Nick to let him know she was leaving. She ignored his demand to wait for him and took the elevator to the parking garage. Since it was a beautiful night, she planned to wait for him outside. The minute she stepped into the garage, though, she almost bumped into Aiden. "What…?"

Stepping back, she spun around looking for someone to help her, then glared at the aggravating man. With a smirk on his face, he tried for a casual lean against the post and missed. He was barely able to catch himself in time.

Lia burst out laughing. "I told you they were dangerous."

Dropping his gaze, he said, "I know. I'm not alone. My cousin, Jaime, is here." He looked back over his shoulder and Lia saw the man who stood there look down at his feet and shake his head.

"Well," she said, "at least you're smart."

Aiden looked chagrined. "I thought I had a brain tumor. Thanks for contacting me."

Lia's right eyebrow rose, but she kept her voice even. "You're welcome."

When she started to walk away, Aiden hurried to catch up, lost his balance, and went hurtling toward a silver SUV. Lia reached out to help but missed.

He would have been okay if his wrist hadn't connected with the broken side mirror. "Ow!"

Jaime came running over and helped him up. "Hell, Aiden, you're cut."

Aiden wrenched his wrist away and covered it with his hand, but blood spurted out through his fingers.

Lia reached over. "I think you nicked a vein. Let me see."

"I'm okay."

"Fine. Go ahead and bleed all over yourself." She made as if to leave.

Jaime had ripped his shirt to make a tourniquet.

Lia stopped and said to Jaime, "I can fix it."

Jaime turned a stormy glare on his cousin. "Give her your wrist."

Darkened eyes and compressed lips made Aiden look like a stubborn little boy, but he shoved out his right hand to Lia.

She gave him her best pissed-off face and took hold of his wrist. As she closed her hands around his wound, her eyes strayed to the muscles in his arm. *Ooh, very nice.*

A few minutes later, she saw that the bleeding had all but stopped. She kept his wrist in her hands for a little longer than necessary, enjoying the sensation.

When she gave him back his hand, and he didn't say anything or show any surprise, she said, "No thank you?"

Aiden's face showed interest but not amazement. He knew what she was.

Jaime, on the other hand, was excited. "She's just like…" He never finished the sentence because Aiden whipped his hand across his neck signaling Jaime to stop.

Lia tilted her head waiting for more, but Jamie kept quiet. "Just like who?"

Aiden smiled. "My aunt. She's very good with medicinal herbs."

Lia knew her features reflected the irony in her voice. "Oh really? She can heal a wound in minutes with a poultice?"

Aiden shrugged.

Lia backed away, looked at Jaime, and said, "Watch him. They won't stop trying until the twenty-four hours are up."

With a derisive backward glance at Aiden, she strode away trying to conceal the strain of healing. Her insides melted as his voice purred in her head, *Thank you, Lia.*

****

Lia kept her meeting with Aiden to herself. She didn't want Nick to launch into a tirade. But when she saw Alex in the kitchen later, she couldn't resist. "Hey, come out back with me for a minute."

Alex followed her out onto the patio. With a little laugh she said, "What's up? What is it that you don't want anyone else to hear?"

Lia tried to suppress a smile. "Oh, nothing."

"Come on, Cuz. You're bursting with it."

Lia allowed a tiny grin. "I saw him tonight. He was at the hotel."

She didn't have to tell Alex to whom she referred. "God, Lia, you're like a needy schoolgirl, dying for the sound of his name. What was he doing there?"

Lia looked down at her hands and swung her shoulders back and forth. "He came to thank me."

"For what?"

Lia squirmed with excitement. "For saving him from the gremlins."

Alex paused for a second, probably remembering the pain those gremlins had caused her, and then laughed. "I figured that's who it was. They must have lit into him."

"They certainly did, and I knew it was Aiden. He must have seen me sitting there." She gave a toss of her long hair and managed a sexy smile. "He couldn't resist."

"I don't understand. How could you save him? You can't stop those little buggers."

"I sent him a message."

Alex's face showed her confusion.

"I sent it by telepathy!"

"What?"

"Apparently, that's one of his powers because he heard me." She touched Alex's arm. "The poor guy was horrified. He thought he had a brain tumor."

"No wonder he wanted to thank you."

"He's so cute. He tried to lean against one of the posts in the garage and slid right off. Then he cut himself on a piece of glass and I had to heal him."

Lia smiled and gazed off into the distance, but Alex was frowning. "So now he knows about your powers. You better hope he isn't the enemy."

"No way. He's too cute to be a bad guy."

Alex shook her head. "Not good. Your libido is going to get you into trouble."

****

Kane was disgusted with himself. Yesterday's attack on the two women with the amulet was a grave mistake. He'd underestimated them and had to use a cloaking spell to get away. Now they'd be on guard. The next strike had to work. He coughed out a jeering laugh. He had a plan.

His temporary Narragansett rental, though small, had served its purpose. He gathered his crew there in front of the altar: Gianna, now out of the hospital, Jago, and Tapper. They needed an edge, so he pulled the last magic trinket from his safe. Not as powerful as the amulet, but it had a little oomph. With the help of Gianna, he repeated the spell he'd used on the amulet to add extra enchantment.

A look at the clock told him he didn't have much time if he wanted the element of surprise.

On the way to Newport, he gave a brief outline of

his plan. "We'll know more when we get there." In the silence that followed, Kane felt the rhythmic beating on the back of his seat. "Stop it, Tapper." The man couldn't keep his hands or feet quiet for a minute.

He wished he could leave the hyper toad with the car, but Gianna, whose wounds precluded her help on this job, would have to do the driving. When she dropped them off at the old mansion's overgrown lane, he told her to wait up the street for his call.

Tonight, the cool air held no moisture. He sent Jago and Tapper ahead to the ruin he'd discovered behind the Stuart's. "I'll do a quick check on the house."

The rain had hidden him the other night while allowing him to smell his prize. Tonight, he took more care as he scouted the area. Once he confirmed the amulet's presence, he circled back to his men.

"Okay," he said. "This dump is located between the two families who have the amulet. I need to get into the Stuart house, so I want you to create a diversion. I'll grab the amulet, and we'll get out of here."

"Can't you use your magic?" Tapper said.

Kane considered inflicting an itching spell on the little toad. Instead, he settled for a hard pinch. When he spoke, it was to Jago. "The people in these houses possess their own powers. I don't know what they are, and I don't want to find out. If you do as I tell you, we'll be out of here before they know what happened."

Kane led Jago along the riverbank to the far side of the Brendani home. He stopped in the trees and crouched down to explain the plan. Handing Jago the charmed coin, Kane jogged back to Tapper. It was a little before one a.m. when he arrived. Looking at his squat partner, he wished he had anyone else with him. With a snarl,

Kane snatched the two branches from the drumming fool. “I want silence.”

Chapter Nine

Aiden slammed around the motel room, throwing electronic equipment into the bag. When one of his men suggested they ought to give up on the surveillance for now, he snapped, "Do I have to remind you that someone killed Smitty? The guy who bailed us all out when we got busted for *drunk and disorderly* at his own wedding. Or, that someone used magic to kill him?"

"Hey, be careful of that equipment. It doesn't come cheap," Jaime said.

His cousin turned on him. "Do you agree we should stop?"

"Hell. We don't even know what we're looking for, never mind who."

"So, we give up then. Is that it?"

"For crying out loud, they're on to us. You don't think that little gal didn't run straight to Stuart to tell him we were there last night?"

"All the better if she did. He won't expect us to be back. Even if he does, I will find out what happened to Smitty." He stopped filling the bag and looked around at his men. "I'm going back there tonight. Who's coming with me?"

The one who'd questioned their return stared at him, then looked away. Jaime shook his head.

"Well?"

With an exasperated expression, the first speaker

said, “I’ll put stuff in the truck.” The non-magical team member helped him.

Jaime didn’t wait for an invitation. “You know I’m always with you.” Under his breath, he mumbled, “Even if it is a stupid idea.”

Aiden reached back to grab something from the bed and smashed his hand against the metal base of the lamp, which went sailing toward the equipment on the floor.

Jaime leaped over and retrieved the monitor. “It makes it a lot harder when we have to babysit for you.”

Aiden managed a crooked up-tilt to his lips. “Yeah, remind me to thank you for that.”

A beautiful starlit night guided them to the beach they’d used the previous evening. Jaime and the others hauled the boat and supplies to the water, leaving their leader in the truck for his safety.

In the last twenty-three hours, Aiden had developed a healthy respect for labyrinthian lore and gremlins.

Unable to wait any longer, he left the truck and followed his men. Muffled curses disturbed the quiet as he tripped and slipped his way down the beach. He checked his watch. Fifteen more minutes until one o’clock, the witching hour. He swore he’d never take his good health for granted again.

Without the wind and rain, the shoreline flew by. Jaime’s voice was the only sound above the engine as he turned to Aiden. “Hold on, will ya? I don’t want you to slip overboard and drown. It’s not twenty-four hours yet.”

When they reached their destination, it was five minutes past the curse deadline. Aiden should be okay now. He took a deep breath and jumped from the boat. When he managed to stay on his feet, he sent a thumb’s up sign to his men and a celestial thank you to the gods.

He took one end of the boat, Jaime the other and they hauled it to the covering they'd used the night before. Keeping his voice low, Jaime gave him a friendly shoulder punch. "Good as new."

Knowing Stuart might be on alert, Aiden signaled stealth as they spread out to make their way back to the spot behind the deserted mansion. As Trent set up the gear, Aiden used the hand-held monitor to detect any movement. He found nothing significant at either house.

As they'd done the night before, Jaime observed the Stuart home while Aiden checked out Lia's. He took care to stay far away from the neat lawns and that devil's spiral. He'd learned a hard lesson. Their detection system must be part of the labyrinth.

Lia's late-night foray told him she enjoyed the wee hours of the morning. No wonder her work schedule began in the middle of the day. The urge to move closer tugged at him. Lia Ferguson was too much of a distraction. Aiden had to force himself to put her out of his mind and concentrate on the job.

No sooner did he sit down than he received a message in his earbud from Jaime. "We've got movement near the back of the Brendani house."

He took out his binoculars. Lia. She stood for a minute before taking a path toward an outbuilding on the other side of the house. A cat streaked out in front of her.

Jaime's voice sounded again. "We've got new movement. Far-left perimeter, one person."

"Copy." He put his binoculars up to his eyes and scanned the area. Jaime had given coordinates which put the new person near the building where the cat had been heading.

Going into a crouch, Aiden closed in. He had to skirt the gazebo and follow the river to the line of trees extending behind the structure.

Jaime's voice came again. "The first person is moving in your direction."

Checking his monitor, Aiden saw Lia striding toward the building. He slunk back into the bushes, wondering if the person in the woods was a guard. His earbud came to life again. "The one in the trees just moved inside."

Aiden made a snap judgement and entered Lia's mind. *A man just entered your building. Is he one of yours?*

The response was immediate. *No.*

****

Lia, always the last one to retire, stood by the balcony door in her bedroom. Too keyed up from the day's events to sleep, she decided to ignore the orders to stay inside. The problem last night had been Aiden, and she knew he wasn't a threat. She needed fresh air to restore her sanity, and a little time with her plants.

Standing on the back patio, she inhaled the familiar salty-sweet scents. A slight breeze tickled her neck, and she spun her hand to freshen it. She took a deep breath. This was what she needed. Her connection to nature. She hugged herself before turning toward the greenhouse. A familiar meow caught her attention. "Hi, Annie." The cat blinked up at her before speeding ahead. Annie often accompanied her mistress at night.

Scraping sounds in the bushes caught her attention, and she paused, hoping to see a rabbit. They loved playing in the dark. This time of night was her favorite, with the quiet only disturbed by small animals scurrying around and night birds claiming their territory.

She stopped to savor the atmosphere when Aiden's warning burst into her head. For a second the sound of his voice made her smile. He was back. Then she realized what he said. Someone was in her hideaway. As she looked across the lawn, her nose twitched. Smoke. Coming from her refuge. *Oh no!* Light shone where none should be. For a second, she froze, before shouting out a psychic call for help. *Fire. In the nursery.* But she knew they'd never get there in time.

She raced toward her haven. As she neared the building, she heard a plaintive mewing. Annie! She saw her sweet little face inside the window, clawing to get out. She had to stop the fire. Screaming the cat's name, she swung her hands up in a frantic motion, demanding rain. As the drops turned to a downpour, a man leaped out at her.

****

Aiden watched in horror as Lia sped toward the smoking hut and the intruder.

He screamed in her mind to stop, but she only paused, raised her arms, and flexed her hands. A cloud appeared and rain poured down on the fire. He experienced a moment of surprise and pride until a figure charged at her with something in his hand. Aiden's heart pounded as he watched him raise his arm. With no time to use his powers, Aiden yelled a warning at Lia, but he was too late.

Lia turned toward him as the rock crashed down on her head. Her eyes widened and then closed as she crumpled to the ground. He called her name, but she didn't move. Golden hair spread around her on the grass, but close to her skull, a bloom of scarlet bubbled up.

By this time, others had arrived. When he saw women tending Lia, he changed direction. A fiery rage exploded in his chest as he chased Lia's attacker. If the bastard thought to find safety in the trees, he was wrong. Aiden hadn't been here when Smitty needed help. He'd damn well avenge Lia.

The surprise in the scum's eyes as he took him down brought Aiden some satisfaction. His mind filled with the image of her, her radiant eyes closed and her unmoving body. He let out a roar as he slammed his fist into his opponent.

So intent on crushing the man, he didn't see the blade until it was almost too late. He ducked, but the son of a bitch caught him in the ear.

Liquid tickled down the side of his neck as he smashed the man's head against the ground and tossed the knife away. When a solid blow to the guy's nose produced a spurt of blood, he grimaced in satisfaction. The wily snake was tough though and retaliated with a knee to Aiden's gut.

As he doubled in pain, his prey tried to scramble away. Aiden could have brought him down with a flick of his wrist, but he wanted his hands on this low life. He grasped the creep's leg, climbed over him, and held him by the throat. His fingers had a mind of their own as he began to squeeze. He might have killed him if people hadn't intervened.

Strong arms hauled Aiden away as Nick pinned his opponent. Aiden struggled in the grip before he recognized Duncan, who said, "You've been spying on us."

Jerking out of Duncan's grasp, Aiden let his own anger rip. "You're lucky someone was."

When he saw Nick's look of triumph as he subdued the attacker, he bristled. "I softened him up for you."

His anger vanished, however, when his gaze moved to Lia. He ignored everyone else and drifted to where she lay. Dropping to one knee, he just missed the yellow cat who circled nearby. As he watched the two women bathe Lia's beautiful face in their tears, he understood the severity of her injury.

One woman held Lia's head in her lap and rocked back and forth as she keened. Blood still flowed from her head. The other ripped her shirt for a bandage and held it against the wound as she sobbed. "Oh, dear God. Lia's the healer. There's no one else to take care of her."

Aiden heard her words, and something clicked in his mind. Going still, he sent an urgent message to his father. *Wake up. I need Aunt Maeve. Now! Get the helicopter and bring her to these coordinates in Newport. It's a matter of life and death.*

****

Kane watched in satisfaction as his plan to retrieve the amulet progressed. Curls of smoke drifted above the trees to his left. Panicked voices followed. Seconds later, people burst out of the back of the Stuart house, running off in the direction of the fire. Time to get his property.

Ordering Tapper to keep watch, Kane jogged to the back door. The knob turned beneath his touch. In their rush, the fools forgot to lock it. With a thank-you to the goddess, he slipped in. He followed the acrid trail of dark magic to an office with bookshelves and a large desk. He ripped open the drawers, scattering the contents, but found nothing. The amulet was no longer in this room. His keen sense of smell led him to a nightstand in a second-floor bedroom. Nothing.

Again, the amulet had been here, but no more. The bastard had taken it with him. In his fury, he smashed his hand onto the small table, knocking the lamp to the floor. At the sound of breaking glass, he twisted his lips in a sneer. Everything on top of the bureau went next.

Then Tapper appeared at the doorway. "We need to get out of here. Someone's coming."

Knowing he'd failed, again, he screamed at the fool, "Go. Out the front."

Choked with fury and no time to use a destroying spell, he decided to leave a little calling card on his way out. As his knife sliced across a painting of a beautiful wild garden, he unleashed a guttural cry. "Let him know I was here."

After racing down the hall and out the door, he leaped into the waiting car. "Where's Jago?"

Gianna lifted her shoulder. "Don't know. Never saw him."

"Then get out of here."

"But…"

"Forget him," he yelled. "Drive."

Kane originally planned to secure the amulet, dump the rental car, then sever all relations with the men he'd recruited. That all changed now. He needed help. Tapper might not be an ace in the deck, but he was loyal. Movement from the back seat distracted him. He slammed his fist on the center console and glared at Tapper. "Stop bouncing your foot."

Blessed silence followed his outburst, and he was able to think. If Jago had been captured, the Narragansett location was blown. He checked his phone for twenty-four-hour motels. Once he cleaned out the rental, he wanted to hole up somewhere and think.

****

Aiden glared at the bloodied face of the assailant. It was all he could do to keep from killing him.

More important things took precedence. The helicopter pilot would need directions. Aiden instructed Jaime to set up lighting and lead him in. Then as the smell of smoke and charred wood clogged his nose, he gazed at Lia. She was breathing but her pulse was erratic. She'd taken a terrible blow to the head. Her beautiful hair lay bloody and matted across her mother's lap. When Bree reached out to his mind, he gaped at her, astounded at the second intrusion in as many days.

He looked up at Bree, sending back the message, *How are you able to contact me?*

I don't know. But I can feel your pain for my niece. Thank you for caring.

Although Aiden hadn't realized it, he'd been caressing Lia's hand.

Nick gave a savage kick to a nearby rock. "Dad just made contact from the house. The bastards got in, but the leader got away.

"The amulet?" Bree asked.

"Safe. Dad has it."

Ready to snap, Aiden let go of Lia's hand then leaped up to stand nose to nose with Nick. "What are you talking about? What amulet, and who the fuck are *they*?"

Nick didn't back down. "Who are you with your magical powers?"

Bree quickly intervened. "Nicky, he isn't the enemy but an ally. He tried to save Lia."

Nick visibly deflated with Bree's words. He looked down and scuffed his foot along the grass. Finally, he raised his head to meet Aiden's gaze. "I guess you have a right to know. The kid who killed your brother-in-law stole some artifact that gave him unbelievable power. We took it for safekeeping. The people who were here tonight want it back."

"Oh. So, you decided to keep this deadly artifact a secret?" Aiden blasted. "Now it belongs to you?"

Nick squared his shoulders. "The amulet is too dangerous to fall into the wrong hands. We've been trying to get it to the right people. We even tried to get someone to bind its powers, but the thing has a protective spell around it."

"Nice story."

Scowling, Nick said, "It isn't a story. This fire must have been a diversion to steal the amulet. Thankfully, it didn't work."

Bunching his arm muscles, Aiden jabbed a finger at Nick. "You didn't think I deserved to know what or who killed my brother-in-law?"

Bree whispered, "Calm down, Nicky."

He gave her an exasperated stare then turned to Aiden, both hands up in surrender. "We knew your group had power and you were at the murder scene. We didn't know who to trust, so we trusted no one."

Duncan appeared out of the dark. He knelt beside Franki, who still caressed Lia's forehead. "The ambulance will be here soon."

Aiden spoke up. "I've got a helicopter on the way with my Aunt Maeve."

Confused looks swiveled in his direction. He lifted his shoulders and forced out the admission. "She's a healer."

****

Having already directed his men to set out lights on

the lawn as a landing guide, he watched the helicopter touch down a few minutes before the ambulance. Aiden recognized his aunt's red ponytail as she jumped down and ran over to Lia. "Thanks, Maeve." He indicated Franki. "This is Lia's mother."

His aunt knelt, nodded to Franki, and began touching Lia. "I'm Maeve Kennedy. I'll take good care of your daughter." Then she cupped Lia's head in her hands.

Franki kept Lia's hand in hers, never taking her gaze off her daughter's face.

Aiden listened with admiration as his cousin soothed Lia's mother. Though Maeve had no children of her own, she often found it easy to take a parental role. He gazed down at Lia and knew they were lucky. Maeve was a powerful healer whose touch had saved many lives.

The sight of Lia's beautiful face still and white made him ill. Her mother had wiped away the drops of blood from her skin, but her vibrant, sunny hair stuck together in clumps as if bathed in a rich wine. He prayed her injury wasn't as bad as it looked, but Maeve was frowning. Finally, she said, "She has severe trauma to her brain. It will take time."

He tried to ask how serious, but she waved him away. The medics had arrived.

Maeve touched Franki's hand. "She's stable now." Then she leaned toward the distraught woman, her voice seeming to beg forgiveness. "I hate to ask you this, but please let me pass as her mother. I need to stay with her."

Aiden saw pain flash across Franki's face, but she agreed. "I only want what's best for my baby. I'll let the others know."

He fought the urge to leap into the ambulance with

them. As the vehicle drove away, he stretched his hands and rolled his neck. For the first time in his adult life, he had no plan.

****

Aiden insisted on accompanying the Stuarts to the hospital. Ignoring Nick's objections, Lia's aunt Bree invited Aiden to hop into the back seat with her. A young woman named Alex sat in front with Nick.

During the ride, Aiden tried to wrap his mind around the latest information. What a cruel twist of fate to have magic, something his clan had been given to protect innocents, be the cause of his best friend's murder.

No one spoke on the ride, giving Aiden the opportunity to watch the two in the front seat. Nick and Alex couldn't keep their eyes off each other. Lia had been telling the truth. Nick wasn't her boyfriend. The realization hit him like a burst of sunlight. Now, if only Maeve could heal her.

At last Bree spoke. "Why couldn't Lia wait for help? That damn prophecy came true."

"Oh, my God, you're right," Alex said. "She ran right toward the burning shed."

"Lia will be fine." Bree sounded like she was trying to convince herself. "Remember what Josiah said."

Aiden tried to follow the conversation and failed. "What prophecy? Who's Josiah?"

Alex explained about the painting and the agent's words.

"You know this guy, Josiah?"

Nick whipped his head around. "He's someone we can trust."

Aiden wanted to know more, but not now. Later. He'd also find out what else they'd been hiding.

Concerned about Lia, he contacted his aunt, *What are her chances?*

I don't know all the answers. I'll stay with her as long as she needs me.

Her words only enhanced his pain. *Please. She has to come out of this.*

A soft sigh. *I'm doing everything I can, sweetheart.*

****

The atmosphere in the waiting room outside the Intensive Care Unit pulsed with psychic frustration. Aiden knew these people had always relied on Lia to heal their wounded. Now, her life lay in a stranger's hands. All he could do was reassure them that Maeve was a skilled healer.

He couldn't sit still. As he paced the tiled floor, he overheard Nick and Duncan discussing plans to find the persons responsible for hurting Lia. He left them to it. His concentration fluctuated between worry for Lia and disgust with himself for not being able to protect her. If only he'd stopped her from moving forward to the fire. If he hadn't been so caught up in watching her, he'd have intercepted that devil before he hit her. Self-loathing washed over him. He'd taken too long. When he couldn't stand it any longer, he contacted his aunt to see how Lia was doing.

If you want her to survive, don't disturb me again!

Maeve's angry retort didn't faze him. All he cared about was Lia. When Duncan came up to Aiden to say that he and Nick were going home, Aiden felt none of his usual emotions, no territorial aggression, no fear of losing control. He felt only gratitude for the extra help.

"Why don't you come with us?" Duncan said.

"No. You don't need me. I'll stay here."

Duncan put his hand on Aiden's shoulder. "I haven't thanked you for capturing Lia's attacker. We all owe you."

"Yeah. Too little, too late."

"You couldn't have done anything to save her. Stop blaming yourself."

Aiden shrugged off the man's hand.

Duncan lowered his voice. "She'll be fine. I trust your aunt. We'll hear the news when anything changes."

Aiden didn't want to leave. Smitty was dead and the woman who dominated his mind fought for her life. As his gaze strayed toward Lia's room, Duncan spoke. "You're just going to drive yourself crazy here. Come back to the house. We'll go to the police station, and you can take out your aggravation on a deserving soul."

Aiden stopped and considered his options. He let his jaw relax. What was he doing here? He hardly knew the woman. An image of her flashing eyes and golden hair almost undid him. "You're right. Thanks."

"Your aunt is a very impressive woman," Duncan said as they walked to the elevator. "She never questioned or hesitated, just jumped from the helicopter and hurried to Lia. She treated her like a precious possession, refusing to leave her side."

In the elevator, Nick said, "Hey, O'Connor, what did your guy say about our prisoner?" Aiden had left Jaime in charge until the police arrived.

"The name's Aiden and give me a minute to find out"

Aiden contacted Jaime, then said, "The police took him in. They'll charge him with arson and attempted murder."

"Did he say anything before that?"

Aiden turned a piercing glare to Nick. "You want something from me? How about giving me some information? The whole story. From the beginning."

Before Nick could answer, the doors opened to the lobby. Aiden blinked. Men in blue uniforms looking distressed and disheveled filled the room.

"What the hell?" Duncan said.

Nick went over to one of them, followed closely by Aiden and Duncan. "Hey, man, what's up?"

His friend swiveled his head, took off his hat, and wiped his sweaty soaked brow. "Jesus, Nick. We had a fire at the station. A couple of people got burned."

Nick sucked in his breath. "How'd it start?"

"Don't know. All of a sudden, piles of paper just burst into flames. First on one desk, then another. That's when guys started yelling because their shirts caught on fire. It was crazy. We don't know what the hell happened." He lowered his gaze. "Sorry, Nick. Your guy got away."

Aiden knew they'd discover nothing else there. Their enemy possessed powers strong enough to worry even him. They had to stop them before they hurt anyone else. "Let's go."

On the way back to the car, he brooded over the magic connected with Lia's family. He recalled the image of Lia calling down the rain. Who were these people? He didn't push, though. Aiden's family had their own secrets.

Chapter Ten

Nick peeled out of the parking lot, snapping Aiden back against the seat. They were all on edge. It was time to get some answers. He contacted Jaime. *The prisoner escaped. What did you get out of him?*

The answers meant nothing to him. Although he wanted to shout his aggravation, he kept his cool and posed his question to Duncan who'd taken shotgun position in the front. "Who's Kane?" Duncan looked puzzled and shook his head.

"The attacker's boss?"

Duncan's shoulders sagged. "I never heard that name." He glanced back at Aiden. "I'm sorry. I didn't dare tell you about the amulet." His eyes held a plea for understanding. "I didn't know you, but I felt your power, and I knew magic killed your brother-in-law."

Aiden felt rage pinch his face. "You think I killed a member of my own fucking family? Smitty was like a brother to me."

Duncan sighed and continued. "Whoever has the amulet can make objects do whatever they want. The little creep who stole it killed your brother-in-law, forced a security guard to shoot himself, and injured a friend of mine. To keep it safe, we took it." Releasing a deep breath, he continued. "Since we didn't trust you—or anyone for that matter—we kept quiet."

Aiden grunted and looked out the window.

When they arrived at the Stuart house, Jaime met them in the kitchen. Aiden introduced his cousin to Duncan and Nick, then asked him what he'd found out.

"I had time to talk to him and check him over—his name is Jago by the way—before the cops arrived. No weapons and no *special* skills, so I persuaded him to talk to me."

Aiden grinned and turned to Duncan. "My cousin is good at that."

Jaime continued. "Jago's boss is a warlock called Kane. He came here to retrieve his property, a magic disk stolen from him. After that, he clammed up. This Kane dude scares the crap out of him. Oh yeah." He leaned in, giving Aiden a knowing look. "Jago lives in Narragansett."

Aiden shook his head. "Where is this incredible artifact?"

Duncan took it out of his pocket and unwrapped it.

Aiden stared at it for a minute, then murmured, "I've sent this image to my father." When he reached for it, Duncan pulled it back. "Are you kidding?"

Duncan conceded. "You're right but be careful. It will try to control your mind."

When Aiden touched it, the psychic strength pulled at him. Anger dominated his thoughts. He glared at Duncan, wanting to prove his dominance and slam him into the counter. He'd lifted his hand before the realization set in. In his exhausted state, he'd almost succumbed. Thankfully, his inner guardian recognized and neutralized the demonic influence.

He shoved the cursed medallion back in its covering. "Keep it. You're right. It screws with your mind. This thing's dangerous on an apocalyptic level."

Duncan rubbed his hands over his face. “I know. I underestimated the lure of its dark energy.”

****

By two-thirty on Tuesday morning, Kane’s rambunctious neighbors at his Narragansett rental finally quieted down. Lights from the party still burned, but the occupants had crashed. To make certain, though, he closed his eyes and picked out the human signatures. All asleep.

Stationing Tapper in the car, he and Gianna spent the next twenty minutes collecting their things. Kane threw his clothes in a suitcase and told Gianna to wait in the car while he cleaned out the basement: altar bowl, candles, knives, and incense. To ensure no trace remained, he whispered a cleansing spell.

Kane’s employer sent him on these missions because of his ability to recognize obscure artifacts that had dormant traces of enchantment. His specialty was amplifying their magic, as he did with the coin he’d given Jago. But the amulet was different. When he’d heard its whispered promises, Kane wanted it for himself. He’d struck a deal with the trapped demon. The entity promised to reveal his name if the strengthening ritual worked. Kane knew that knowledge would give him control over the beast and allow him to use the demon’s abilities against any witch, warlock, or wizard.

The spell worked. Agamorth gave up his identity, and Kane felt the power flow into the relic. Freedom, wealth, and supremacy were within his grasp. Then Gianna, the nosy witch, picked up the amulet and caused the car to crash.

He kicked the door closed and stalked to the car. He would get Agamorth back.

First, he had to find a chink in his enemy's armor. After that, he'd close in for the kill.

****

Kane received a phone call from his missing associate as they headed to Newport. Jago gave him a brief rundown of his capture, then went into detail as he described setting fire to the station and the cops inside. "This coin is awesome."

Though Jago had escaped the police, Kane heard the nerves in his voice. He'd talked. The only reason Kane accepted him back was that he still had the coin.

Kane, Gianna, and Tapper holed up in a dingy Newport motel room, waiting for Jago to return. Poor lighting failed to hide the worst of the crummy pit. Kane tried not to inhale. The place stank of stale cigarettes and whatever the former occupants had stuffed in their faces. Something garlicky and rank. A little purification magic cleared the worst of the smells.

Though less than stellar, the accommodation worked for now. Kane expected to be gone before the end of the week.

When Jago joined them, Kane explained the rules. "Until I get the amulet, we're on lockdown. No one leaves without permission, and no one knows where we are. That means no phone calls." He glared at Tapper. "Got it?"

The fleshy thief's eyes widened. "Yeah. No problem."

Kane didn't trust Gianna to stay off her cell, but a psychic suggestion later would keep her in line.

"What happened to you?" he asked Jago.

Though Jago emphasized he'd accomplished his goal, getting everyone to the fire, a lookout caught him.

Kane listened again in angry silence. But when Jago finished his story, Kane grinned. The stupid fool had provided the answer. His bargaining chip for Agamorth. The trouble-making bitch in the hospital.

****

A short while later, Tapper's foot twitched. "We're going now?"

Kane closed his eyes to control his anger. He needed everyone. Jago kept quiet, but the toad couldn't let it go. Tapping the tips of his fingers together, he said, "But we've been up all night."

Kane pinned the little shit to the motel wall. "Are you questioning my orders?"

Tapper, whose eyes looked like they were about to burst, couldn't speak. He gave a panicked head shake. When Kane let him go, Tapper lifted his hands in a surrender signal. "No. I-I just thought you could use a little sleep."

The audacity of this creature amazed him. Before he could mete out more punishment, Gianna's whine saved him. "Where are we going to put her?"

Kane wondered what he'd ever seen in the stupid witch. She couldn't form an independent thought. Disgust filled his voice. "We have two rooms. She'll share ours."

He ignored her angry pout and pointed at Tapper. "You'll drive."

****

As Aiden and Jaime walked out the Stuart's back door, Aiden asked his cousin to continue monitoring the grounds. A howl of rage sent him running into the hall where Duncan stood, fists clenched and a vein popping at the side of his neck. His anger was directed at the remains of a large painting now reduced to tattered strips of canvas.

"Son of a bitch," Duncan said. "He was in this house. He must have searched for the amulet, realized it was gone, then slashed my mother's favorite painting."

While Duncan fumed, Nick swore long and low. Aiden waited until Duncan calmed down. "Did he ruin anything else?"

"Oh, Lord, I don't know. I better take a quick look around."

After he left, Nick slammed his hand against the wall. "I'd like to kill him."

Aiden empathized with them at the vicious destruction, a nasty piece of vengeance that said a lot about the perpetrator.

"It's ravaged," Nick said. "My grandmother doesn't need to see this." He flicked his hand to lift the ruined painting from the wall and let it float it to the floor.

Aiden stared in shocked surprise, not at the act of magic, but at what he saw on Nick's wrist. He captured Nick's arm and stared at the pink glow beneath his watch.

Nick tugged his hand back. "What the fuck. Let go of me."

"Interesting mark on your wrist. It seemed to glow when you used your power."

"That's none of your business."

Duncan returned from his search saying, "I found nothing…" He stopped and stared at them. "What's going on here?"

Aiden answered. "I was just admiring your son's wrist tattoo. I don't suppose you have one also?"

Duncan's eyes widened as he shoved his hand

behind him.

Nick's voice held a warning. "I told you, Aiden, it's none of your business."

"Oh, I think it might be," Aiden said, and laughed. Before the situation escalated, he thrust out his own wrist.

Duncan leaned closer, moving his arm next to Aiden's. "Identical."

Nick rubbed his chin. "I thought we were the only ones."

Duncan grinned. "I guess not."

It all made sense now to Aiden. The reason he could use telepathy with Lia. Why Lia and Maeve were so alike. The power he'd sensed, so similar to his own. He looked at Duncan. "Watchers?"

Duncan nodded and smiled. "It seems we're family."

Aiden needed to know more. "Who are your ancestors?"

Duncan gave him a brief rundown of his people in Scotland. He included Lia's Italian relatives in his story. Aiden disclosed his own Celtic heritage. Each Clan traced its origins to the Knights Templar and their refuge in Scotland. It was the Templar cross that burned on their wrists. Both Clans had taken the same oath to conceal their ancestry, watch over Templar possessions, and protect the innocent.

Aiden listened in fascination as Duncan described an attack last year in the Convent House. "Someone from our past came after the treasure. He learned to control the demon and turned it against us. We still don't know how he did that or discovered our secret."

Duncan's words clicked. Aiden now understood

why the amulet seemed so familiar. His Clan guarded similar objects housed in the Nipatucket Museum. They'd check to see if this trinket was part of their ancestor's property, but he needn't wake his father now.

Turning to Duncan, he said, "How did you know about the curse?"

After Duncan described Alex's vision, Aiden told them about his Clan's responsibility. "I think it's time my father checked the museum's inventory."

"Excellent idea," Duncan said. "First, I suggest you get some sleep. I'm guessing you and your men have been up all night. I'll take the first watch and wake you in a couple of hours. Nick can go over to the Brendanis and let them rest."

After Nick left, Duncan flicked a finger to lock the door and turn off the lights. Aiden laughed. "No more hiding our powers." With a flip of his hand, he gestured toward the ottoman. When it reached his chair, he boosted his legs over the stool and closed his eyes.

While Aiden made himself comfortable, he received a telepathic message from Maeve.

Hi honey. I'm taking a break from the healing, but I wanted to let you know what I just told Franki. Although the procedure is slow, requiring extreme delicacy, the healing process has begun. The internal bleeding has stopped, and the swelling is receding.

Aiden sighed with relief. *Thank you.*

I'm happy to do it. Now, tell me. What's so special about this girl?

Aiden didn't know what to say. He didn't even know himself. Instead of answering, he said, *Shouldn't you be resting?*

All right, I get it, but we will discuss this another

time.

With Maeve's news warming his heart, he leaned back and fell asleep.

A while later, he jolted awake as a scream ripped through his head.

****

Slight chirps from the monitoring equipment cut through the quiet in the hospital room. Twisting hoses, like invasive snakes, angled into the blonde's slim form as she slept. The redhead in the chair twitched as if busy in a dream.

Kane smiled. Deserted corridors stretched in either direction, the steady cadence of mechanical devices, the only background noise.

He'd spotted the night nurse behind the tall desk, a magazine in her lap and eyes closed. He'd flicked his fingers and recited a spell to lengthen her sleep.

The patient looked bad. He wanted to take her as a bargaining chip, but with a head wound and all the tubes keeping her alive, he decided against it. If she died, she'd be no use to him.

The one next to her must be some kind of family. She'd have to do. He admired her fiery hair. A shame she was too valuable to play with. He brought out the needle. Jago stood on the other side, ready to restrain her.

Kane's thumb caressed the plunger. She stirred when he touched her arm but didn't wake until she felt the bite of the needle. When she lurched up, Jago held her and covered her mouth. "Don't worry," Kane said. "We're going to take good care of you."

She struggled and then collapsed.

Jago picked her up and put her in the wheelchair they'd confiscated.

"She looks dead," Gianna said in a panic. "They'll never let us out." Maeve lay slumped over, her bright ponytail splayed along the side of the chair. Jago propped her up and smoothed the strands that had come undone.

"Stop whining," Kane said. "I'll take care of any problems." His fingers itched to punish. These nothings should be grateful a high-level warlock allowed them in his presence, especially the one who called herself a witch.

He'd found scrubs for her, a white coat for himself, and sent Jago ahead to pave the way. No one would question a physician and his nurse with their patient.

Kane put a superior frown on his face, ignored everyone, and led them outside to the waiting car.

As they transferred their hostage to the vehicle, Kane allowed himself a nasty grin. Now who had the upper hand?

****

Aiden jumped up, ready to fight. A dream? Someone inside the house?

"What's wrong?" Duncan said.

Aiden realized it was in his mind, a psychic cry for help. He sent repeated messages to his aunt. Nothing. She'd told him not to bother her, but his frantic bombardment should have roused her. "Something's happened to Maeve."

"Let's go," Duncan said. "We'll pick up Nick on the way."

The three men charged into the quiet hospital, ignoring the elevator, and running for the stairs. Their noisy race down the corridor disturbed the entire floor.

Aiden didn't care. Lia lay on the bed, her beautiful eyes closed. A brief second of thanks turned into a soul-searing laceration as he scanned the room. “She’s gone.”

He tried, once again, to contact his aunt. The knot inside him twisted at the lack of response. Nothing since that first scream. They must have drugged her. As the nurse tried to usher them out, he heard a tiny moan.

“Lia.” Aiden reached her first and squeezed her hand.

Duncan leaned over her. “Can you hear me?”

Lia’s eyes fluttered, and she made a sound of pain.

“She wouldn’t have seen anything,” Aiden said. He wished there was some way to ease her suffering, but only his aunt could do that. Rage choked him. “We’ve got to do something.” An image—his hands around the throat of Maeve’s kidnapper—provided temporary satisfaction. “They’d better not hurt her.” His aunt had nothing to do with any of this. She’d only come because he’d asked her.

Two men with tasers arrived. Hospital Security.

Before Aiden could tear into them, Duncan placed a hand on his arm and whispered in his mind. *Let me explain.*

Aiden clenched his teeth but backed off.

“We think someone kidnapped his aunt from here this evening. We need to see your cameras.”

After a brief argument, during which Duncan explained he was a lawyer, and it would be in the best interests of the hospital to work with them, the officer agreed.

Aiden paced as the footage on the monitor played out. “Stop!”

Three people left the elevator. A nurse with an empty wheelchair followed the other two. They went into Lia’s room. Minutes later, they reappeared, pushing an unconscious Maeve. Aiden groaned as he recognized the bastard who'd attacked Lia.

Nick muttered, "That son of a bitch."

Aiden turned to the guard and yelled, "How could they do that? Why didn't someone stop them?"

The officer seemed horrified. "I don't know, but I'll find out. I don't understand, though. Why would someone want to abduct a visitor?"

Aiden knew why. He kicked the desk and glared at Duncan. "A trade."

Chapter Eleven

In the quiet of her hospital room, Lia dreamed of being in her garden. She often went outside to commune with the stars; tonight was no different. The sky looked so spectacular that she slowed her steps to gaze up at the constellations. When she felt Annie's soft fur brushing against her legs, Lia bent to pat her, but the cat streaked off into the trees.

"Annie. Come back." Lia ran after her little shadow, calling, "Here kitty, kitty. Come on." She made little sounds with her mouth, trying to lure the animal back. Taking a breath, she prepared to call again when she heard someone whisper her name.

She froze, scanning her surroundings. No one. She listened to the silent night. At a crackling sound in the bushes, she spun around.

"Meow."

"Annie!" Lia's hand went to her chest as she laughed. "You scared me." She scooped up her baby, turned and screamed. A shadowy figure stood there.

Clutching the now squirming cat, she side-stepped, trying to get around the man and run, but he held out his hand. "Don't go, Lia. I won't hurt you."

His soft voice and non-threatening stance calmed her. When he stepped into the moonlight, Lia saw his strange eyes, one blue and one green and the hard lines of his face, but he smiled, and she instantly knew she could trust him. "My cat ran away, but I found her. Her name is Annie." She looked down at her empty arms. "Where…?"

"I've got her."

She reached out to take the cat, but he pulled away and laughed.

"Please, give me my…"

She stopped speaking and covered her mouth with her hands. Something was happening to his face. It looked like dough frying in oil, bubbly and changing shape. Unable to move, she watched the bones in his face become more prominent and his eyes darken and elongate.

Annie yelped.

"You're hurting her." She reached out for the cat. "Give her to me."

The movement caused pain in her head. Both the man and the cat disappeared, and Lia heard noise, people talking. She tried to open her eyes but could only manage one. She saw the ceiling, felt the soft mattress beneath her body. Another dream? She didn't think so.

She peered at the blurry figures near the door. Was one of them Aiden? Her head throbbed. With a groan, she closed her eyes. Images flitted through her mind—her greenhouse on fire and her cat. She tried to sit up. "Annie?"

"Annie's fine, sweetheart." Franki's gentle hands eased her down.

She relaxed at her mother's touch and opened her eyes. "Mom?"

"Yes, sweetheart. Now lay back and rest."

Her father, Aunt Bree, and Alex also hovered around her bed. She looked for Aiden, but he and the other men had disappeared. The effort hurt her eyes. She forced out the words. “What’s happening?”

Franki sighed and sat beside her. “Someone attacked you, and you suffered a severe head wound.”

The thing Lia had always feared—she, the Clan healer, injured and unable to help herself. “The hospital?”

Franki’s eyes filled up, and she had trouble speaking. “You might have died if not for Maeve.”

Lia tried to focus on her mother’s words, but she was so very groggy. “Who?”

“Aiden’s aunt. She has your gift.”

“Aiden?”

Before Lia could get more answers, the nurse came in and demanded the visitors leave.

As ill as Lia felt, her mother’s reaction amused her. Franki’s nostrils flared, and her voice dropped to the dangerous level Lia always heeded. “I beg your pardon? After what happened here this morning…”

Bree patted her sister’s shoulder. “Calm down. I’ll take care of this.” Then Franki took Lia’s hand and recounted the events of the night, but Lia had trouble taking it all in as she fought to stay awake. She missed some of the story, but Aiden’s name pulled her back. He’d saved her? A bubble of warmth filled her chest. The rest was confusing.

Franki squeezed her hand. “I’ll tell you all about it later.”

The pain in her head had been building, and Lia leaned back, trying not to moan. Too much was going on. She didn’t understand. The return of Duncan, Nick, and Aiden to the room didn’t help.

The sound of Aiden’s angry voice dug into her head.

"They took her."

"Who?" Lia whispered.

No one answered her, but her mother's shoulders straightened. "That's why we have to take Lia with us tonight. She's in danger here."

Before Lia could ask another question, a nurse appeared, checked her, and injected something into her intravenous line. Someone said, "She needs it for the ride."

The next time she woke, she was at home.

****

The familiar touch of sunlight encouraged Lia to open her eyes. Her bedroom. She lifted her arms for a leisurely stretch and stopped when a flash of pain cut into her head. Memories surfaced—the hospital, her family standing around her bed and Aiden's angry voice.

She struggled to sit up and heard the jingle of jewelry before her mother reached the bed. "Easy, honey. Try not to make any sudden movements."

Her throbbing head convinced her to accept the help, but she hated being powerless.

"Take this pill and some chicken soup. You'll feel better."

Though she disliked taking conventional medications of any kind, she complied. "I'm starving. What time is it?"

"It's afternoon. One-thirty. Dad stopped in earlier before he left for work."

Lia finished the soup, handed the empty bowl to her mother, and relaxed back into her cool blue sheets. "Thank you."

The familiar space calmed her. On the wall above the fireplace hung one of her mother's paintings, a gift from Franki to celebrate Lia's inheritance of her ancestral powers three years ago. The crashing white foam erupting against a rocky coast spoke to her on an elemental level. Each time she looked at it, she reveled in the imagined sting of wind-driven salt spray.

The breeze floating in from the balcony doors held the accustomed scents of summer, sweet flowers mixed with the tang of seaweed. A small seating arrangement, the color of a quiet ocean, looked out on the gardens, labyrinth, and busy river beyond. If she had to take time to recuperate, she couldn't have a better place.

Franki smoothed her hand over Lia's forehead. "How do you feel, sweetheart?"

"Like someone played kickball with my head." At Franki's frown, she added, "But a lot better than last night."

Her mother pulled up a chair beside the bed. "Let me bring you up to date on everything."

When she learned about Maeve's unselfish response to her injury, then her kidnapping, Lia wanted to scream. Her own self-centered actions had caused it all. Aiden must hate her.

"Now, darling, do you feel up to some company?"

"Who?"

Franki motioned to the door. "He's just outside."

Lia couldn't imagine Nick or Duncan or any other member of her family waiting for permission to enter. She started to nod but a sharp pain in her head made her think better of it and said, "Sure."

Her mother's formality seemed ludicrous until she saw Aiden walk in. Lia's hands fluttered to her hair, where her ring snagged on a bandage. *Rats! I must look horrible.*

Aiden had seen and grinned. "Your hair looks fine."

Damn him. What a conceited jerk. She hoped her night gown was sexy but didn't dare check. He'd know.

She gave her mother a dagger-like stare for allowing him to see her before she was ready. She hated this feeling of helplessness, but she wouldn't let *him* know that. Trying for casual unconcern, she shrugged her shoulder and said, "What brings you to Newport?"

"Can't I come back to see you?"

"Why? You know who was responsible for your brother-in-law's death. What else could you want?"

Her mother interrupted them. "I'll step out, let you two have some private time. See you later, sweetheart."

Lia cringed. Her mother's ploy to leave them alone was so obvious.

Aiden chuckled. "I think your mother approves of me."

She felt herself blush. *It must be the drugs.* She ignored Aiden's comment and asked, "Is there any news on your aunt?"

The smile slipped from his face. "Nothing yet. I'm sure we'll hear something soon. I'm glad she worked on you before they took her."

With that, he plopped himself on the side of her bed. She wanted to swat him and tried to ignore the sensations his proximity caused. That he needed a shave made him more desirable. Lia loved the bad-boy look. As his spicy scent flowed over her, she realized her head injury had nothing to do with the rest of her body.

"Where were you going that late?" he asked.

She knew he meant last night. "My greenhouse." Her hand flew to her mouth. "Is it still there?"

"It might be, but I don't think you'll be able to use

it for a while."

She reached out and brushed her fingers over his arm. "Thank you for saving me."

Aiden's lips lifted in a sensual smile. "My pleasure."

His reaction made Lia's throat go dry. She swallowed. "I feel terrible about your aunt."

He sat back and rubbed his hand over his mouth. "I'll make the bastard pay."

"Please be careful. You can't imagine how dangerous they are."

His eyes turned cold as he looked at her. "They don't know how dangerous I am."

"You don't understand…" She never finished her sentence because Aiden took her wrist, flipped it over to reveal the tattoo, and placed his own next to hers.

The Templar cross? She reached over to touch it, brushed her fingers along the outline. "You're one of us?"

He leaned over and kissed the tiny mark on her skin.

The simple gesture sent a shock of heat through her system—and understanding dawned. "The telepathy. That's why I could contact you."

The sweet moment dissolved, though, when Aiden reverted to type and winked. "Great minds. And speaking of that, you might want to refrain from using yours right now. Want me to get you a bell?"

She laughed. "I've got an excellent set of lungs."

"I've noticed." When his gaze dropped to her chest, her breath hitched, but Aiden was unrepentant. His smile widened as he leaned down and brushed a soft kiss on her lips. "I'll be back later."

She lay there, mouth open but, for once, no comeback. After he left, she could still feel the heat from his touch. She grinned and hugged herself.

Twirling a stray curl around her finger, she replayed Aiden's actions. Then her hand strayed to her lips, and she smiled. Aiden might be the perfect boyfriend. Since Rich died, she'd never considered her beaus as anything but temporary. Given her abnormal family, no ordinary relationship had a chance of surviving. She'd never understood her parents' union, and often wondered how her human father had accepted this crazy family. With Aiden, however, he not only had *special gifts* like her, but he had the same ancestors. Lia smiled and hugged herself. She'd better make herself more presentable in case he came back.

She flicked her hand toward the small mirror on her bureau. When it didn't move, she frowned and tried again until the sharp pain in her head stopped her. Her breathing slowed. Icy tendrils gathered in her chest. She turned to her bedside table and tried to summon her glass of water, then a pen. The stabbing pain turned into a churning knot in her stomach. Panicking, she wrenched around to the open window, ignoring a spike of agony in her head, and swirled her hand in the air, commanding the wind to rush into her room. Nothing happened.

****

As Lia leaned back on her pillow unable to use her gifts, terrible thoughts twisted in her mind. Images of her life without magic. She'd brought it on herself. If only she hadn't gone outside. She tried blinking, hoping the loss was only a dream, but nothing changed. The powers she'd always taken for granted were now gone. How could she live without the most important part of herself? Without her gifts, she was no one. A cipher. An empty vessel. She didn't think she could survive.

Clutching her mattress, she tried to send a telepathic call for help to her mother. Her wound revolted, and she cradled her head. As the pain subsided, tears trailed down her cheeks. Whether from the knife-like spasm or her lost identity, she wasn't sure.

She'd been told to stay in bed. She understood why when she tried to get up. Her head spun, bile rose in her throat, and her vision blurred. Eyes closed, she laid back down wanting to scream. Her feeble attempt produced another fiery spike in her head. Defeated and helpless, she closed her eyes.

Thoughts of Aiden tormented her. *Today! Handed the gift of a relationship on the same day I lose my powers.* She didn't miss the cruel irony. For years, she'd avoided a serious relationship, unwilling to introduce an ordinary man to her family's powers. Now she was the one with no gifts.

A knock on the door brought her head up. Terrified it was Aiden, she sighed in relief when her cousin Alex looked in. "You decent?"

Lia reached for a thin smile. "Sure. Come in."

"Can I get you something? To drink or eat?"

"Thanks. I need my cell, the hand mirror, and a bunch of aspirin. I'm still a little woozy."

Alex brought them and sat. "So, how are you feeling otherwise?"

About to pretend everything was fine, Lia stopped. She couldn't hold in all the misery, and Alex was a safe receptacle. The old Lia would have glossed over the situation, but now her karma had changed, her run of good luck finished. With her phone clutched in her hand, she fought the urge to smash it against the wall. This small piece of technology represented a lifeline now, the only access she had to her family.

But the mirror was different. One glance at the shaved spot and the huge bandage on her head, and she flung it across the room. No wonder Aiden had left. She looked like a helpless freak rather than a prospect for romance.

Alex's eyebrows shot up and her mouth dropped open, but she said nothing.

Feeling like a child, Lia apologized and twisted her lips. "I'm not doing all that well."

Alex took her hand. "What is it?"

"Well, let's see. Aiden came for a visit, and I look like hell." Before Alex could speak, Lia held up her hand. "And then he kissed me and said he'd see me later."

"That's wonderful. Why are you so upset?" Alex tipped her head toward the broken mirror on the floor.

"I couldn't get the mirror or the cell or the aspirin."

Alex shook her head in confusion.

"Alex," Lia said, then held up her hands and wiggled them. "I couldn't get my things."

Alex sighed as she understood. "Your magic will come back once you heal. It's been less than twenty-four hours."

Lia cried, "I can't even use telepathy!"

Alex put her arms around her cousin. "You've had a serious injury, and Maeve didn't finish the healing. Until we get her back, you'll have to rely on time and nature. You'll be fine in a few days."

Lia hugged Alex back. "Do you think so?"

"Of course. You need to be patient." Alex laughed. "Something you're not used to."

Glad she'd confided in Alex, Lia smiled. Her cousin

was right. Patience wasn't one of her strengths.

"So," Alex said with a grin, "Tell me about Aiden."

After Lia described his visit, Alex told her how worried he'd been before they'd taken Lia to the hospital, and how he'd paced while they waited for the doctor.

Although Alex cheered her up, a tiny sliver of fear stayed lodged in her chest.

The topic turned to Maeve and the Clan's attempts to discover where they'd taken her. Aiden's people in North Kingstown were checking facial recognition from the hospital video, though they wore surgical masks. "So far, they've found nothing and there's been no call with demands."

All her own worries faded in the face of Maeve's plight. Aiden's aunt had dropped everything to save her. Ashamed of her earlier tantrum, Lia said, "She wouldn't be in danger if it weren't for me. I wish I could help her."

"We all do, but don't worry. Once we hear from her captors, we'll get her. We've got two Templar Clans working on a plan. He doesn't stand a chance."

****

Lia woke later to see her mother peeking into her room. Franki drifted over to her. "Did I wake you, sweetheart? You look tired. I don't think you need another guest right now."

Her mother's efforts to dissuade a visit piqued Lia's curiosity. Although she didn't want more company, her mother seemed too willing to retreat. "Who is it?"

Franki pursed her lips in distaste. "Josiah Warren."

The Templar agent? What was he doing here? As the door slid open, she recognized the well-dressed gentleman. She recalled his last visit to the house, his inability to bind the amulet, and the strange spark they'd exchanged when he touched her shoulder.

Would the man who purported to be another Templar and who recognized her Clan's powers perceive her psychic change? She fingered the razored wreckage of her once-beautiful hair, sighed, and gave her mother an inquisitive smile. Before the attack, that look would have precipitated a message from Franki. Lia's heart squeezed at the loss.

"How can I help you, Mr. Warren?"

"Ms. Ferguson. Lia. I'm so sorry about your injury."

Franki stepped forward and glared at Warren. "She was attacked. By someone with one of your damn demon traps."

Josiah dropped his shoulders in a sigh. "I feel terrible. That artifact should have protected itself and killed the thief. I'm trying to figure out where the amulet was located and what went wrong. Once we discover that, we'll be able to follow a trail and find out who is going after our treasures."

"What do you mean? You've lost others?" Franki asked.

"We've lost smaller relics here in the Northeast. Although they all have tremendous value, this one is the most disturbing."

"How do you know all this?" Lia asked. "Who do you work for? Where are they?"

"You don't need to know that now, but I'll keep you informed."

Lia didn't believe that for a minute. His calculating gaze told her he would remain as close-mouthed as before.

She itched to talk to him about the connection she'd felt when he'd touched her, but not until they were alone without her mother, who looked to be gearing up for a tirade. "Mom."

"Mr. Warren can visit you later."

"No. I want to talk to him now."

When Franki's face showed surprise, Lia reiterated her request. "Please leave us alone for a while."

With a guarded look at Josiah, Franki said, "I don't think that's a good idea." She stood ramrod straight and compressed her lips. Lia could sense her mother channeling her gifts. "I'll sit over here." She pointed to the chair by the balcony. "Mr. Warren came here to talk to Duncan." She turned to the agent. "He'll be here soon."

With a last parental *We'll discuss this later* glare, Franki strode to her seat.

Josiah seemed contrite. "I'm sorry your mother doesn't trust me, but I hope I can convince you."

"About what?"

"Ah." With his hands out, palm up, he said, "I'm concerned about the amulet and your family. If you give it to me, I'll make sure it's safe."

"Sorry to disappoint you, but we can't do that."

"You're making a mistake." He straightened up. "I'd like to speak to you about the other day. I felt a kinship, and I know you also experienced it."

Lia gave a careful nod. When he moved closer, a pulse of strength reached out. Lia endeavored to meet the power with her own but failed. An understanding passed between them. *But how could he know?*

Josiah moved to Lia's side. "I'd like to assess your wound. May I?"

"What are you going to do?" Franki surged out of her seat.

He dropped his hands. "Evaluate the damage."

"Mother. He won't hurt me. You're right here." She turned to him. "I'm fine with this."

Franki stayed next to the bed. Although Lia trusted Mr. Warren, she was glad when her mother took her hand.

Josiah nodded, then held his hands a few inches from her head. He hissed in a breath, but only said, "It's healing."

He paused, as if considering. "With this amount of damage, you shouldn't be as healthy as you are. Someone with medicinal gifts has already treated you."

For her whole life, Lia's inner guardian had given her knowledge and strength. No longer. Her chest squeezed against the hole left by its absence. Still, she sensed his sincerity. As a Templar agent, he knew about Clan powers, so she told him about Maeve.

"Ah. You're concerned about your own abilities."

Her eyes stung, and she sucked in her breath. Crying wouldn't help. "That's right."

"Brain injuries are difficult."

She pulled her gaze away, unable to disguise the pain of her loss.

"I'd like to touch you, if I may?"

She blinked. "Why?"

Franki interrupted. "That's enough. I think it's time for you to leave."

Lia squeezed her mother's hand. "Wait a minute, Mom. Let Mr. Warren speak."

Her mother's snort conveyed her displeasure, but all she said was, "Fine."

Josiah answered Lia's question. "I sense a special essence in you I'd like to evaluate."

Unable to disguise her frustration, Lia said, "You mean there *used* to be something there?"

He smiled and said, "It is still there," then turned his ring around on his finger and pressed the bloodstone into her hand.

Lia felt a slight shock before heat pulsed through her arm. She looked up as his gaze probed hers. For a moment, she felt the strange sensation of a puzzle piece about to click into place. Then pain.

He dropped her hand. The connection ended, and her distress lessened. "I apologize. It's too soon."

She took a calming breath and asked, "What's too soon?"

He stepped back, shook his head, and gave Lia a sad smile. "I'd like to come back when you're better and we can talk again. You need the healer."

Disappointment and anger colored her response. "No can do. They kidnapped her."

Something like fear flashed across his face. "What? When did this happen?"

Surprised at his concern, Lia hurried to reassure him that her family and Aiden's would take care of it. They'd get Maeve back.

Josiah's eyes darkened as he spoke, "Let me guess. They want the amulet in exchange."

His words, delivered in a cold and emotionless tone, surprised her. She pulled back. With no more powers, she was helpless, but her mother wasn't. Lia could feel Franki gathering her strength as she said, "I'd like you to leave. Now."

But Warren paid no attention to her. He spoke to himself. "They can't do that," and then he mumbled something about not knowing the truth.

With a start, he came back to himself. In a more amicable tone, he said, "Sorry," then tilted his head toward Franki. "I'll come back later." He took a package from his jacket pocket and handed it to her. "In the meantime, these herbs will help her."

Lia's gaze fell on the plastic bag and then moved to the retreating figure. "Wait." Too late. The door closed. *The man moved fast.* Her mother followed him out.

Lia sat there stewing, hating being stuck up here with no way to monitor anything. What was the heat Warren had sent through her? He'd turned his ring around before taking her hand. Why? Impatient, she needed to talk to him again. And then a sobering thought. What if she'd misread him? He wanted to take the amulet. Was he an agent of the Templars? She knew nothing about him and could no longer trust her instincts. What if Josiah Warren wasn't who he pretended to be?

****

When Aiden heard Josiah Warren was at the Brendanis' home, he hurried along the back path from the Stuarts. As he neared the house, a charred wood smell fouled the air, a nasty reminder of the previous night. The sight of the blackened ruin caused a stomach-twisting memory of Lia, surrounded by blood.

That scheming louse! He'd gone for the most vulnerable. Thank God, Lia had survived. Now, Aiden would get Maeve back, and then he'd deal with her captors.

The kitchen was empty, but loud voices echoed down the hall. He followed the sound to the living room door. He didn't recognize the man whose angry tone dominated the room. "The artifact must be protected, no matter the situation."

"It's safe here," Duncan said.

The second man countered, "Not for long. I know you're planning to trade this piece of silver for one of the O'Connor Clan. You can't do that."

Aiden stormed into the room. "Who the hell do you think you are?"

Duncan explained the situation. Unconvinced, Aiden said, "I'd like to see some identification. Why should we believe you?"

The man stepped back to face his opponent. "You're an O'Connor, I take it."

"Damn right, I'm an O'Connor and one who values his aunt over any lousy magic trinket."

Aiden had more to say, but Duncan interceded. "I was just about to explain to Mr. Warren what we intend to do."

"Wait a minute," Aiden said through gritted teeth. "Before you give away our plans, I think you should make sure he isn't part of this whole thing. How do we know we can trust him?"

Duncan said nothing but sent an inquiring glance toward Warren.

The agent stepped back and took a long breath. "May I remind you that you contacted me? Where did you get the number?"

Duncan turned to Aiden and explained how Rosemary had contacted him.

"He could be an imposter." He turned to Josiah. "Where can we corroborate your credentials?"

Josiah snorted. "We're a secret society. The less you know, the easier it is to keep you safe."

"And how's that working out?" Aiden said.

Duncan gave Aiden a quelling look and turned to

Warren. "What do you suggest we do?"

"I'm waiting for more information on its origin. If you hand this demon back to the thief, innocents will suffer. If what I suspect is true, none of us may survive."

Chapter Twelve

Though it featured two queen size beds, the motel room proved too small for Kane, Maeve, and Gianna—a detail not lost on the surly witch. She stopped whining—only after he sent her a nasty glare. Her sour mood was like a stone in his shoe begging to be expelled.

"Go to sleep."

The growled order did the trick. Giving her pillow a healthy punch, Gianna turned away from him. Only after her huffs of irritation turned to light snores, could he finally think. The drug he gave his prisoner should keep her quiet for now, but she'd need supervision. And this hovel would not work because he needed space to think and plan. He couldn't afford to make a mistake. They'd have to move.

Three hours later, the alarm he set went off, and so did Gianna. Her waking screech pierced his brain. With a few mumbled words and a flick of his fingers, he sent her back to her dreams.

His captive was still asleep, but she needed another injection. After replenishing the medication, he regarded her, from her freckled nose to her shapely legs. She was lovely. In her mid-thirties, he guessed. Unable to keep away, he let his fingers slide across her forehead, dislodging a few fiery curls, before trailing down her body. With a sigh, he gave an annoyed glance at Gianna. Soon, he'd rid himself of the annoying witch.

A disastrous night on a cheap mattress had tormented his body. To get out the kinks, he stretched his arms toward the ceiling and planned his day. Coffee first, then a new rental.

****

The next morning, thanks to Maeve's initial healing, Lia felt well enough to go outside. Her mother refused to admit Josiah's medicine may have also helped—Franki still didn't trust him.

The stairs took a while to navigate. In the garden, Lia rubbed the leaves of her herbs to release her favorite scents: lavender, peppermint, and lemon. Their pungent aromas renewed her faith, and a tiny hope flourished that the magic of the labyrinth might awaken her powers.

The moment she stepped onto the swirling, sand covered path, a sense of comfort enveloped her like a warm blanket on a chilly night. When she reached the center, she drew in a deep breath and aimed a silent plea to the heavens before sinking onto the bench. A gnawing welled up inside her as she braced to try her powers. One last prayer, and she attempted to send out a greeting to her grandmother.

Searing pain hit. She clutched her head, hunched her shoulders, and let the tears flow. Her magic hadn't responded. She'd been so sure. Time to face the truth. She'd lost her lifelong talents.

A sharp voice startled her. "What are you crying about?"

She popped her head up in surprise at the sound of Kitty, her grandmother's irreverent ghost. "How can I hear you? My telepathic powers are gone."

Lia heard a snort. "I'm a ghost in a magical labyrinth. I can make anyone hear me."

Her grandmother's derisive tone didn't deter her. "And you can hear me speak?"

"What is wrong with you, young lady? Have you lost all your senses? Of course, I can. I'm not deaf."

Leave it to Kitty to pull her out of her self-pity. Not your typical grandmother, alive or dead. The woman cut through emotional baggage like a samurai swordsman.

"Sorry, Kitty. It's just that I…"

"Who's the young man sending steamy vibes your way?"

"What?" She spun her head around, then stopped when the pain hit again. Aiden. *Why is he here?* His gaze locked on her, and a flutter started low in her belly. She furtively wiped her cheeks.

"Well, invite Mr. Hot Stuff in," Kitty said. "Ooh! I can feel his power from here."

Knowing Kitty's words never left the labyrinth, Lia called out to Aiden, "If you're coming in, stay on the path. Don't tick off any more gremlins."

Kitty's voice purred in Lia's ear. "So, he's the one who crossed the stones. Interesting."

"He's also the one who saved my life the other night."

"Looks like a keeper to me."

As Aiden walked the ever-diminishing circle, Lia's breathing quickened. Her gaze drifted from his lips to his strong shoulders to his muscular jean-clad thighs. When he paused and gave her a suggestive grin, a wanton heat rushed through her. She hoped Kitty didn't notice.

She didn't know whether to stay sitting or stand, but when he reached the labyrinth's center, she popped up from her seat.

His lips curled in a wry smile. "You look a lot better

than you did yesterday." With a glance around him, he said, "Strange place. If that damned curse hadn't almost killed me, I'd think the twisty path to get here was ridiculous."

Lia frowned. "The path isn't what you think. In today's world, it's used as a journey to acquire peace of mind. The original labyrinths, like this one, were steeped in magic and often contained the bones of ancestors. People walked them hoping the gods would smile on their requests." She held her hands up to encompass the mystical circle. "We come out here when we have to work through tough decisions."

His smile made her want to touch his face. He tilted his head. "What difficult problems do you have?"

"Ahem!"

As Aiden jerked his head around, Lia said, "Um. We're not alone."

His eyebrows shot up.

"My grandmother…"

"I'm Kitty," her grandmother announced in her most imperious tone. "Keeper of the Labyrinth. Don't tell me I'm your first ghost."

As the words floated through the air, Aiden looked all around them, his mouth open in shock. "I-uh-How do you do?"

Kitty's laugh swirled around them. "I do just fine, thank you. I like him, Lia."

Lia knew Kitty was just getting warmed up. She'd move from pleasantries to embarrassment at any moment. "Time for us to go. Great talking to you, Kitty."

"So soon? Well, it was wonderful meeting you, Aiden. Do come again, with or without Lia."

Aiden mumbled something about it being his

pleasure, and Lia nudged him toward the path.

Once outside the labyrinth, he gave a quick look over his shoulder. “Was she there when I walked across the stones?”

Lia chuckled. “Kitty’s the one who blew the whistle on you.”

Rubbing the back of his neck, he said, “Is she dangerous?”

Sometimes I wonder. At the concern in his voice, she suppressed a grin. “Don’t let it worry you. Kitty rattles most people.”

She tilted her head, grateful that simple movement no longer caused searing pain. “Did you want something?”

“I wanted to check on you. Should you be doing so much so soon?”

Checking on her? Then she thought, *He’s worried about me.* “It was my head that was injured, not my legs.”

He raised an eyebrow. “You’re not tired?”

“Nope.”

Warmth spread through her as his gaze swept down her body. “Then do you think your legs might enjoy a walk?”

Lia’s spirits rose—until she remembered the labyrinth hadn’t restored her powers. She knew she shouldn’t encourage Aiden now that she no longer had her gifts. Could she even be part of the Clan?

“Why so quiet? Something wrong?”

“No. Just surprised to see you here. Don’t you have work to do?”

He grinned. “You think I’m dogging it—trying to get out of work?”

"Of course not." She hurried to reassure him. "I only wondered… I mean, your job is way out in North Kingstown." *Oh, Lord. She sounded like a fool.*

He laughed and pulled out his phone. "I keep in touch." Then he got serious. "I'm waiting until the thief contacts Duncan."

She had to stop this inane chattering. It was his damn eyes. So weird, yet so fascinating. She looked away. "You haven't heard anything?"

"Nothing," he said as he kicked the grass. "I don't understand. He wants the amulet. Why hasn't he called? I'll bet that damn Warren knows something."

"Josiah?"

"That's right," he said in an ah-ha tone. "I heard he came to see you and gave you some medicine. What was that all about?"

"He wanted to help me."

"You don't know if you can trust him. Wasn't he supposed to bind the amulet?"

"He tried, but he couldn't do it."

"What a surprise."

"No. He tried, but the metal sent out a huge spark. It's cursed."

"Tell me you didn't fall for that. He could have used any spell to cause that result."

Ignoring his jab at her intelligence, she said, "The curse is real. The kid who stole it died."

"Don't be a fool. Josiah Warren is a charlatan."

A fool? "You know what? I do feel a little tired. I think I'll go in and rest."

****

Aiden watched her march off—head high, golden mane swaying below her scarf in rhythm with her taut little butt. Damn! He'd hoped to spend some time with her to explain he'd be leaving later for Smitty's wake. The funeral was tomorrow, so he wouldn't be back until Friday. She was so stubborn. He hadn't meant to call her a fool, but even her mother didn't trust Warren.

A few seagulls screeched overhead as he headed back to Duncan's place. He might as well leave now, although he hated having to face his grieving sister. According to his father, she was heavily sedated, and his mother was working overtime trying to care for her.

Then there was Maeve. He'd dragged her here to help Lia, so it was his responsibility to find her. His family would want news. He wished he had some.

****

Lia relaxed into the slow cadence of the porch swing and gazed out at the deceptive calm of the sleepy river. A few lonely bird calls and the buzzing of industrious insects were the only interruption to the comfortable silence. *Oh, wait a minute.* With a quick grin, she added the sound of her cat's soft snoring to the list. Annie's light breathing and the soothing rhythm of her swinging perch almost lulled her to sleep.

A sharp ringtone destroyed the tranquility and drew an annoyed twitch from Annie. The phone, an instrument previously relegated to Lia's purse, now functioned as an indispensable appendage since her telepathic powers were on the fritz. She checked the screen. Alex's face.

"Hi, Cuz. What's up?"

With a grin and a raised eyebrow, she said, "You've got a visitor. Mr. Warren is here and wants to see you. You up for company?"

Lia took a moment to decide. She'd watched her mother head to her studio earlier, so she wouldn't have that argument, and she hadn't seen Aiden since she left him outside the labyrinth. Lia understood Franki's distrust emanated from her role as a mother, but this new suffocating protective manner drove her crazy. She wasn't stupid. Josiah wasn't some stranger. He was a Templar agent who bore the mark. She liked him. And, yes, she harbored a secret hope he could help her.

Still, caution prevailed. She asked Alex for her psychic impression of him. After her cousin's "All clear," Lia said, "I'm on the back porch. Give me a few minutes, then bring him out."

She hurried to the kitchen for a pitcher of lemonade. A few minutes later, Alex arrived with Josiah and gave Lia a conspiratorial wink before she left them alone.

Josiah thanked Alex then gazed at the surroundings. "A beautiful place to heal."

Lia gestured toward the nearest chair and invited him to sit. "It is and I'm grateful."

He smiled, the first genuine expression of pleasure she'd seen on his face. As soon as he sat, the cat rubbed against his leg and meowed. He chuckled and reached down to give her golden fur a scratch. A loud purr rumbled in response.

That did it for Lia. If Annie approved, the man was okay. "Thank you for your special herbs. Since using them, I've felt much better."

"Good. How are you otherwise?"

She sighed, knowing he referred to her lost gifts. "No different."

He closed his eyes for a moment and then said, "May I examine your wound?"

When she removed her scarf and turned, Josiah stood over her, his hands near her head. She heard a soft chant before he returned to his seat. "Much better. You're lucky the healer started right away."

At the reference to Maeve, Lia cringed. "We've got to save her, but we've heard nothing. I don't understand."

He spread his hands, palm up. "I can only think of one reason. Whoever is in charge either knows about the Clan or can sense the magic surrounding you and your family. I'd guess he's trying to develop a plan to protect himself."

"That doesn't explain why he hasn't contacted us."

Josiah's eyes narrowed. "Are you certain he hasn't?"

She nodded. "Positive."

While he mulled that over, Lia offered him cold lemonade.

His brow cleared as he accepted a glass. "Thank you." After a sip, he reached into his pocket. "More herbs for you."

Lia accepted the clear packet containing leaves that resembled large pieces of oregano. Then he asked about her abilities, and she lowered her gaze. "Anytime I try to invoke them, extraordinary pain slices through my head."

When his expression turned pensive and he glanced toward the water, Lia dared to hope. "Can you help me?"

Instead of answering, he reached down to a briefcase he'd brought and withdrew a large manila envelope. He held it for a moment as if rethinking his actions, then handed it to her.

She undid the clasp and peeked inside. "What is this?"

"I hope the start of your education."

No matter what she'd been expecting, it wasn't this. "I don't understand."

Josiah leaned forward, elbows on his knees. "From the start, I've sensed in you a kindred spirit. It began with the spark when I touched your shoulder in the living room the night I saw your mother's painting. Tell me about your gifts. What are they? How do you use them?"

The hollow ache growing in her chest was replaced by anger. "There's no sense in talking about them. They're gone."

Josiah reached over to touch her, and warmth spread along her arm. "Your powers are as much a part of you as breathing. In time, they'll return." He sat back. "Please. Your gifts?"

The rush of heat reminded her of their connection. After taking a cleansing breath, she revealed what she considered the best part of herself or former self.

He nodded his thanks, saying, "Your gifts are impressive." Although his tone was polite, Lia wondered at the excitement in his eyes. "Until they return, let's see if we can substitute some basic spells. I've assembled a few in that envelope. While your special skills lie dormant, my ring tells me your inherent magic still sings in your blood. We can work with that."

His words gave her hope. Could this man whom Aiden and her mother mistrusted help her get her powers back?

****

Kane looked out at a dirt road that was almost obscured by endless rows of potato plants. The dust swirls and the small striped bugs made his skin crawl, but it was the best he could do on short notice—this place was only fifteen minutes from downtown Newport. He'd rented the four weather-worn cottages lining the back lot to discourage prying eyes. Behind the shingled structures that were little more than sheds there was nothing but scrub pine and oak trees.

He had a bit of trouble opening the cracked and swollen door and cringed as he previewed the inside of the first cottage. Although clean, faded linoleum covered the floors and dingy, second-hand furniture filled the space. A lumpy sofa and matching recliner sagged against one wall, two chairs with a coffee table faced the front window, and a small maple dining set abutted the tiny kitchen.

A lovely two-bedroom retreat, my ass!

Gianna's loud complaints as she flounced around the seedy room echoed off the dark-paneled walls. On the way from the motel, she'd taken the liberty to paw through their captive's purse. "Her name's Maeve," she sneered. "What is that? Irish?"

He was tired of her constant criticism. "This place is a dump. I can't believe we have to sleep in these bedrooms. They're so….I don't know—common."

"Take whichever one you like," he said. "I'll sleep with the woman."

"What?"

Kane's jaw muscles tightened hard enough to crack a tooth. "I have to monitor her."

Damn! He'd chosen this witch for her looks. Big mistake. No matter, she'd soon be gone. *I think I'll leave her with a little gift. A couple of warts on her pretty face.*

He turned his attention to his prisoner. He'd placed her in the chair instead of the bed so he could keep tabs on her. Gianna sat sulking on the sofa. While they waited for the others to join them, she played on her phone.

When Jago and Tapper arrived, Kane led everyone to the table, opened his laptop to a satellite view of Newport, and pulled out sketches he'd made. "I've found the perfect place for the switch."

Part of his plan included Tapper driving a boat. Kane silenced the expected arguments. "I'll give you a few lessons before I cast a spell. You'll be fine." He confiscated the pencil Tapper had been bouncing on the table and continued. "We'll do a dry run this afternoon. Gianna can stay with the prisoner."

"Me?" she whined. "Why do I have to babysit?"

"Enough," he roared. With a twitch of his fingers, Gianna's voice disappeared though she kept trying to speak. When she realized what had happened, panic filled her eyes, and her face paled.

Kane nodded toward the couch. "Sit there and remember your place. If you behave, I might return your voice."

About ten minutes later, Gianna flew off the sofa and slammed into Kane, waving frantically at the chair by the window. He whipped around, his hand ready to attack her, when she pointed at Maeve, groggy, but awake.

****

Lia stared across the porch at Josiah and wrinkled her nose. "What spells?" She'd never had to recite witchy incantations. Anything she ever needed had come with a flick of her fingers.

Before Josiah could answer, Aiden came up the steps and glared at Lia's companion. "What are you doing here?"

Neither she nor Josiah had seen him approach.

Lia slid the envelope between her arm and her side,

then put on a welcoming smile. "Hi, Aiden. I believe you know my friend." She saw Josiah's brief grin.

"We're acquainted," Aiden said. "I didn't expect to see him here again."

Lia sat up, frowning. "Mr. Warren…"

"Josiah. Please," the agent said.

Lia smiled. "Josiah has been helping me heal. His medicine is working wonders." As she spoke, she showed him the packet of herbs. Josiah settled back with a satisfied smile. She was glad he wasn't caving under Aiden's boorish behavior.

Lia enjoyed watching Aiden try to regain control. "We were just having lemonade. Would you care for some?"

Tossing a semi-sincere smile to the agent, he turned to her. "Thanks. I'd like that."

"I'm afraid you'll have to fetch a glass in the kitchen."

The smile slipped from his lips, and she thought he might change his mind, but after a momentary scowl, he went inside. She leaned over to whisper to Josiah. "Don't mention the spells."

He nodded as the door opened.

Lia wanted to smack Aiden for the interruption. Her fingers twitched with the urge to open the envelope. His sociable attitude as he pulled up a chair to join them made her wary. He might have been attending a tea party the way he complimented Lia on her sundress and asked how she was feeling. Oozing with civility, he turned to Josiah. "Don't let me disturb you. Please, continue your visit."

Josiah tilted his head. "I was just telling Lia how sorry I am about her injury and assuring her I will do anything in my power to help her with what little healing skills I possess."

"What about you, Aiden?" Lia said. "What have you been doing?"

"I've just come to say goodbye." He glanced at Josiah. "Smitty's wake is tonight; his funeral tomorrow."

With all that had happened, she forgot about Aiden's brother-in-law. She leaned over and touched his arm. "I'm so sorry."

Josiah dipped his head. "As am I."

Aiden's chummy facade slipped a little. "My brother-in-law was the first victim of that deadly piece of metal." He turned to the Templar agent. "I don't want my aunt to be the next."

Lia jumped in. "I'm sure Josiah wants to find her as badly as we do."

Aiden offered her a cold frown. "Somehow, I don't think he cares about Maeve as much as her family does." He surged out of his chair. "I'll let you two get on with *whatever* I interrupted." As he turned to leave, he stopped as a surprised look creased his face.

"What's the matter?" Lia asked.

He ignored the question and raced off toward the Stuarts. Clearly, he'd received an important message and wasn't sharing.

Josiah frowned. "Something's happened."

"Yes. I think so. Do you mind if we finish this later?"

"Of course not." He pointed to the envelope at Lia's side and, with a snap of authority, said, "Don't attempt the spells by yourself."

The abrupt change in his demeanor reminded her she barely knew this man.

After exchanging cell numbers, she walked him out. As soon as the front door clicked shut, she called Alex. "Hey, Cuz, what's going on with Aiden? I saw him receive a message that upset him."

"Let me check. I'll let you know as soon as I find out."

Lia, never big on patience, fidgeted until Alex called back.

In a frightened voice, she said, "It was a cry for help from Maeve."

****

Lia toyed with her lunch at the kitchen table while listening to the conversation about the latest development in the kidnapping. Although relieved to hear Maeve was strong enough to use her telepathy, everyone worried about her abrupt silence after the one message.

What was the kidnappers' plan? Why hadn't they contacted them about a swap? They'd had her for two days.

As Franki, Bree, and Alex discussed the problem, Lia's thoughts turned to Aiden. Nick said Aiden planned to return sometime tomorrow after the funeral. She tried to bite down the smile that threatened at the thought of seeing him again then scolded herself. If she didn't regain her gifts, she'd have no relationship with Aiden. Still, she continued to cherish a spark of hope.

A few hours later, Josiah returned. She took him out to the gazebo, her new refuge since she'd lost her former haven in the greenhouse. Life in a household with four gifted women could be combustible. This simple wooden structure afforded a peaceful, secure space. The white Victorian octagon, overlooking the now restless

Sakonnet River renewed her energy. A freshening breeze ruffled her hair and tempered the aggressive rays of the sun. How she yearned to increase the wind's velocity. Instead, she bowed her head.

Josiah approved of their classroom. "Peaceful and unobtrusive." The voice of a lone seagull caught their attention. Josiah's gaze followed its flight before he said, "Let's begin. First, about this ring." He held up his hand. The vibrant red stone seemed to pulsate. "Before I explain, you must promise to protect its secret and never reveal it to anyone."

Lia shook her head. "I won't lie to the Clan about using my powers."

"Not the spells. I'm talking about the spark you experienced when the ring came in contact with your skin. That connection signifies that you possess a rare legacy. A special skill whose existence must remain hidden in order to protect you and others who share this gift."

Lia held up her hands in a *stop* gesture. "What are you talking about?"

"Even if you decide to reject this boon, you must promise to never divulge what I tell you to anyone. Lives are at stake."

Although the idea of a special power sounded exciting, the "Lives are at stake" bit made her nervous. "Will I be in danger knowing it?"

"No. Just forget what you heard."

"All right. Unless I suspect something doesn't add up."

"Fair enough." He held the ring up to catch the sunlight. "It's called Seeker. Only a few Templar descendants have the ability to trigger the ring's gifts.

The chosen one receives the knowledge and strength to ferret out and defeat any who threaten our kind."

Lia rubbed her arms. That spark from his touch the first day he arrived, and the warmth in her arm. Did he mean her?

Josiah tilted his head and whispered. "Don't look so nervous. You felt it."

She shook her head. Not possible. She knew what her gifts were and none of them involved chasing criminals. "You're wrong. My gifts are healing and manipulating the air. I'm no paranormal detective. Besides, I don't have any powers now. I can't challenge anyone."

He stood up and contemplated the river. When he turned, his gaze pinned her. "You're wrong about your gifts. They will return. And, along with them, an ability to detect evil in all its forms. Once touched by the bloodstone, you can't ignore its presence."

Lia gave the ruby an icy stare. She had a life she loved—her work, her plants, her family. What was he suggesting she do? Her healing was important. She wasn't about to go looking for trouble.

Involved in her thoughts, she missed his next words. "I'm sorry. What did you say?"

"I said you can try to deny it, but you can't escape your destiny. I'll work with you and help you in any way I can. What are you afraid of? Commitment? The job isn't twenty-four hours, seven days a week. If it's the potential for danger, you won't be alone."

Lia didn't want to be a Templar divining rod. She took a deep breath and changed the subject. "What about the spells?"

All affability disappeared as he flattened his lips.

"Fine. But we'll take this up again."

Lia had no plans to discuss it later.

He opened the envelope. "Let's try this spell."

A slight flutter teased her stomach and surprised her. She'd known magic all her life, but this was different. This work today might decide her future.

"First, picture your intent. Then, recite the incantation using hand movements to enhance it." He demonstrated by twitching his fingers, then handed Lia an incantation and a twig. "This is a simple fire spell. Envision lighting the stick, say the three words, emphasizing the last, and move your hand like this."

Lia gripped the stick, praying she'd pronounce the Latin correctly. Taking a calming breath, she pictured a burning twig. "*Lignest ignatio. Nara*!"

She sensed a tingling from the Templar mark on her wrist before a rush of heat swept down her arm. When the twig in her hand caught fire, she let out a screech and dropped it. Josiah laughed, swept his hand, and the fire died.

Lia forgot her angst and hugged herself. "I did it! I still have my magic."

He shook his head, but Lia ignored him.

She must be better. Without thinking, she flipped her fingers in a call to the wind. The only response was excruciating pain. The warm glow of power from her recent triumph dissolved, replaced by a raw, spreading void. She dropped her chin to her chest. Why? How could this other magic work when her gifts failed her?

"You don't listen," Josiah said in a harsh tone. "Stop tormenting yourself. This magic is different. Because of your Templar heritage, you have inherent psychic abilities. Although your special gifts are unavailable to you at this moment, Templar magic still sings in your blood, allowing your intent mixed with the simple words to affect an enchantment."

He threw his hands in the air. "Stop feeling sorry for yourself. We have work to do."

She glared at him as she straightened her shoulders. Ignoring his callous indifference to her pain, she plucked out a wooden box that was smaller than her cell phone.

She may have lost her incentive, but curiosity impelled her to investigate. Carved into the soft pine cover was a majestic eagle. She brushed her fingers across the engraving before opening the box. Empty but for the spicy scent that drifted out. "What do I do with this?"

He handed her another spell, explaining the gestures. "Ready?"

Lia blinked at strange words like *intwint* and *stiptust*. "Wait a minute."

First, she tried out each word until she felt confident, then ran through the finger-spinning, trying to ignore Josiah's impatient stare. Despite the cool breeze, she felt hot. Magic had never been this difficult.

It took two tries before she felt the tingling in her fingers that signaled success. When she saw no change in the box, she looked at Josiah. Hating to beg for approval, she said, "Well? Did it work?"

"Open the box."

She tried to lift the lid, but the top held firm. "Oh. I sealed it."

Josiah replaced the box in his case. "A binding spell. Simple, but it does the job."

Lia perked up. She wouldn't give Josiah the satisfaction to witness her pleasure, but inside she smiled. *Look what I did.*

"Only one more."

Lia focused on the pleasure of her success before picking up the last slip of paper. Another alien phrase: *Kaeso* and *santur wornum.*

By this time, the wind had died down, and long shadows crept across the lawn behind the house. She wiped sweat from her forehead and waited for Josiah to hand her an object.

Instead, he pulled out a knife and cut his finger. "Recite the spell."

Lia's mouth dropped open as she watched blood drip from his hand. She reached over to heal him until she remembered.

He stared into her eyes. "The spell!"

She pulled herself together and began. On the last word, she flicked her hand as he'd taught her, and the small slice closed.

A burst of warmth filled the void in her chest. She could heal again.

"Will this spell work on any healing?"

She guessed the answer from his ugly frown.

"No. This is more of a quick fix. Besides, to use any spell, you need to carry around a "How To" of magical secrets or memorize the words. If you knew Latin, you could create your own."

Some mentor. His disparaging attitude hurt. She'd never been treated like this. Not even by her high school Chemistry teacher, who'd always chided her for socializing rather than listening to his lectures. At least he'd always finished with a smile.

She realized Josiah was getting ready to leave. "Is that it? I want to learn more."

"Why? We know you can work the spells but don't understand the language. I can't anticipate your needs to set up incantations."

Lia didn't like Josiah, but believed he was on their side.

As she walked him back to the house, he asked her about the amulet.

She gave a helpless shrug. "What do you want to know?"

"I want to understand how the demon's magic leaked out. It was bound hundreds of years ago and sealed in a secure area."

"You know what it is?"

He paused for a second, then nodded. "The protection ceremony you and your cousin witnessed shouldn't have enabled him to unleash the beast's tricks. The demon is more powerful than I thought. We must stop him."

"How?"

Josiah played with the ring on his finger. "By keeping the amulet away from him."

"But—" she began.

"No. Listen to me. The day I saw the artifact I felt its strength. The demon wants to escape. You can't let that happen."

Chapter Thirteen

Aiden's insides churned as he rushed along the now familiar path to the Stuarts, paying little attention when bluestone and lush grass changed to the rough sand and scrub brush skirting the deserted mansion. *Someone had cut off Maeve's message!*

All attempts to reconnect with her failed. He flexed his fingers, imagining them around someone's neck. His only consolation was the knowledge she was still alive. He began to run.

Before he reached the Stuarts, his father's voice entered his mind. *We received Maeve's message. What else do you know?*

I've had Jaime working from that end, he sent back. *Check with him, and I'll see you this afternoon at the wake.*

The thought of the calling hours, common before the actual funeral mass, brought him to a stop. Memories swamped him. He'd known Smitty for most of his life—riding bikes, discovering girls, and Smitty's drunken declaration at his bachelor party, "You're the best friend a guy could ever have." Pain dug into his chest and his throat closed as he swiped at his tears. He'd never see Smitty again. By the time he reached the Stuart home and spoke to Duncan, he'd stuffed the pain away and was ready to concentrate on Maeve.

"What did she say?" Duncan asked.

"She managed to tell us she was in a cabin near a field. I've got Jaime doing a search for any properties that meet that description. I'm headed home now. My brother-in-law's wake is at six o'clock and the funeral is tomorrow morning. I'd like to come back here afterward—if that works for you?"

"Of course. We're glad to have you. I'm so sorry about everything—your brother-in-law and Maeve. Let us know if we can help. We'll work on this end, checking for areas that fit her description."

"Thanks, I appreciate it."

He started to leave, then stopped, letting disapproval tinge his words. "By the way, did you know Josiah Warren has been visiting Lia?"

Duncan's headshake set Aiden off. With his emotions a jumbled mess, he threw his hands in the air, then took a deep breath to control his tone. "What do we know about him? Other than he and Lia are thick as thieves."

Duncan placed a reassuring hand on his shoulder. "I understand your confusion and your fear. We worried about him until Nick used his talents to do a bit of investigating. Josiah Warren wasn't lying. He knew nothing about the amulet." The encouraging grip on Aiden's shoulder remained as Duncan continued. "That doesn't mean we aren't watching him. We'll take care of Lia. You look after your family."

Although he still didn't trust Warren, Aiden had to let it go for the moment. He had enough on his mind without adding Lia to the list. *Damn! What was the matter with that woman? She seemed to enjoy playing with fire.*

He'd saved her once, but this threat was more subtle.

****

In order to deal with Maeve, Kane had to shove Gianna aside. Before he uttered a word, an energy blast slammed into his chest. He flew backwards, crashing against the table, and ended up on the floor among his scattered papers. Gianna and Tapper scurried away into the bedroom. Enraged, Kane tried to scramble to his feet but had to duck to avoid an airborne Jago who'd also tried to stop their prisoner.

Damn! As she struggled to shake off the drug, she prepared for another attack. He'd underestimated the woman's strength.

The words, "*Nunc somnum*," and a flick of his wrist froze her hand in midair. The determined expression dissolved, and she slumped back into the chair. A slumber spell. He should have used it earlier. Much easier than drugs. He could wake her and control her mind when necessary.

Jago stood up and stretched his neck. "What the hell did she do?"

Kane ignored him and walked over to the woman. With a sigh, he reached out to capture one of her curls, running it through his fingers. *Maeve.* It was the name of a mythical warrior queen. *Fitting,* he thought. *As fiery as her flaming hair.*

Gianna and Tapper earned a scowl as they slunk out of the bedroom. Ignoring them, he kept his focus on Maeve. *If I could find a woman like her, we'd be unstoppable.*

****

The dinner conversation was bleak. Lia repeated Josiah's concerns to her family which precipitated an anxious discourse. All agreed releasing a demon would create disaster, but their decision was simple. Maeve's life was more important. Safety for their own came first.

"Besides," Bree said as she put down her fork, "we will stop this *warlock*. His magic will be nothing against our combined gifts. We can save Maeve and the amulet. It's our only option."

Her aunt sounded so positive. Lia wanted to believe her and convince Josiah the plan would work, but she worried. Knowing that her own fears stemmed from her lack of powers didn't help. She had to trust her Clan. They'd prevailed against devastating odds last year. They could do so again.

After cleaning up, she gravitated outside. The slow rhythm of the porch rocker, cool air, and the magnificent star-filled sky failed to soothe her as dire thoughts spiraled through her mind: fear for Maeve, what to do about the amulet, and Josiah's creepy ring. Then, there was Aiden. She believed he could be the one, but it depended on reclaiming her powers, and only Maeve could help with that.

"Hey. Want some company?"

Lia smiled at Alex and pointed toward a chair. "You're always welcome. Especially since I can't quiet my thoughts."

"I know what you mean. I can't forget that giant snake last year, and Nick keeps telling me not to fret." With a toss of her head, she said, "Fret? Where did he come up with that?"

Lia grinned. "You're not alone. After our battle with that red-eyed demon last year, the mere mention of the 'D' word makes me shiver. Never mind that nasty warlock who's after the amulet. Poor Maeve."

"At least we know she's alive, but I feel so sorry for

Aiden. First his brother-in-law and now his aunt. How's he coping with this?"

"Anxiety and anger. I wish he wouldn't take it out on Josiah, though."

"Yeah. Aiden doesn't seem to like him much. Did you learn anything about our close-mouthed agent? He makes me nervous—which reminds me. What were you two doing in the gazebo?"

"You don't miss much."

Alex grinned. "I try not to."

"We were working on spells."

"Your powers are back?"

"No." She paused, then said, "I have some other Templar boon, separate from my gifts."

Alex leaned forward. "What do you mean?"

Lia shifted in her chair and looked out at the darkening sky. "He sensed I have other magic."

Alex gaped at her. "Like what?"

Relieved to discuss it with someone who'd understand, Lia told her cousin about the spells. When she finished, Alex touched her hand. Worry creased her face as she asked, "He didn't do any summoning? Nothing dark?"

Lia reassured her cousin. "Of course not. I'd never allow that."

But why couldn't she tell her Clan about the ring?

****

The early morning stillness held a sense of expectancy. Not even a tiny wisp of air disturbed her bedroom curtains. The usual birdsong seemed muted, and the rhythmic splash of waves a memory. A warning? Lia shook off the sensation. She no longer had an affinity with the weather. Her apprehension mirrored her dread of the future.

She tipped her head, inspecting the ugly scar there and the frizzy hair that sprouted around it. When the doctor had proclaimed the wound was healing nicely, she'd wanted to scream, "But what about my gifts?"

Snatching up her scarf, she tied it over her hair, looked at the clock, and sighed. Seven a.m. A formerly unheard-of hour for her. With her late-night forays canceled since the attack, she had no reason to stay up. Her mother intercepted Lia as she left her room. Franki, usually the sweetest of women in the morning, pursed her lips and tossed her head.

"What's wrong?" Lia said.

"He's here again."

"Who?"

"That Warren man. He wants to see you. After I told him you were still sleeping, do you know what he said?"

Lia couldn't help but grin. "What did he say?"

Franki just glared at her. "Wake her up."

Lia laughed. Her mother had warmed to the protector role, and Josiah was pushing all her buttons. "It's okay, Mom. I want to talk to him. He's helping me."

"With...*spells*?"

"Come on, Mom. You can't believe I'd go to the dark side. Wiccans use spells, and they aren't evil. You know I only ever want to help others." She gave her mother a kiss and headed downstairs.

Josiah met her in the hall, took one look at her, and nodded. "At least you're up. We have work to do."

"Good morning to you, too. I'm getting something to eat. Why don't you join me?"

"I've eaten."

"Fine."

Stopping by the breakfast room, Lia filled a travel mug with decaf and scooped up a couple of blueberry muffins to take to the gazebo.

In the absence of wind, a fine mist clung to the shore. Josiah sniffed the air. "Something's coming."

Lia's back stiffened as her earlier concern about the unnatural stillness reemerged. "It's just a quiet summer morning."

Josiah's eyebrows rose. "Is it?"

A sudden chill shook her. She took a bite of her muffin and handed the other to him.

He ignored the offering. "We have little time. Now pay attention." He described the secret to spell casting: purpose, magical intention, and channeled energy.

"You can create your own spells. They don't need to be in Latin. Picture what you want, gather your inner magic, say the words, and use your hand to direct the spiritual force."

Lia looked at him in disbelief. First, he said she couldn't use English and second, what mystical force was he talking about?

He glared at her. "Let's not go there again. Yesterday should have convinced you. Your ability grows with each use. Now, let's get started."

He handed her a twig. "Light it with your own words, using the formula I gave you."

Okay, she thought, *Here I go*. She pulled up an image of the tip on fire. Finding the right words proved difficult, so she said, "Ignite this twig," and flicked open her fist. Nothing happened. She looked at Josiah.

"What did you forget?"

"I did everything you said." She detailed her actions. "I guess I can't do it."

Josiah's look of disgust made her angry. She'd tried.

"You didn't pull the magical energy from here." He rapped his fist against his chest. "Now try again."

By lunchtime, Lia had lit the twig and healed a cut, but binding the box, which had worked yesterday, was beyond her. Josiah told her she didn't have enough confidence in her ability.

She knew he was right. Since the accident, she'd felt like a powerless husk, a burden to her Clan. This was her chance to change that.

"Once you stop feeling sorry for yourself, the magic will find you. I should have information for your Clan this afternoon. In the meantime, practice. We'll talk later."

Oh boy. She couldn't wait. Fun with Josiah, part two.

****

By that afternoon, the sorrow and pain of Smitty's loss had eaten a hole in Aiden's gut. His sister had collapsed at the gravesite, then his father's back gave out when he tried to lift her. When his mother rushed to help them, she twisted her ankle and went down. Aiden rescued his sister but was unable to help either parent. His two brothers took over parental assistance. This family couldn't handle another loss. He had to get Maeve back unharmed.

After dropping his things in the Stuart guest room, he found Duncan working on his computer in the study.

"Aiden, I'm just going to send this lesson in for my criminal law class. Then we can talk."

There wasn't much to discuss. Duncan had started making inquiries about rentals in the Newport and Narragansett areas, but with people gearing up for the

Fourth of July festivities, he'd been unable to contact all the property owners. Aiden, too, came up empty.

"I'm going over to the Brendanis," Duncan said. "Josiah Warren called. He wants to meet with the Clan in a couple of hours. We'll be getting together before that to discuss our options. Care to join us?"

"Thanks. I will. In the meantime, is Nick around?"

"Let me check." Duncan paused, closed his eyes, then smiled. "He's in the kitchen, waiting for you."

Nick had his head in the refrigerator when Aiden walked in. In a muffled voice, he asked if Aiden wanted a sandwich.

"Sure. I can always eat." The simple camaraderie he experienced with Duncan and Nick helped lighten his sorrow, and now that he knew Nick wasn't interested in Lia, he could see him as a friend.

As they scarfed down the food, Aiden asked Nick about his reading of Josiah Warren, emphasizing his concern about Lia working with the *so-called* Templar agent.

Nick reassured him. "The guy's been honest with us so far. He's not very personable, but it seems like he wants to help. I heard he was working with Lia to try to retrieve her powers." When Aiden gave him an incredulous stare, he shrugged. "Her gifts aren't back yet, but he gave her some kind of herbal medicine."

Aiden's powers had always been part of his life, like his hearing or sense of smell. He imagined that for Lia, the loss of her gift would be devastating.

Half an hour later, Aiden joined the trek to the Brendanis. When he spotted Lia's bright blue kerchief among the flowers, he veered off the path. "I'll see you guys later. I want to speak to Lia."

“Right,” Nick said with a grin.

Aiden ignored his teasing tone and wandered over to the garden. Today she wore white shorts that emphasized her long legs. He paused to watch her clip blooms for her basket until she noticed him.

She straightened. “You’re back.”

Her smile touched a chord inside him. “Like a bad penny.”

“I’m so sorry for everything you and your family are going through. I wish I could help.”

When she touched his arm, he felt the heat of her hand and inhaled her sweet fragrance. His protective instinct took over. “How are you feeling?”

“Fit as a fiddlehead fern.”

“What?”

She laughed. “I don’t know about musical instruments, but I know about plants.”

Her delight was contagious, allowing him to bury his sorrow and anxiety for a moment. He enjoyed being with her.

She paused, stared into space, then heaved a sigh. “I understand loss. My cousin, Tony, died last year in that decaying monstrosity we call the Convent House.”

“I didn’t know. I’m sorry.”

The corner of her lips lifted in a sad smile. “He used to tease me a lot, but in a pinch, he’d always stick up for me.” With a tiny chuckle, she said, “He risked his life to save me and a tiny bird.”

As Aiden squeezed her shoulder, his own memories surfaced. “I get it. When Maeve was seventeen, she used to babysit for us. I was seven, the adventurous one, but when I climbed out on the roof one day, I got too near the edge and panicked. Although she was afraid of heights, she managed to inch her way out and drag me back." He shook his head. "She never told my parents."

"We'll get her back."

Embarrassed by his emotions and wanting to change the subject, Aiden brushed an imagined speck from his shirt. "Heard any more from Warren?"

She slid the basket on her arm and planted a hand on her hip. "And that's your business, how?"

Damn! He wished he'd kept his mouth shut. Even in anger, her eyes were beautiful. Feigning innocence, he said, "Just trying to catch up on any news."

"I consider Mr. Warren a friend to the Clan, and I enjoy his company. He'll be here this afternoon to give us an update on his research. I hope you plan to be there."

"Ouch! Didn't mean to touch a nerve. Sorry. I'll listen to him and try to keep an open mind." He smiled and tilted his head. "Friends again?"

Lia's stance softened. "I apologize. My mother's been giving me grief, and I got a little carried away." She gave him an impish grin. "I am glad to have you back."

He brushed his fingers across her cheek. "You're much prettier when you smile."

Whether pouting or laughing, those lips tempted him. He wondered what she'd do if he kissed her. Before he could act on that impulse, a message from Duncan interrupted his thoughts. *Time to discuss plans.*

****

They walked into the Brendani kitchen to the smell of baking. When Aiden stopped to look around for a tasty tidbit, Lia gave him a poke. "You'll find the goodies in the living room. Don't worry. I'm sure my mother made plenty."

Franki greeted them, and Aiden grabbed a handful

of chocolate chip cookies as he walked by. When he popped a whole one into his mouth with obvious pleasure, Lia made a mental note to get her mother's recipe.

Aiden's smile of appreciation soon faded, and she remembered the reason he was here. Not to flirt with her, but to rescue Maeve. The last of the Clan arrived, and Rosemary cleared her throat. "Although we've heard nothing yet, we know what the kidnapper wants. We need to be ready."

As heads nodded, she continued. "We don't know where the exchange will take place, but we can prepare. I've come up with a plan of sorts. Once we hand over the amulet, Alex and I will trap the kidnappers inside a shield, allowing Bree to get into their heads. The second line of attack will be Duncan, Nick, and Aiden. They'll stop anyone who escapes our net."

Lia listened in silence, acutely aware that she had no place in the plan.

Rosemary, seeming to understand, turned to her. "Until you're well, it's best that you stay here. We want you safe."

Lia got it. Powerless, her presence would only add to the danger. She blinked and jumped up to leave, but the sound of the doorbell stopped her. She headed to the door, swallowing her feelings of inadequacy, and ushered Josiah Warren into the living room.

He cut short the greetings and laid out his argument for them retaining the amulet in their possession. "Based on the unique carvings, I was able to do a deeper search on the medallion. Centuries ago, your ancestors used it to imprison a demon named Agamorth. Though summoned to protect a Templar treasure and kill the one who tried to steal it, something went wrong.

"I found an old first-person account. After the demon emerged from the amulet, instead of killing the thief, he slid into his body then transferred to one of the knights and caused him to turn against his brothers. Bloodshed and death followed before the Templars imprisoned the entity."

Rosemary spoke up. "Why didn't they send him back to hell?"

"I don't know, but if he escapes again, innocents will die. And once he's free, as a higher demon, he can slice a rift between worlds, allowing lesser fiends access to our realm. We can't let that happen."

Chapter Fourteen

The next morning in the kitchen Lia stretched before pouring herself another cup of decaf. She missed her usual energy boost but, until they defeated the warlock, any mind-altering substances were prohibited.

During last night's discussion, which continued into the early hours, Josiah had regaled them with demonic possibilities. As an enormous yawn seized her, she bristled. Thanks to his graphic descriptions, red-eyed monsters had clawed their way through her dreams. She needed fresh air and the feel of the water on her toes. Outside, the intermittent sound of fireworks reminded her that the Fourth of July was just three weeks away. Some overeager kids always started early.

At the water's edge, she slipped off her sandals and waded in. On days like this, the river felt like a living soul, caressing her feet while whispering to her in soft murmurs against the shore. In the silence following the scream and crack of a nearby rocket, the sound of Aiden's voice triggered a surge of excitement.

"Hey, beautiful."

She turned. For just a minute, with the brilliant rays of sun surrounding him, he appeared heaven sent. She suppressed a chuckle. Aiden was no angel.

He scrambled down the rocky berm and gave her a crooked grin, half closing one eye, the blue one. "Kind of a noisy morning."

Lethargy forgotten, she checked her scarf and smiled. "You noticed."

Stooping to pick up a handful of pebbles, he skipped one across the water. "Josiah made some good points last night."

Lia shivered. "I'll say. He gave me nightmares."

"I think Rosemary's plan will work, though. We've got more than enough power to capture the warlock." As he whipped another stone into the water, his tone sharpened. "First, we make sure Maeve is okay."

Lia knew his inability to help his aunt was killing him.

"Absolutely." She lifted her face into the wind. Something scraped her ankle. A piece of seaweed. As she bent to remove it, she thought of her Clan. They'd save Maeve and the amulet. "I can't wait to see the warlock when they spring the trap."

Aiden spun toward her. "What?"

"I want to see his eyes when he realizes we have him."

"You won't be there."

She stepped toward him and planted her feet. "Of course I will. I may not have my powers back, but I intend to be there with my Clan."

Aiden flung the rest of the pebbles to the ground and narrowed his eyes. "That's ridiculous. You're still recovering from a serious wound. It's too risky."

"Are you kidding? With all that psychic power floating around, I'll be more than safe."

"Forget it. We don't know what we'll be facing, and I'll be too busy to protect you."

Oh no! Treating her like a victim wouldn't fly. She lifted her chin and glared at him. "Who asked you? I'll have you know…" She paused when she realized he wasn't listening to her, but to a telepathic message.

When he tightened his lips and turned to leave, she clutched his arm. "Wait a minute. What's wrong?"

"He called. It's on. I've got to go."

"Now? Aiden, take me with you."

With one hard head shake, he said, "It's too dangerous." She sensed his anxiety as he turned and put his hands on her shoulders. "You're not going."

"I'll stay in the background. You can't expect me to wait here without even telepathy to hear the news."

He just shook his head and walked away. *Oh, no you don't.* She scooped up her sandals, scrambled up the bank, and hurried after him. Jogging to keep up, she tried to figure how to insinuate herself into the rescue party. At a time of crisis, she belonged with her Clan.

Everyone had gathered in the kitchen. She leaned against a counter and kept quiet. The swap was in two hours at Sayers Wharf in Newport. Not much time. Summer traffic on a Saturday would slow them down.

Nick pounded his fist on the table. "Are you kidding? There's a big craft show there this weekend. The lot will be crammed with people. We can't use magic around normals."

"No doubt that's the reason he wants to meet there," Duncan said.

While everyone argued, Lia told Aiden that she'd be right back. Since she couldn't convince anyone to take her to the exchange, she'd figured out another way. Reaching for her phone, she called Josiah. While voices rose in a heated discussion, Lia snuck outside.

The background staccato of firecrackers jarred her nerves as the grim coincidence sliced into her. Last July, she'd helped her Clan save Alex from a magical enemy. They were successful, but in the process, two of their Clan had died. Today, she could only watch and pray.

****

Lia spotted Josiah's car and hurried to get in.

He didn't bother with niceties. "I don't like this. Without your gifts, you won't help anyone, and you'll only slow me down. Give me the directions and we'll talk later."

"No." She turned in the seat to check behind them. "Drive off before they come out."

Josiah's scowl matched the growl in his voice. "Poor way to start a partnership."

"If that's what you intend for us, then let's discuss what that does and doesn't mean. Partners share with one another. One doesn't dictate to the other."

"Yes, but in this instance, only one has the requisite strength and skills to do the job. The other is just a hindrance."

Lia wanted to hit him. She wondered what powers he had other than the ring. Her voice dripped with ice. "Well, the powerless partner has the address."

"Fine. Where do I turn?"

"Take a right at the next street."

"Newport?"

"Mm hmm."

"All right. When we arrive, do exactly as I say." He turned to her, eyes hard and lips compressed, as he waited to hear their destination.

His glare made Lia cringe inside, but she said, "Okay. We're going to the wharf area. We'll have to park at the hotel. Newport is crazy right now." Under her breath, she muttered, "Disrupting the plan."

Josiah snorted in disgust. "Clans always think their gifts will prevail. How can you throw a shield over one person in a crush of people? You better hope your aunt can cloud his mind."

He slowed down as traffic increased. "I think you'll find that psychic powers are no match for superior cunning."

****

The deadline didn't give them much time. When Aiden insisted on being part of the plan, and Rosemary asked him about his powers, he balked. He'd never divulged their existence to anyone outside of his Clan, let alone spoken of their use. He hated to let his guard down, but this Clan wasn't the enemy. "The same as you. Psychokinesis. Energy bolts."

"Oh yeah?" Nick said. "What about the hypnosis?"

Aiden spun around. "How do you know about that?"

"Video surveillance when Lia caught you in Dad's office."

He shrugged. "I can use my ring to mesmerize someone, but it only works within eight to ten feet."

"Okay," Rosemary said. "We'll have to leave soon. Maeve's fiery hair should stand out in the crowd. Most of you have also seen Jago."

Aiden would never forget the thug's rotten face or nasty reptilian tattoos.

"What I suggest is we each take a specific area of the wharf." She stopped to explain the layout of Sayers to Aiden before continuing. The plan relied on Bree and Alex controlling the warlock's mind while Rosemary kept him in her snare. They'd never be able to go on the offense with energy bolts amid a vast group of tourists.

Suddenly, Aiden realized Lia hadn't returned and

went looking for her to say goodbye. Smitty's death had taught him a wicked lesson: you never knew if you'd see someone again. After checking the entire house, he couldn't find her.

He spoke to Duncan. "You don't suppose she's outside?"

"Damn!" Duncan said. "She wouldn't leave and miss the discussion. Let me check." After a minute, he said, "Kitty says she hasn't seen her since you two came rushing to the house. And she sees everything on the property."

Aiden cringed. He knew what that ghost saw.

Duncan raised his voice. "Lia's missing. She's probably on her way to the wharf. Let's keep an eye out for her when we arrive. She doesn't even have her telepathy, so she'll be vulnerable."

Aiden felt sick. Maeve was in danger. They couldn't use their powers. And now, a defenseless Lia was running headlong into a deadly situation.

****

Hundreds of voices, along with fireworks and boat horns almost drowned out Kane's instructions to Jago and Gianna. He'd left Tapper in a speedboat by the public dock, drooling over the fancy yachts. Too worried about tipping over, he forgot about tapping.

Gianna, still peeved because she'd been relegated to watching their redheaded captive, kept gazing at the various craft tables scattered about the fair.

Kane pinched her chin. "Ignore those cheap trinkets. Pay attention to Maeve and your phone. *Do not* leave this food tent. Do you understand?"

She pulled her face away. "Yes. Whatever you say."

He gave Jago his instructions.

"No problem, boss. I'll take care of it."

Kane positioned himself to wait. He'd checked out Stuart and his family online. They were a prominent group with lots of pictures posted to various sites. He'd recognize them the minute they entered. He allowed himself a smile. They knew nothing about him or what he had in store for them.

****

Aiden's anger boiled. From the waterfront restaurant to America's Cup Avenue, the Sayers Wharf parking lot resembled a mob scene. A small band played in the far corner next to the food tent, with the rest of the real estate crammed with crafters' tables. He blinked, trying to adjust his eyes to the constant flow of people as he tried to find Maeve.

Franki and Bree stood with him near the walkway to Bannister's Wharf. Rosemary and Duncan were at the street entrance, and Nick and Alex had the Scott's Wharf access.

Each group sent telepathic messages as they moved into place. Since they believed Maeve was drugged, they figured she'd be seated or in a wheelchair, so they looked toward all the people sitting down: those listening to the band and a large group eating in the food tent.

Moments later, Duncan answered his cell and relayed the news. *It's the kidnapper. He spotted me. Check for people using phones.*

Right, Aiden thought. *That narrows it down.*

While he scanned the area, hoping to catch someone watching Duncan, another message came through. *He wants the amulet on the end table.*

Aiden followed as Duncan pushed his way through the crowd, stopped at a small table, and spoke into his phone. He knew Duncan was demanding proof that Maeve was there before handing over the amulet. Then Duncan picked up something from the table. His eyes widened, and his body stiffened. Seconds later Aiden received a telepathic image—a picture of Maeve at the food tent with a gun to her head and the words, *Leave the amulet or she dies.*

Aiden's stomach dropped as he tried to find her. He didn't dare attempt a rescue until they had the warlock under their control.

He saw Duncan tug the amulet from his pocket and toss it onto the table.

****

Lia and Josiah arrived at the event before the Clan. She was furious when Josiah insisted she wear a hat. His reasoning? He wouldn't have time to save her if her attacker recognized her.

Nice. Josiah Warren might be a Knight Templar, but he was no hero. She wore the hat, ignored Josiah, and glared at the packed area. People moved in all directions, making forward progress difficult. Some wore shorts, some jeans, while others wore patriotic garb. The ambient noise was almost deafening. Excited chatter, music, and an occasional loudspeaker challenged her concentration.

Josiah leaned in close to be heard above the din. "She'll probably be under sedation in a wheelchair. I'll check around the bandstand. You head over there. He pointed to an area with people eating lunch under a canopy."

The bustling throng made it difficult to move. When she caught sight of Aiden across from her, she ducked her head and followed the smell of fried clam cakes. In the shade of the food tent, she blinked to adjust her vision before checking the crowded tables. Now to look for Maeve.

With her attention focused on finding Aiden's aunt, she accidentally cut into the food line and got a rude shove. As she backed off, she spotted two women, one in a wheelchair. If only she had her telepathy. She tried a quick message to let the others know and grabbed her head. Not yet. As she closed in on the couple, she saw a bright flash above them, then a steamy trail. The canvas was burning.

Without thinking, she flicked her hand to call for rain, causing another stab of pain. Fire broke out all over and people began panicking. She had to fight to get to Maeve, elbowing and cramming her way forward. At last, she made it, but the other woman had vanished, leaving her unconscious prisoner alone. Lia checked Maeve's pulse. She was okay but sparks continued to fly all around them; smoke had invaded her nose. Boxed in by a metal fence, she held onto the wheelchair and started yelling for help.

****

Josiah wasn't searching for Maeve. He'd leave that to the others. He'd spotted Duncan and knew he had the amulet. Rescuing the Templar artifact was his goal. He followed Duncan to the back of the lot where the only outlet was the harbor. *Of course!* He thought. *The warlock will make his escape by water.*

He saw Duncan put his phone to his ear. He'd made contact. Josiah watched him look around, and when he placed the amulet on a table, Josiah made a dash for it, but before he'd taken two steps, it disappeared. Apportation. Strong magic. A warlock with that ability had serious power.

Someone yelled “fire!”, and people began to panic. Then, from the corner of his eye, he saw a man heading toward the harbor unconcerned with the ensuing commotion. That had to be his quarry.

Josiah followed him to the dock where a nearby yacht hosted a rowdy wedding reception. As the party craned their necks toward the pandemonium behind him, the man flicked his hand in their direction, and a bright spark hit the bride’s dress. The fluffy concoction burst into flames. Her screams added to the overall chaos as she jumped into the water. Moments later, an insane, fuchsia-colored fire dance followed as bridesmaids in flaming gowns leaped after the bride into Newport Harbor.

Josiah ignored the clever diversion to focus on his goal. As he’d suspected, the getaway craft was manned and ready. Knowing he was no match for the warlock’s powers, he grabbed his phone to take a picture. Easy, when the man, sensing an enemy, turned and glared at him.

Prepared for an assault, Josiah invoked a protection spell. When the warlock’s curse hit, he staggered, almost plunging in with the screeching females.

Cries for help from figures splashing in the water and the smell of sulfur surrounded him as he tried to maintain his balance on the slippery dock. The damn warlock packed a powerful blast. Josiah decided his enemy must be older than he’d thought. More dangerous. He sent his photos to headquarters before tucking the phone in his pocket and weaving his way back through the drenched and sobbing partygoers. Although in a hurry to leave, Josiah checked on the Clan. He read anger and frustration on their faces. Stupid to underestimate the enemy.

He hated to duck out on Lia, but he had to stop the demon. He hoped he was wrong about the amulet, but the full moon was Tuesday, only three days away. If they didn't stop the warlock before then, he feared all hell, literally, would break loose.

****

Lia tugged at the wheelchair, but it wouldn't move. The smoke swirling around her increased in intensity, bringing on a spasm of coughing. Finally, she found and released the brakes. Sparks landed on Maeve and then Lia's arm. When they hit Maeve's straw hat, Lia tossed it to the ground along with her own. She shoved the wheelchair, but it bumped up against the metal barrier. Then she grabbed the damn fence, trying to move it, all the while screaming for help. Behind her, flames chewed up the paper tablecloths and bit into the wooden tables. The wheelchair was too bulky to maneuver. She tried to pull Maeve over the fence, but the dead weight was more than she could handle, so she started kicking at the obstacle. Just as her strength wavered, strong arms ripped it away.

"Come on, Lia. I'll get Maeve." Aiden dragged her away from the tent, then rolled his aunt to safety.

"Thank God," Lia said. "I couldn't get her out." She rubbed her hand over her face, surprised when it came back wet.

He gave her a brief, tight hug. "It's okay."

As he knelt next to his aunt, Lia's family arrived. Franki enveloped her in a fierce embrace before beginning a familiar lecture. In the past, Lia would laugh and say she could take care of herself, but, to her horror, she'd learned the meaning of helplessness.

When Alex squeezed her shoulder, she asked her about the amulet.

"We had no chance to do anything. The warlock used apportation. The amulet just disappeared. We never even saw him."

"What? I didn't think that was even real."

Alex nodded. "Neither did I. Then we had to help with the fires and the hysterical crowd. He got away with it."

Lia wanted to scream. All their plans and superior powers meant nothing. He'd outsmarted them. She looked around. Most of the people had dispersed when the fire fighters appeared. Vendors scrabbled among overturned tables to retrieve their merchandise. What a mess.

EMTs caring for those who needed help tended to Maeve and assured them she should come around soon.

Aiden wanted them to check Lia, but she laughed. "I'm fine. Still a little shaken, but otherwise, good."

He took her hand. "I can't thank you enough for protecting my aunt. You risked your life."

She shook her head. "Just a few burns."

Franki put her arm around Lia. "All right. Time to go. You can talk back at the house." She turned to Aiden. "You're coming back?"

"Yes. I want to make sure Maeve is conscious before I drive her home." He leaned in and gave Lia a kiss on her forehead. "Thanks again for taking care of my aunt."

As Lia watched him wheel Maeve out, her mother gave her shoulders a squeeze. "I think he's smitten."

Lia frowned and shook her head, but inside, her

heart sang. "He's just grateful."

"Is your car at the hotel?"

"My car?" Then she remembered Josiah. She stopped and looked all around. Nothing. Would he have left by now?

"I came with Josiah. Have you seen him?"

Franki's frosty "No" told Lia all she needed. She was in for another maternal scolding. In the meantime, she wondered what had happened to their strange Templar agent.

****

Kane's fingers itched to destroy the intruder as he slipped through the dripping throng. *Who the hell was the man with the camera, and how had he detected me?*

He couldn't be part of the magical group. None of those holier-than-thou people would refuse to help drowning women.

Damn! And now they had his picture. The amulet begged Kane to use it, but he didn't dare comply. If Agamorth escaped before Kane's spell released him, he'd be out of control. Kane had to let his enemy go.

The trip through the harbor with Tapper was hairy. When a wave hit them broadside and the boat rocked, Kane shouted at him. "Stop looking behind you. No one is following. We're safe. Unless you capsize us. Slow down."

Tapper didn't pay any attention, his knuckles whitened as he clutched the wheel. Kane had to use a calming spell on the fool to keep the boat under control.

They made it to the dock where they'd left their cars. Kane told Tapper to wait for the others and meet him at the cottage. Although he no longer needed them, he had to make sure they'd keep quiet. He might leave Jago on his payroll and dump the other two.

The amulet, secure in his pocket, pulsed with Agamorth's energy. Soon, that power would be his. He wouldn't need anyone. Nothing would stand in his way. He smiled as he thought of the Templar Council in New York. All their secrets and treasures would be his. But the jewels and gold were nothing compared to the ultimate prize. He was certain they harbored the Cup of Immortality. With the Holy Grail, he'd live forever.

Chapter Fifteen

Before they left Newport, Bree invited everyone back to the house for lunch and brainstorming. Lia called Pizza Palace to deliver food. After a day filled with shock and disappointment, she could use some carbohydrate comfort, and knew she wasn't alone.

Back home, after changing out of her smoky clothes, Lia sent a text to Josiah asking if he was okay. He didn't answer. No surprise. She jabbed the *off* button and hurried downstairs to help Alex set the table.

"So," Alex said. "Aiden saved you again."

Lia checked to make sure they were alone. "And he kissed my forehead in front of my mother."

Alex poked her shoulder. "He's so sweet. Give him a break. You know love doesn't depend on psychic powers. Look at your parents. Besides, Maeve will help you."

When the doorbell rang, two delivery persons arrived with the food, followed by the heady scent of tomatoes and garlic. Lia's stomach gurgled. She'd had nothing to eat since breakfast. The others arrived shortly afterward, with an alert Maeve leaning on Aiden and Duncan.

Nick, in the lead, hollered, "Where's the food? I'm getting faint."

Bree and Franki fell over themselves to find him something, but Alex smacked him in the shoulder. "Get over yourself. We're all hungry."

The dining room smelled like a pizzeria as everyone converged on the table. Lia scooped up a cheesy wedge and saw Maeve laughing with a gooey piece in her hand. The poor thing sighed as she took a bite. "This is wonderful. I don't think I've eaten in the past few days."

Next to her, Aiden growled as he ripped off a chunk of his own slice, spraying a little sauce around. The spots on the white cloth resembled blood.

In between bites, Duncan told everyone what Maeve had seen when she'd awakened. "It sounds like some kind of farm. Our Clan and Aiden's are checking properties that rent cabins."

Lia glanced around the table. With Duncan's news, the mood at the table brightened. Everyone had an idea where to look. When they finished the meal, Rosemary suggested they move to the living room to talk. She positioned herself by the fireplace in the same spot where Franki's prophetic painting had stood almost a week earlier, and Lia winced. So much had happened since then. She chose a seat next to Maeve, with Aiden protecting his aunt's other side.

Rosemary walked a few paces back and forth until everyone settled in. "Today, we discovered a dangerous enemy. One who outsmarted us, retrieved the amulet, and escaped unscathed. We knew he was a warlock, yet none of us thought to investigate his powers. We assumed our gifts were superior." She shook her head and slapped the chair in front of her, sharp enough to make Duncan flinch. "A costly mistake."

She paused and glanced around the room. "We have to stop him before he releases the demon." She held her hands up. "I'm open to ideas."

An uncomfortable silence ensued before Aiden spoke up. "What about Josiah Warren? Shouldn't he know about warlock powers? Doesn't he have any resources?" He turned and stared at Lia. "What happened to him today?"

All eyes locked on her. "I don't know," she answered truthfully. "He isn't answering my texts, but I'm sure he'll get back to me. He said he needs us to defeat the demon."

She glared at Aiden. *Did he blame her? Rosemary was the one who called him.* But Aiden's anger didn't bother her so much as the disappointment she saw in his eyes.

Rosemary sounded desperate. "It's imperative we find the warlock."

Aiden's lips curled as he said, "We don't know what he looks like or where he came from. How the hell do we start a search?"

He looked at Maeve. "Do you remember any more about him?"

She shook her head. "He was dark. Hair and skin. Angry black eyes. He looked to be in his late thirties. It was all so quick. I'm sorry."

Duncan sighed. "Don't be. It's more than we had. If we can find where he kept you, we might get something else."

"I'll try to remember more."

Lia squeezed her hand. "You've done great."

With nothing new or helpful to add, the meeting broke up.

When Maeve leaned toward Lia and suggested they go outside, Lia could have hugged her.

****

She led Maeve to the back porch and watched as the woman's whole body came alive, reaching out to the sun like an eager flower. Maeve's green eyes brightened, and her movements were more assured.

A welcome shaft of air ruffled Lia's hair. She rested her elbows on the railing and embraced the safety of her home. She'd never experienced the fear she'd felt today—defenseless in the face of danger. At least with the fire in her greenhouse, she'd had her gift to summon rain.

Maeve leaned down beside her and took a deep breath. "It's beautiful out here. The fresh air is a balm to my soul. It feels as though I've been cooped up forever. I can't remember anything other than waking up in the cabin." She stood up and smacked the wooden rail.

"Four days is a long time." Lia shivered. "I hate that you went through that because of me, but I'm grateful you answered Aiden's call. If you hadn't, I might have died."

"Don't be silly. It's what we do. Besides, I have it on good authority that you saved me today."

Lia shook her head. "I tried, but Aiden saved us both."

"He's a good kid." Maeve smiled and tilted her head. "But what a brat. He didn't think ten years' difference gave me the right to *boss him around*."

She leaned her back against the railing. "He seems anxious about you."

Lia, who never blushed, felt her cheeks heat. "He's a caring person."

Maeve nodded. "He is. But he couldn't stop talking about how brave you were protecting me from the fire. That's not like him."

Nervous flutters teased Lia's chest. She could only say, "Oh." Then, before she could stop herself, she blurted out, "He doesn't have a girlfriend?"

Maeve chuckled. "He says he's too busy."

Yes!

Trying not to seem too interested, Lia said, "I forgot about his business. I guess he'll have to get back to it right away."

"Not really." Maeve turned with a grin. "Aiden insists Jaime's got a handle on everything, so he can stay here and channel his efforts into finding the warlock."

Lia felt her mouth go slack. He was staying? In a rush of pleasure, she smiled and stretched her shoulders. But she'd forgotten she wasn't alone, and her companion was a perceptive healer. When she caught Maeve's knowing expression, she cleared her throat and changed the subject.

"I'm excited to meet another healer. I thought I was the only one. I didn't even know other Watcher Clans existed."

Maeve nodded. "Nor did I."

"Do you have gifts other than healing?"

"Yes." She nodded towards the lawn. "I have an affinity with the earth and everything that grows there."

Lia leaned forward, excitement in her voice. "Wonderful. Can you control plants?"

"I can, but only when necessary."

"Have you ever had to use your gift in self-defense?"

Maeve looked unhappy and said nothing for a second. Then she nodded. "Once, when someone accosted me while I was hiking in the woods. I knew I was in trouble, so I petitioned the trees for help. They obliged by sending out roots to bind him while I escaped."

"Cool. I would have loved to have seen that." As she pictured it, Lia imagined the face of the nasty thug who'd burned her greenhouse. "My gift is also part of nature. Air." But as soon as she spoke, the ache of her loss dampened her pleasure.

Maeve must have sensed the emotional shift. "What's the matter?"

"I-it's not back yet."

Seeing Maeve's look of pity, Lia wished she hadn't spoken.

"It will return."

Lia hoped she was right as she gazed across the yard. Neither woman spoke for a few minutes.

"Lia?"

She brought her focus back to Aiden's aunt.

"What's the story with this Warren person who's gotten under my nephew's skin?"

Before Lia could answer, the screen door opened, and Aiden walked out. Putting his hand on Maeve's shoulder, he said, "Time to take you home. I've been getting pointed messages from both your mother and mine."

He turned to Lia. "Sorry about the outburst. I know it's not your fault. I guess I hate being helpless."

With a sardonic smirk, she said, "I know the feeling."

Her pointed retort hit the mark, and he apologized again. "Look, I'm coming back here after I bring Maeve home, and I'd love some company on the trip. Want to take the ride with us?"

Her insides sang. She wanted nothing more, but she

looked at Maeve. "I'm sure you two have a lot to catch up on. I don't want to intrude."

Maeve tapped Lia's arm. "Don't be silly. I can always talk to him." She flipped her hand in Aiden's direction then smiled at Lia. "We can continue our conversation on the way."

****

During the trip to North Kingstown, the two women sat in the back seat for a private discussion. Lia described how the attacker destroyed her greenhouse. "He set it on fire and burned all my babies. Thinking about the shriveled and charred plants makes me sick."

"What a horrible experience." Maeve patted Lia's hand. "You come over to my place when you're ready, and I'll let you replenish your stock from my nursery. If you don't have room for them now, Aiden can bring them later."

Lia wished Maeve lived closer. Not only did she enjoy her company, but she was eager to talk to another who had her special gift. Since Aiden had the radio on and seemed immersed in driving, Lia broached the topic of Josiah. "Every time I try to use my gifts or my telepathy, a pain cuts through my head, but someone taught me to use spells. And they worked. Without causing me pain. Have you ever done anything like that?"

Maeve shook her head. "I've never needed to try something different. What spells, and who showed them to you?"

Lia peeked at Aiden, hoping he couldn't hear. At Maeve's questioning look, Lia realized Aiden had filled Maeve in on the amulet and the warlock but not Josiah. "He's the Templar agent they were talking about in the living room.

"He answered some secret phone number and came to help us with that deadly piece of metal, hoping to bind it. But he couldn't. When he discovered I'd lost my powers, he told me about the incantations. He taught me one for healing." Lia hugged herself. "It made me feel as though I had my gift back."

Maeve's expression darkened as she said, "I've always suspected people who use spells. What did you have to do?"

"It was simple. I pictured the outcome, spoke the words, and wiggled my fingers."

"What language?"

"Latin, I think." She'd memorized the healing spell, so she repeated it for Maeve.

Maeve tilted her head and brushed wisps of red from her eyes. "Doesn't sound so bad. Speaking of healing, let me see how you're doing."

"Isn't it too soon after, you know, your experience?"

She laughed. "For me, food is the great healer. I feel much better." She lifted her hand toward Lia's head. "May I?"

"If you think it won't be too much."

Lia liked Maeve. Not once had she played the *victim* card. No tears, droopy shoulders, or sad expressions. No *poor me*. Lia wondered how well she'd behave under the same circumstances, not only being held for ransom, but having a horrid chop job to her gorgeous red hair. Lia's own shaved spot, although growing out, drove her crazy. But the uneven cut to Maeve's hair couldn't discourage a few fiery tendrils that curled around her face.

Maeve's fingers sent a wave of warmth through Lia's head. How strange to be on the receiving end of someone else's magic and experience the soothing medicine she'd offered to others. She prayed this woman's gift would revive her own.

"It's coming along. A few small areas of scar tissue might be the culprits blocking your powers. I've tweaked a couple. Wait until tomorrow and try something."

Maeve peered out the window. "Here we are." As soon as Aiden pulled into the driveway, people streamed out of the cottage.

An older woman with red hair hurried over and leaned in the window to hug Maeve.

Laughing, Maeve said, "Hi, Mom," as men, women, and children converged on her.

To Lia, she said, "Looks like I have a welcoming committee. You two coming in?"

Aiden waved at his relatives. "It's been a long day. Best if we get back."

Lia, who'd gotten out of the car to say goodbye, found herself engulfed in a smothering hug from Maeve's mother before she could slide into the front seat next to Aiden.

As he put the car in gear, he grinned. "They're a little excited."

With a chuckle, she said, "I think I felt ribs crack when her mother squeezed me."

"That's my grandmother. She's big with hugs."

Lia enjoyed watching the loving family. She leaned back with a sigh of contentment but couldn't help a wry smile as she thought about Kitty, a definite non-hugger.

Aiden's matter-of-fact voice snapped her up straight. "Okay. Now you can tell *me* what Josiah's been teaching you."

****

During the ride home with Aiden, Lia wished she were anywhere else. She'd hoped for time alone with him, but all he did was question her about Josiah.

Her *private* conversation with Maeve had been a farce. He'd heard everything. Damn the Templar's acute hearing.

Sarcasm dripped from his lips as he said, "I thought you couldn't use your gifts. That trying only caused you pain. Josiah cured you?"

Flustered and angry, she said, "You don't understand."

"Yeah? Why don't you enlighten me?"

Ooh. He sounded like a teacher who'd caught her in a lie. "What do you have against Josiah? He works for the Templars, for crying out loud."

"You only have his word for that."

"What are you, a conspiracy theorist? Josiah answered the secret Templar number, has the mark, and has been helping me."

"How?"

She wanted to explain about the Seeker thing, but she knew he'd never believe her. "Spells. He taught me a few simple incantations. And before you start, one was for healing."

"You know who uses those things? Warlocks. Our Clans don't. You know why?"

Disgusted, she said, "Because we don't need them?"

He ignored her words and said, "Because that way leads to evil."

"Oh, come on," she yelled.

"It's too easy to use it for your own ends. Black magic is full of dangerous, even lethal, incantations. How do you know what other things he wants to teach you?"

This was too much, and Lia laughed. "Are you jealous?"

The car swerved as he spun his head toward her. "Don't be ridiculous. He's sixty if he's a day."

The horror on Aiden's face when she accused him of jealousy amused her, and she didn't want to argue anymore. "Look, Aiden. All I know is that I won't be powerless if Maeve can't help me. It felt good to regain healing gifts. How would you feel if you'd lost your powers?"

In a more reasonable tone, he said, "I guess you're right. I'd do anything to regain my skills. But that's just why it's so dangerous. How far do you go?"

In a decisive tone, she said, "I'd never dip into the dark side. I'm smart enough to know the difference. Why don't you join us the next time he shows up, and see for yourself?"

"When is that?"

"I don't know. He disappeared today, but I'm sure I'll hear from him soon."

"Yeah, he disappeared, leaving you and Maeve in danger."

"He knew the Clan would help us."

He turned to face her. "It was too close."

"Could you please keep an open mind until you talk to him?"

After a long pause, he said, "I'll think about it."

She giggled. "Could you smile when you say that?"

His soft laugh preceded a wide grin, and Lia's heart leaped.

When they pulled into the Brendani driveway, the atmosphere in the car had brightened. Aiden escorted her to the door.

She opened her mouth to thank him and caught her breath as he leaned in. He cupped her face in his hands and touched his lips to hers. As his arms moved around her, she melted against him. Heat pulsed through her. His kiss became more insistent, and she met it with her own passion. Her whole body was aflame. She wanted more, but he pulled his head back, their bodies still fused. His ragged breathing matched hers.

The husky tone of his voice thrilled her. "This isn't the time or place." Then he grinned. "We'll continue this conversation later."

He leaned down and captured her lips for one more brief, but intense, moment. "Good night, Lia."

Her answer came out on a breathy sigh.

As Aiden drove away, his voice entered her head. *Take care, sweetheart.*

****

The sharp ping of sand attacking his expensive ride infuriated Kane. A burning sensation crawled into his throat. "Damn backwoods cow path!" He couldn't wait to get out of there.

The fire in his gut had begun earlier that day as he was making his escape. Pleased his plan had worked—Agamorth safe in his pocket and all the do-gooders fighting fires and saving innocents—a sudden tingle of alarm had made him turn in time to see some old fart taking his picture.

Who the hell was he? Kane had sensed no power emanating from him and no sign of the other group's magic. When he'd sent out a deadly spell, the man rebuffed it. How had that nobody protected himself?

Kane clamped his lips together and slammed his

hand against the dashboard before rubbing the inflamed spot burning his chest. He'd have to get a potion from Tetchy. The old witch could cure anything. He grinned. When they'd first met, and he'd asked her how she got her name, she'd snapped at him. "I'm tetchy about who I give my magic to."

At the cabin, he turned the car off with a satisfied grunt. Tuesday, with Agamorth's help, he'd be invincible. Now, he had to clean up loose ends.

He opened the cabin door with a bang. Tapper leaped up, Gianna dropped her phone, and Jago raised his eyebrows. "I thought you'd beat us here."

"Gassed up." He smirked. "I see you all kept from getting caught. Good for you. You completed your part of the deal and I'm here to keep mine."

He tossed an envelope to each one. "Your money." He pointed to the men. "Now I want you to forget you ever met me. Understand?"

They nodded. Tapper smiled as he bounced the envelope against his hand.

"Enjoy. Jago, could you wait in the car for Tapper for a minute?"

"Sure." Jago headed for the door as Tapper's eyes widened. He began moving from foot to foot.

"Relax," Kane said. "I just want to thank you for the transportation earlier."

Tapper's "Okay" sounded like a plea for mercy. Kane walked over to him and touched his arm. "And you won't remember any of it. You'll enjoy your money but forget where it came from."

Tapper blinked his eyes as Kane walked him out the door. The warlock then turned and regarded the useless witch who resembled a frightened bird. When he smiled at her, she fidgeted with her earrings. "You're coming home with me."

She calmed down a bit when he held out his arm to her. "I just need to do a cleansing. Don't want anyone tracking us." While he stood at the door outside to intone the spell, Gianna leaned in to listen and bumped into him.

He spun around and yelled, "Get in the car."

She tugged her hand from her ear and almost fell off the steps as she scurried away.

****

On the ride to Gianna's New York apartment, Kane applied his charm. With only three days until his transformation and the absorption of Agamorth's power, he realized he needed her. As they chatted, he sensed Gianna's confidence returning. He played to her vanity. By the time they reached her driveway, he was certain she'd forgiven him.

He carried her suitcases inside and heard a scraping noise on the tile floor. A streak of black careened around the corner and skidded to a halt. Green eyes blinked at them. "Meow!"

Kane smiled.

Gianna bent down and scratched the cat's chin. "Did you miss me, Brim?"

"Nice to see you again, Brimstone," Kane said. As he spoke, the cat rubbed up against his legs. Kane reached down and scratched the cat's back.

"I'm surprised he likes you," Gianna said. "He's usually nervous around men."

"Brimstone and I understand each other." He gave the cat a last pat. "Cats have always gravitated to me."

She looked up through her lashes and smiled. "I can understand why."

He laughed and took her in his arms. "I hate to leave, but I have things to do at home. I want everything to be perfect for our work. It'll take a few days. I'll pick you up on Tuesday." With an insolent grin, he said, "Make sure Brimstone has plenty of food. We may get very busy."

She answered with a sensuous smile, stroked his chest, and leaned up for his kiss. *This was the witch he'd first met*. He ran his finger down the side of her face. So soft. Lovely. He almost wished he could keep her.

****

Early Sunday morning, a loud conversation downstairs dragged Lia from her latest Aiden fantasy. She'd been replaying last night's kiss in her mind and wondering how to arrange an encore. As she tilted her head to listen, her chest expanded with little bursts of pleasure. Was that his voice she heard?

Although she'd been up for a while, she checked her image in the mirror, applied a quick dab of lipstick, and hurried downstairs. The voices came from the kitchen. When she opened the door, she stopped in surprise.

The entire Clan, plus Josiah, crowded the room. Josiah held the floor. "I'm telling you we have to find this guy before Tuesday night. It's the full moon. That's when he'll do it. We must stop him."

"How?" Duncan said. "We don't even know who he is."

"I've got his picture, and we know he's a warlock. My research team is on it."

"What picture?" Aiden said, "Let's see it."

As soon as Josiah pulled the photo from his pocket, Aiden snatched it from his hand, glared at it, then passed it around. No one recognized the man. Lia peeked over her mother's shoulder at the warlock's image and pulled back, repulsed. Hatred seemed to radiate from him.

"We'll check our computer." Aiden used his cell to send a copy to Jaime then turned to Josiah. "When did you get this?"

The Templar agent frowned. "I knew he'd be leaving by boat yesterday, so I walked that way and saw someone set fire to the bridal party. I knew it had to be him."

"If you'd told us," Aiden said, "we could have caught him."

"No time. You were busy rescuing people. Plus, he's dangerous. When I took this—" Josiah held up the photo "—he threw a powerful curse at me. Thankfully, I expected it and saved myself."

Duncan's phone rang, and he walked out of the room to answer it. When he came back, he said, "I think we've found where they held Maeve." He looked at Aiden. "Can you get her here to check it out?"

"Wait a minute." Aiden paused, then said, "She's already on her way. She'd planned to come over today for Lia." He turned to Lia and gave her a cheeky wink that sent heat searing through her. As she pondered whether she could get Aiden alone for a bit, Josiah touched her arm. "I'd like to talk to you for a minute."

Rats. She'd wanted to talk to Josiah, but not right now.

"Let's go outside," he said.

She swallowed her disappointment and followed him to the garden. He looked around. "This should be fine. It's time for you to begin your training."

"Now? In the middle of all this?"

"You're the only one who can help."

What was he talking about? “Me?”

“I’ve told you a little about your potential abilities.”

“*Very* little.”

“I didn’t think we were up against a seasoned warlock. You’re the only one who can track him.”

Lia sucked in her breath. “I can’t go up against a warlock without my powers.”

With a sour expression, he said, “I doubt you could do it even with your powers. Since we don’t have the luxury of time, I’ll give you the basics and help you along the way.” Without waiting for a response, he handed her a small velvet bag. “Put this on.”

Her thoughts whirled as a necklace slid onto her hand. The stone winked in the sun. A dark ruby color. The same as Josiah’s ring. She hesitated. This was too soon. She wasn’t ready to complete something she didn’t understand or even want.

“Your ancestors chose you,” he said. “Please.”

Wow. She never thought to hear that word on Josiah’s lips. If this was something given to her by her ancestors, she couldn’t reject it. In the battle with the demon last year, ancient Knights had materialized to work with her Clan. How could she refuse them? With a quick prayer, she lifted the necklace over her head. The sparkling stone hung between her breasts, heavy enough to remind her it was there. She expected to experience some kind of revelation like the transformation she’d felt on receiving her powers.

Nothing.

“Am I supposed to feel different?”

“Not until you find a monster.”

She backed away from him, shaking her head. “I’m not ready.”

He stopped her from removing the necklace. "It's your destiny. I'll teach you to protect yourself."

"How?" she yelled. "I have no gifts."

"Listen to me. When we go to the cabin where the warlock held Maeve, the ruby will allow you to feel his essence and understand how to track him. We're all counting on you."

Her insides cringed. This guy was insane.

"You'll understand when you get there," he said. "I'll be here for you. Every step."

A deep voice interrupted. "Every step where?"

Aiden placed himself between Josiah and Lia. "What crap are you trying to sell here, Warren?"

Josiah looked up and sighed. "You are a royal pain, O'Connor. Why do you distrust what you don't understand?"

"Then enlighten me, Mr. Templar agent."

Josiah straightened his shoulders and glared at Aiden before assuming a long-suffering tone. "I think Lia has a gift that may allow her to recognize the warlock's signature. I'm trying to help her with that. We'll see when we get to the cabin."

Aiden's expression went from frosty to deep-tundra glacial. "You want to put her in harm's way? Not going to happen."

"She'll be fine with all of us there."

Aiden opened his mouth to speak, paused, and then said, "They're ready. Come to the house with me, Lia."

Though she appreciated Aiden's protective streak, his controlling attitude irritated her. She touched his arm. "Thank you for worrying, but I want to see if he's right. We're coming with you to the cabin."

****

Sun filled the cheery kitchen, and the smell of warm muffins made Lia smile. Her mother had found time to go blueberry picking. One of Franki's coping mechanisms was baking. Last year during the trouble, she'd loaded the kitchen counters with muffins, pies, and cookies. Interrupted from their cozy chat, Franki, Rosemary, and Maeve looked up from the table. Maeve beamed at her. "Good morning."

Lia returned the grin and introduced Maeve to Josiah.

Instead of his usual brief acknowledgment, he made a slight bow. "It's a pleasure to see you safe and back in the fold."

Lia blinked. Where had this impatient dictator found such courtly manners?

With a nod to the women, he turned to Lia. "If you'll excuse me, I need to talk to Duncan."

"Living room," Franki said. From her mother's curt tone, Lia knew Josiah's civility hadn't won her over.

Maeve turned to Lia and asked if she was going to the cabin.

"Yes. After what happened, I can't wait to help catch this guy. Shall we join them?"

Before they left, Franki reached for Lia's necklace. "What's this?"

She'd forgotten the stone. "I'll explain when I get back." Knowing her mother wouldn't let it rest, Lia hurried out.

They were taking two cars. With Nick, Alex, and Bree in Duncan's car, that left Lia, Maeve, and Josiah to ride with Aiden. To make the trip more uncomfortable, Maeve insisted on sitting with Lia in the back seat to continue her healing. Josiah's mouth puckered as he headed for the front. She squelched a smile. No more refined gentleman.

Warmth swirled through her head as Maeve's healing hands did their work. After a few minutes, Maeve's pleased voice broke the silence. "This looks much better. Did you do anything last night?"

Lia's lips quirked as Aiden turned to grin at her. Then she remembered the telepathy and her whole day brightened. With all her mooning about Aiden last night, she'd forgotten. Her chest filled with pride as she sent a message to Maeve.

"That's wonderful." Maeve's voice alerted the others.

"She's better?" Aiden said.

Lia giggled as she used her mind to update Aiden. *I have my telepathy back. I got your message last night.*

She met his smoky gaze in the mirror and caught her breath as heat flared deep inside her.

****

The ride to the cabin took less than fifteen minutes. They pulled into a driveway leading to a weathered shingle ranch surrounded by pine trees. The landlord's home. Some Aquidneck Island farmers augmented their income by renting summer cottages.

Duncan's car turned onto a dirt road, where the tree line ended to reveal rows and rows of leafy green potato plants. "Oh!" Maeve whispered. "I thought it was a grassy field."

"You did great," Aiden said. "We found it, didn't we?" They stopped in front of a group of cottages and got out. Duncan pointed at the structures. "The owner indicated he rented them all, but let's start with this one. I think Maeve should go in first." He opened the door and led her inside. When she stopped and held Aiden's arm, Lia moved close, ready to lend support.

In the shabby room, Maeve pointed to a chair by the window. "There. As I woke up, a woman threw herself at an angry man." She paused and shivered. "His eyes were so cold. When he lifted his hand, I reacted and sent him sailing backward. Another man came at me. I threw another energy bolt and then…" She closed her eyes and shuddered. "That's all I recall."

Aiden wrapped his arm around her shoulders. "That's all right. You don't have to remember anything else. You're safe now."

Duncan had searched the tiny cottage. "It's clean."

Josiah pulled Lia to the side. "Hold your necklace and try to sense any signature left behind. Anything that doesn't belong here."

She blinked at him. "What?"

"Just do as I say. You should feel a lingering essence of the warlock."

Aiden interrupted. "What are you talking about?"

Josiah's voice hardened. "I told you. Lia can discover traces of paranormal beings."

Duncan took Maeve outside while the others finished searching the different cabins. Aiden wrapped his arm around Lia. "I don't know what you're trying to pull, old man, but I'm going to stay with her."

Although it was nice to have Aiden holding her and fighting for her safety, she had to step in. "It's all right, Aiden. I have another gift. If I can help hunt this warlock, I want to try." She patted his arm. "This is the perfect place to attempt it while I'm safe with you."

He huffed, "Fine," but gave her a comforting squeeze before backing off.

"Go ahead," Josiah said. "Just move around and touch things."

She walked to the chairs first, touching each. Nothing. Then to the sofa and table. Again, no hits. In each bedroom, she did the same. Still no spark.

"I guess this doesn't work," she said, holding up the ruby.

Josiah's nostrils flared as he scanned the place. "Nothing?"

"Not even a twitch."

"He must have used a cleansing spell."

"Or she isn't a monster hunter," Aiden said.

Although the thought of chasing demons didn't thrill Lia, she felt a little disappointed. Then she remembered her gifts were returning and moved out to the porch. Lifting her fingers, she called up a light breeze—and felt no pain.

Her powers were back.

A strange impulse made her step down and kick the dirt. Something glinted in the sun. She picked it up. A gold earring. The minute her fingers touched it; she felt a tingle. Could it be? She wrapped her other hand around the necklace and concentrated. A picture formed.

Dark hair and eyes, a beautiful face, and fear. The woman's terror reached out to Lia, then she recognized the face—the same one from the car crash where the kid stole the amulet.

Chapter Sixteen

As the image of the beautiful woman faded, Lia found Josiah staring at her. “What did you uncover?”

Fingers of cold slid down her spine. A dark aura had surrounded the woman. Josiah’s question alerted the others. Aiden slid his arm around her waist. “Are you okay?”

She leaned into his warmth. “I’m fine. Thank you.”

“Of course you’re fine,” Josiah said. “Now, what have you got there?”

When she opened her hand, Josiah let out a satisfied breath. “I knew it. He wiped the inside but missed this.” He peered into Lia’s eyes. “You saw something.”

She hated to admit it. She wasn’t ready for her life to change but, judging from Josiah’s expression, it was already too late. ‘Yes.”

“Wonderful! Let’s discuss it when we get back to your house.”

Aiden spoke to her mind. *What’s going on? What is he talking about?*

She smiled at him. *I’m not sure. Let’s wait for him to explain.*

Back home, Josiah took her arm. “I need to know what you saw.”

Aiden refused to let her out of his sight. With a pointed glare at Warren, he reclaimed Lia and led her into the living room where the Clan waited. He confronted Josiah. "Tell us what's going on."

"Fine." Josiah's expression was anything but friendly as he looked around, then motioned to Lia. "Tell everyone what you found."

At that moment, Josiah's voice entered her mind. *Mention nothing about the ring or Seekers. Discuss your vision.*

His warning alarmed her. She didn't want to keep something so important from her family. She hated secrets and wrestled with what to say. Then, in uncertain tones, quite unlike her, she said, "An earring."

Josiah raised his voice, "Come on, Lia. You know what I'm talking about. The attack uncovered a hidden gift." He peered at her. "What did you see?"

"Stop browbeating her," Franki said as she went to hug her daughter. She leaned in and whispered, "I can make him go away."

Lia managed a faint smile. "It's okay, Mom. I don't have a choice."

Franki glared at Josiah. "There's always a choice."

Nick piped up. "That's right, brat. We're behind you no matter what you do."

The familiarity of Nick's teasing helped her recover her confidence. "Okay. I picked up this." She showed them the earring. "A woman's image came to me. I think she was the same woman from the accident where the amulet was stolen." She glanced at Josiah.

He took over. "I sensed something special when I met Lia. It's a different gift from the others she has, and I think the accident amplified it. I was hoping she'd use it to give us information on the warlock. Although he erased all traces inside the cottage, Lia found the jewelry outside. The warlock missed it."

Lifting her hands in resignation, she said, "That's it."

Rosemary turned to Josiah. "All right, Mr. Warren, now it's your turn. Explain." Her tone brooked no opposition.

Josiah glanced at the expectant faces and moved to what Lia recognized as his battle stance—feet apart, arms crossed. "Part of my duties as a Templar agent to protect our membership include scouting for Clan members who possess special skills, abilities that often go unrecognized. It's happened before."

"How did you discover Lia's talent?" Franki said.

"I told you. It's part of my job. Now, it's time to strengthen her gift. If you'll excuse us?"

Her insides trembled. A picture of a guillotine flashed in her mind. Aiden and Franki both insisted on accompanying them, but Josiah refused. "This is a secret Templar ceremony. No one can watch."

His words only made them more insistent, but Lia ended it. "Please stop. This is my decision. I'll be fine."

****

As soon as Lia and Josiah left, Aiden turned to the others. "You're letting her go?"

"You heard her," Duncan said. "It's her decision."

Franki joined in. "But we don't know what he plans to do with her. One of us should be there."

Aiden continued his rant. "What has he done for us? We've lost the amulet, and some warlock is working with a demon who lives inside it. A monster, who—according to Josiah—will rain hell on earth. Warren is ruthless. His only interest is in the amulet. He left Lia on her own yesterday. What makes you think he'll protect her now?"

In a conciliatory tone Duncan said, "He represents our people, and what would we have done differently if we didn't have him?"

"Right," Bree said. "Also, he knew about the demon."

Maeve raised her hand. "Excuse me, but Lia's not helpless. Her powers are returning, and she has all of you behind her."

Aiden exploded. "Oh yeah! And we're all such experts at battling demons."

In the uncomfortable silence that filled the room, Rosemary's soft voice captured everyone's attention. "And yet, we did that last year."

Aiden checked his anger as he perused her troubled face. He remembered Lia telling him about a Clan battle last year, but he hadn't realized they'd gone against a demon. About to ask how they won that struggle, a sad whisper trembled through the air.

"And look what happened." The pain on Bree's face surprised him. Lia's aunt had always seemed so tough.

He saw Bree's anguish reflected on the faces of each Clan member, and his fear for Lia accelerated. The Clan's victory had come at a heavy price. Two Clan members had died. One was Lia's cousin. He wouldn't let that happen to her.

****

Needing a quiet place to perform the ceremony, Josiah and Lia headed to her bedroom. Before they got there, she waved the necklace at Josiah. "Why can't I tell my family about this bloodstone thing? I've never lied to them."

He raised a hand in a quieting gesture. "I'll explain everything."

"Fine." She flipped her hair, almost dislodging her kerchief, and strode into her room. Josiah moved the chairs to face one another. "I'm about to induct you into a sacred Templar faction. One that has endured for centuries. When I complete the rite, your gift will allow you to sniff out your prey as easily as an ant following his predecessor's pheromones."

"But why must I hide it from my Clan?"

"Think of yourself as an undercover agent. Your life may hinge on your discretion."

She wanted more, so she waited, fidgeting and playing with her necklace.

Josiah huffed. "None of these devils want someone alive who can track them. If this warlock discovered your powers, he'd hunt you down and make sure others like him knew of your existence. The knowledge of your presence would endanger other Seekers. As with those before you, you must learn to cloak your gift. Even the name of the Sisterhood has been deleted from our history. Seekers do not exist!"

Spies! Danger! Demons wanting to stalk and murder her? Her terror must have shown on her face, because Josiah's voice softened. "It sounds worse than it is. When you're on the trail of your quarry, you can ask for help as long as you don't reveal how you found the monsters. Once you enter the Sisterhood, you'll learn the secrets you need to protect yourself and defeat your enemies. You'll do great." He patted her hand and pulled out a small, thick, tattered book.

With her Clansmen at her side, Lia had faced trouble before. Knowing she could still count on them in her new role helped tame the pounding of her heart. She dropped her hands to her sides, then noticed the size of the tome

Josiah held. She quirked her lips. “All that for the Seeker rite?”

He flashed a rare smile and tapped the book. “It holds all the special Templar ceremonies.”

She had one more question. “If I do this, will it force me to work for you?”

“No. Although you will find people asking for your help.”

“You mean Templars.”

“Sometimes. Others may request help from the Council. Of course, it will be up to you whether you accept.”

That didn’t sound so bad. At least she could say no.

“Are you ready?”

She took a deep breath. “I guess.”

He instructed her to hold the necklace in both hands while she recited the age-old words. As she spoke, a slow tingling traveled from the tips of her toes to the top of her head. A wave of consciousness poured into her mind—a terrible font of information on all things perverted and otherworldly. The monstrous compilation made her cringe. So many facets of evil. Now she had at her disposal more knowledge than she’d ever wanted. Everything about creatures she never even knew existed. Her insides trembled as a newfound superiority warred with a sickening revulsion. Although the curtains billowing out from the French doors ushered in the familiar scents of her world, and her room remained the same as when they’d entered a short time ago, everything inside her had changed. In addition to an intense new insight, she also felt a profound loss, as if something had been stolen from her. With a shock, she realized what it was. Her innocence.

Society might harbor many with evil intent. She'd seen them, but she'd never experienced their corruption in her very core. What she'd learned in the past few minutes during the ceremony made her want to scrub her mind clean.

She returned her gaze to Josiah when he asked, "How do you feel?"

"Tainted. Disgusted."

He nodded. "I'm sorry for that, but it means you're ready. Knowing who you're fighting and how to exploit the monsters' vulnerabilities will give you the tools for their destruction."

Josiah put the book away and handed Lia a photo.

"What's this?"

"You tell me."

She looked at the picture. The eyes, almost alive with anger and hatred, chilled her. She turned to Josiah. "The warlock? His image pulsates with venom."

He rubbed his hands together. "Good. Wonderful. You feel him. Now, let's find him."

She knew her mouth gaped open, but she didn't care. She flipped up her hands in a sarcastic stance. "How?"

"Use your powers. Keep his face in your mind and concentrate on his location."

Lia inhaled to center herself, closed her eyes, and concentrated on the threatening stare of their enemy. Though an icy wave swept over her, she sensed nothing more. She looked at Josiah. "Nothing."

He frowned. "Are you sure?"

She felt her nostrils flare as she glared at him. "No. He saw me, gave me a great big wave, and pointed to a spot on a map." His surly scowl no longer bothered her, and she waited for him to explain.

"Try holding the stone against the photo while you work the tracking spell."

She surged to her feet. "What the hell is a tracking spell?" When his gaze slid away from her, she threw her arms in the air and let her anger rip. "You need to explain how this works."

Before she could continue, her mother's voice rang in her head. *Are you all right?* Franki often felt Lia's intense emotions. She must have caught the fear mixed in with the anger.

I'm fine. Josiah is a terrible teacher. Give us a few minutes.

Josiah shook his head. "Sorry. We're so close. I forgot. Please. Sit down."

She flopped back down on the chair. "I'm going in blind. How do the other Seekers do it?"

"They all have their own methods—what works best for them."

"I think I need to talk to one of them. You've got me trying to fly here with no wings."

Josiah's chin dipped down as he cleared his throat. "We only have a few Seekers. Most live in other countries."

What the hell? "Some Sisterhood! Why so few?"

Josiah sat back, gazing at something she couldn't see. After a moment, he said. "As you know, the Templars are a secret organization—the full strength of our members accessible only to the Council, and the Council is mostly unknown to the Clans. It's tricky. Can you imagine what would happen if I showed up to each Clan asking for permission to touch them?" He offered an ironic grin as he said, "Look how you people reacted, and you knew I was coming."

The image Josiah's words conjured made her chuckle as she pictured the terrified gray-haired agent running from an irate mob of Templars.

He ignored her mirth and cleared his throat. "Let's try again. Shall we?"

"We?"

He tipped his head, acknowledging her singular role before explaining.

The tracking spell surprised Lia. She didn't have to spout a curious language. No hocus-pocus, just a simple question directed to the object connecting the Seeker to her quarry—the photo.

"Any words to convey the message," Josiah said.

Lia cleared her mind and concentrated on the menacing image as she held the stone against the photo and spoke. "Reveal his location." Her mind filled with a dark, swirling mist that radiated cold. She clutched the stone and tried to force it to work, but the image remained cloudy. Ignoring Josiah's impatient questions, she readied herself for another try.

This time, she squeezed her hands hard enough to cause pain, then made her request more specific by adding in the words, "this warlock." Traces of mist lightened. She detected movement, then a curtain of black descended. She released her hold on the photo and let her eyes flick open. As she tried to focus, wavy lines played across her vision and a furious pounding invaded her head.

"Lia? Did you see him?"

His voice only added to the pain. She pinched her eyes shut to block out the dizzying movement and flapped her hands at him to stop his insistent questions. It took a while for the cacophony assaulting her brain to recede. The noise abated, replaced by a constricting band of pressure around her temples.

She attempted a quick peek at Josiah. Glad to see he, at least, looked concerned, and whispered, "It didn't work." When he tried to ask questions, she stopped him. "I have to lie down. Now."

As soon as Josiah left, her mother hurried in. Franki's soft hand brushed her forehead. Lia squeezed her mom's hand. "Please give me an hour."

"Okay, sweetheart."

But as Lia drifted off, she felt a soft kiss on her mouth. Surprised, she opened her eyes. Aiden. He lifted her hand to his lips. "I'll be back tonight."

As her eyelids fluttered closed, the pain somehow seemed more bearable.

****

After dinner, feeling much better, Lia announced she was going for a swim. Franki's head snapped up. "As in moving through the water using your muscles?"

Lia wrinkled her brows and crossed her arms over her chest. The only reason she never used the pool was that she was always busy with other things. It had nothing to do with disliking exercise. "Since I can't go back to work, and my plants are gone, floating around in the warm water sounds good."

Franki chuckled. "Going alone?"

Lia lifted her chin. "You told me not to go anywhere by myself."

"Ah," Franki said, and gave her daughter a knowing grin. "The decision had nothing to do with you, Aiden, and a tiny bathing suit?"

Before Lia could spout a snappy retort, Franki slipped out of the room. Lia huffed. Her mother knew her too well.

Her irritation abated as she went in search of her new red bikini.

She'd already sent Aiden a telepathic message saying he'd have to borrow suitable aquatic apparel if he wanted to see her tonight.

When he'd asked if it was a pool party, she'd curled her lips and answered, *Sort of.*

****

Moonlight filtered through the clouds, bathing the Brendani property in swaths of soft light. Lia inhaled the sweet aroma of beach roses carried by the wind. A perfect evening. A shiver unrelated to the weather coursed through her. Would he be waiting?

Gravel crunched under her feet and the bite of chlorine teased her nose as she neared her destination. She paused for a moment to control her erratic breathing. Nerves? Ridiculous. No man had ever disturbed her.

The glow from the changing room lanterns almost reached the pool. The flickering shadows on the liquid grew into waves caused by the powerful strokes of the swimmer. Mesmerized by Aiden's straining muscles, desire stirred in her belly.

She swallowed and strolled closer. "I see you made it."

He stopped and looked up, unruffled. She knew he'd been aware of her. Watchers could always sense another's approach. As the silence lengthened, she reached around to the back of her neck, undid a clasp, and let her cover-up slide down. Aiden's sharp intake of breath made her skin tingle.

His eyes darkened as they raked over her body. A slow smile played across his face. "Coming in?"

The deep timbre of his voice ignited her desire. She paused for another moment to enjoy the heat simmering between them. Without breaking eye contact, she lowered herself to the pool's edge and slipped in. The warm water covered all but her bikini top.

"Ooh!" she said as she gazed at him. "It feels so good."

Her body responded to the naked desire blazing from his eyes. She swam past him to the deep end and turned. He hadn't moved, but she felt his penetrating gaze follow her.

Poised there in waist-high water, Aiden resembled one of the ancient sea gods. Her breathing hitched at the sight of his broad shoulders and taut muscles. She couldn't look away as she glided back to him and stood. "You're not swimming?"

With a feral gleam, he said, "I've found something more exciting."

A primitive hunger swelled inside her as he reached out to touch her face. He closed the distance between them, intensifying her need. Rough fingers caressed her neck. His spicy scent added to her mounting flame. She ached to be closer.

When his hands slid down her arms, leaving sparks of need in their wake, she had to touch him, feel his skin, the hard ripples in his chest.

"Lia," he growled as he cupped her face in his hands, then captured her lips.

A desperate need fueled her. He smelled of chlorine, but the sharp tang of coffee laced his tongue. She leaned into the hands that explored her body.

A husky whisper tore out of him. "I've wanted you since that first day."

Aching pulses of heat surged through her. She tangled her fingers in his hair and scraped her nails across his back as he crushed her to him. She felt the pounding of his heart, his ragged breathing, and his lips igniting her skin. She held nothing back as their passion exploded.

As their bodies merged, and they soared toward release, it felt like they were swirling in a magic cocoon. She cried out as the final explosion shattered her.

Gasping for breath, she lay there unable to move. When she finally opened her eyes, Aiden gave her a crooked smile. "What?"

"That's some magic."

"Yes, magical. You were wonderful."

Then she realized she lay in his arms on the chaise. "How did we get here?"

He grinned. "I can't control the wind."

"Me? Oh my God!" She'd felt as if they were lifting in the air. *I guess we were.* She laughed and snuggled into him, excited by the new strength of her magic.

Making love to Aiden differed from anything she'd ever experienced. A new depth of sensations emerged. Sex had never triggered her gifts. With Aiden, she felt no need to control the outcome, keep things light, or say goodbye. She closed her eyes and gave herself a silent hug. All she wanted was to stay in his arms.

He kissed her lips and then the injury on her head. Thanks to Maeve's ministrations, there wasn't even a scar. "When I find the snake who hurt you, I'll destroy him."

Lia, who'd always taken pride in caring for herself, loved that he wanted to protect her. She had no urge to dominate. Imperfections like the stubby hair growing back over her wound no longer bothered her. Nuzzling his neck, she whispered, “My hero!”

His arms tightened. “I care so much about you. It would kill me to see you hurt again.”

“I feel the same way.”

“Good to know,” he said and punctuated his words with a heart-stopping kiss. As her body heated for an encore, he said, “And that’s why I’m worried about Josiah.”

She pulled back, trying to sit up, but his arm held her in place. “There’s nothing to worry about.” Seeing the determined set of his jaw, she took a breath and softened her tone. “I know you don’t like him, but he’s a good guy. A little gruff, I admit, but trustworthy.”

“How would you know? He’s full of secrets.”

“No more so than anyone else.”

He said nothing. In the growing silence, the sound of bubbles from the pool’s aerator filled her head. A sudden knot twisted in her chest as he frowned.

“What is Josiah up to? What are you hiding?”

She sat up, no longer aroused, and tried to convince him. “Templar mysteries I can’t reveal. I wish I could. Believe me. It’s for the safety of us all.”

“You can’t tell your Clan? Your mother? What about me?”

Lia’s irritation dissolved as a hollow void opened inside her. She now understood the consequences of her choice. Thanks to Josiah, her reality had changed. She no longer owed her allegiance to her Clan, but to something bigger she didn’t even understand. The Templar Council. She’d pledged herself to a secret life that would crush any chance of happiness with Aiden.

Her attempted explanation did nothing to change his

mind. With a heavy heart, she untangled herself and reached for her bathing suit. Aiden followed her lead, then held her for a kiss. "I'll see you tomorrow."

As she watched the man who'd carved his name in her heart walk out of her life, a fierce knot of bitterness and regret formed. This new gift had ripped apart her core beliefs and sense of purpose. Tears coursed down her cheeks onto her lips, and she tasted defeat. Falling in love was no longer an option.

Chapter Seventeen

Lia drifted through the empty kitchen, picking up a cup of decaf and some fruit on her way outside the next morning. Sitting on the porch, she tossed grapes in her mouth and chomped them as if they were the enemy. Last night had been so beautiful until Aiden had ruined it. *Why did he have to know every little thing about me?*

When she reached for another grape, the plate was empty. The man had ruined her focus. A yawn reminded her of her troubled sleep. Damn him. A few minutes later, though, his voice entered her head. *Hey beautiful. You up yet?*

Any lingering fatigue and annoyance vanished. *I'm on the back porch.*

Be right over.

She checked her scarf and hurried into the kitchen to scare up something for Aiden.

Returning with muffins and a carafe of coffee, she sat down to wait. Although she didn't want to appear anxious, she couldn't keep her gaze away from the path or control the rapid beating of her heart. No man, not even Rich, had this effect on her.

Minutes later he appeared, jogging toward her. She grinned. Everything would be all right.

Breathing hard, he leaned down for a heated kiss. Then he pressed his lips to the tip of her nose. "I missed you."

She pretended to pout. "Hmm. You better have."

Last night, in the heat of passion, the color of his eyes had changed. The green one took on a tinge of blue. She'd attributed it to the glow of the pool, but the anomaly happened again.

He grinned, sat down, and picked up a muffin. "You bake these?"

With a half laugh, half snort, she said, "Right. I'm a slave to the kitchen."

His voice softened as he gazed at her. "Well, darlin', you do have other assets I admire."

Dear Lord. He had her blushing. She could tell he enjoyed her embarrassment and couldn't believe she was acting like a lovesick teenager. She changed the subject. "What are you planning to do today?"

He linked his hands and stretched them over his head, giving her a superb view of his straining muscles. "I'm going back home for a few hours. It's time to clean out Smitty's desk."

The heavy hand of guilt squeezed her chest. With her attention wrenched between Aiden's lovemaking and the warlock, she'd forgotten about his brother-in-law. "I'm so sorry. I didn't know he worked for you. That won't be fun."

He touched her cheek. "I won't enjoy it, but I'll be all right. Jaime picked up the trail of the bastard who hurt you. I'm hoping we can catch him and force him to tell us about the warlock. Want to go for the ride?" He grinned. "You can check out my seat of power."

She took a deep breath. He wouldn't like her answer. "I'm meeting Josiah. He's helping me with this new gift."

Aiden's good mood disintegrated. With a frown, he

crossed his arms. "What the hell does he have to teach you? More spells? Or is he just trying to pump you for information on the Clans? I know I've said it before, but I don't trust him."

"I hate that's how you feel. He's not what you think." As she spoke, she fingered the stone in her necklace. When Aiden covered her hand with his, she stopped with a start. A flush crept up her neck. He opened her hand and examined the stone.

"This is new."

"No. I'd forgotten about it. I came across it…"

"Stop." His voice softened. "I may not have Nick's ability to detect lies, but I can tell when you're trying to cover up something. Your eyes widen and blink a few times before you embark on your story." He captured her twisting hands. "And you can't keep still."

She dropped her gaze, searching for a plausible answer.

"Look at me, Lia. Why would a Templar agent give you an expensive ruby?"

She tried to speak, but nothing came out. What could she say? Her breathing became strained. Aiden leaned forward, close enough to kiss. "What kind of magic has he given you? Does he want you to face the warlock?"

"I…You don't understand."

He smiled. "You're right. I don't understand, but I want to. Tell me what's going on."

Oh, she wished she could. She wanted to in the worst way. "I can't. I took an oath—a Templar vow." He stood up and slammed his fist against the railing. Lia cringed. Though tears stung her eyes, she joined him and touched his shoulder. "I'm sorry."

He turned and pulled her into his arms. His kiss,

angry and possessive. She met it with an intensity of fear and longing. Her body was on fire. When he pulled back, she wanted to cling to him, tell him everything, but she'd accepted her burden. His hands moved to her shoulders. "I've got to go. Don't let him coerce you into anything dangerous."

Lia only had time to nod before he pulled her into another blistering kiss. She leaned into him, her body begging for more. When he pulled away, she wanted to cry.

He caressed her throat. "I'll see you and Josiah later."

As she watched him go, she tried to convince herself that a nod wasn't the same as a promise.

****

While Lia was daydreaming about Aiden, she received a message from her mother. Josiah was here. Lia's fantasies vanished in the face of cold reality. She had nothing against Josiah, but she wished she'd never met him, and she could do without his acerbic commentary today. Unfortunately, she needed his guidance.

As she led him out to the gazebo, he said, "I hope you're ready for some heavy work. We have one day left."

"Nice to see you, too."

When they reached the octagonal retreat, Josiah said, "I've been thinking about the last time you tried tracking. I believe you found the warlock, and he felt your presence." With a satisfied smile, he said, "He directed a curse back at you. That's why you were so ill."

Her eyes widened in shock as she realized he expected kudos for his deduction.

Heart pounding, she clenched her fists and jumped up. “Are you kidding? You knew about that kind of spell and didn’t even warn me?”

He cleared his throat and licked his lips. “I’m sorry. It’s been a long time since I’ve worked with a Seeker. You’ll have to be patient while I reacquaint myself with the details.”

She stood with her arms crossed. “Oh, thanks. I’ll just take the brunt of your mistakes.”

“I know you’re upset, and you have every right to be, but I’m prepared today. I spent the night researching everything you need to know. Sit. We’ll go over it.”

“Don’t leave me hanging again.”

“I won’t.”

Why am I doing this? I don’t want to spend my life challenging monsters.

She breathed out some of the anger. “All right. Let’s start.”

“Okay. Let’s go over the five safety rules for dealing with these entities. Number one: Believe nothing it says. It lies. Two: Never turn your back on it. Three: Don’t look into its eyes unless you’ve spun a protection spell. Four: Once you’re shielded, don’t look away. Just before it attacks, a black line will slide down its iris. Watch for it. Five: It can be charming and persuasive. It will get into your mind and use your fear against you. Don’t listen!”

She stood up, shaking her head. “No. I can’t do this.”

He patted the air in a gesture to get her to sit down. “You are well-equipped to answer any concerns. Trust your intuition and pull up the insight you assimilated during your initiation. The answers are within you.”

Her body shook, and she had trouble breathing.

He took her hands in his and squeezed. “Take a deep breath and hold your bloodstone. Believe in yourself.”

She swallowed and did as he asked. Then sent up a silent prayer to whatever gods inhabited the ruby. *Please help me discover the information I need to defeat our adversaries.*

A familiar tingling sensation worked its way through her body, and an image appeared in her mind. A large tome opened to two pages. As she watched, writing appeared on the left side with the heading *Warlocks*. The right page title—*Demons*.

Instead of shying away, she felt empowered and wanted more. She squeezed the stone and asked how to protect herself while tracking a warlock. A page appeared with her answer. As she read the words, they became a part of her knowledge. She wouldn’t need that page again.

She looked at Josiah. “Do you have any holy water?”

He let out a breath, then grinned. “You found it? You know what to do?”

She straightened up and looked down her nose. “Of course.” *Whoa! Where did that come from?* “Sorry about that. I think the ruby spoke for me.”

Josiah clapped his hands and grinned. “You’ve got it.”

“Well, yeah. If I know what to ask.”

They stopped for lunch and then continued the lessons.

“I think you’re ready to try tracking him again.”

A brief concern about her previous pain flitted through her head, but she dismissed it. She straightened her shoulders and embraced the newfound lightness flowing through her. The same easy confidence she'd always had with her gifts.

The photo still emanated cold malice, but it didn't bother Lia as she placed a few drops of holy water around its edges and whispered an incantation. Where the water touched, the paper sizzled. As the smoke changed from white to red, a hint of sulfur touched her nose. She held his likeness next to the bloodstone and said, "Find this warlock."

Cold slithered along her arm, and darkness filled her mind. She squeezed the amulet and repeated her demand. When she felt his resistance, she realized her protection worked. The image lightened into a fog. As it dispersed, she saw movement, and then his face. His angry glare crashed into her, but her safeguards held. He raised his hands, mouthed something, and then emptiness.

Lia blinked in surprise before throwing the picture on the bench. "He saw me."

"Are you sure?"

She nodded. "Glared at me, spouted something, and cut off the vision."

"I wish he hadn't seen your face."

Something in Lia's stomach twisted.

Josiah smacked his hand against the wooden seat. "He's on to us. More powerful than I thought."

He picked up the photo. "He'll know we found him through his picture. Although this is only a representation, it captures a trace of the being, thus allowing someone like you to track him. That's why he tried to kill me."

Oh hell. She shuddered at his words. This wasn't a game. The monster was real, and he wanted her dead.

She stretched her shoulders and neck and tried to chase away the fluttering in her chest. Her hand went to the stone, then she lifted her chin. "Now what?"

"We practice."

As Josiah mentioned different methods to fight a warlock or demon, Lia found comparable intelligence within her. For the next few hours, they worked to hone her skills. Josiah threw spells at her, and she resisted them.

"You're getting better, but constantly defending yourself is dangerous. You'll tire and make mistakes. I'll teach you to turn defense into offense. Rather than stopping his assault, you want to echo his attack back at him."

His words brought a smile to Lia's lips. Nice. Protect herself while using her enemy's magic against him? Hell, yes. But she needed some downtime before they began. "Let's take a break first. This isn't easy."

While they rested, Josiah explained trackers could often cause spells to rebound.

"Yes! I like that."

The sound of the restless waves attracted her attention. As they splashed against rocky fingers, trails of lacy foam burst into the air. The tangy scent reinvigorated her. She stood up. "Ready."

"Make sure your shield is in place, and I'll toss them at you. This first one is a freeze spell. It wouldn't hurt you even if you didn't have protection. You'd be immobilized for a minute."

The butterflies she experienced before the lesson, had disappeared long ago. "Okay."

"When you repel it, send it to the side, not at me."

Lia planted her feet, took a deep breath, and nodded.

As the incantation spilled from his lips, Lia pushed out her hand, causing a bright flash.

Josiah's eyes widened, and he stopped moving.

Uh oh. "Josiah?" She leaned over and touched his shoulder. Nothing. Frozen.

"Josiah? Wake up." She held both hands on his chest and called up her healing power. Nothing.

Focusing on him, she rubbed her hands together and apologized. "I didn't mean to do it. I'm so sorry."

About to call her family for help, she heard him groan. "Oh. Thank God. Are you all right?"

He shook his head and glared at her. "I said push it aside. Pay attention. You can't make those mistakes with a demon."

Lia covered her face with her hands. "I don't know what happened. I guess I'm tired." The afternoon sun had moved behind the house, bathing parts of the lawn in shadow. "I think I have to stop."

Josiah smoothed down his shirt. "We're out of time. He'll start the ceremony around ten tomorrow night."

Lia couldn't take any more. "Doesn't matter. I'm spent. You saw what just happened."

He pulled a prune face but agreed. As they walked back, Lia worried about the impending danger if they couldn't track the warlock before he released the demon. Then her gut twisted. What if their efforts succeeded?

****

The minute Kane walked into the pet supply store, his nostrils twitched. The warm space exuded an earthy mixture of grass pellets, animal fur, and cleaning fluid. Then sorrow hit him. The air was alive with it—the anxiety and despair of caged creatures.

He paused and watched the kittens try to scratch

their way to freedom. Poor things. He pushed their desperate cries from his mind and finished his shopping. As he contemplated his purchase, a wave of cold clawed up the back of his neck. He stilled, concentrating on protecting himself. This was the second time someone had tried to invade his mind. He hit back, conjuring a nasty burrowing worm to drive the person on the other end mad.

His superior smile disappeared as a face floated in his mind. With a loud growl, he shut his eyes, clenched his teeth, and squeezed out the intruder. Trying to catch his breath, he leaned on the shelf. He'd seen that woman before. One of the groups who'd stolen the amulet. How had she infiltrated his defenses? Only a superior warlock or wizard could do that. Her magic felt new, almost hesitant. An apprentice? Why not the master?

As he paid the cashier for his purchase, his lips flattened into a grim smile. If they were coming for the amulet, he'd be ready.

****

Despite being tired, Lia had no plans to rest. The walk back to the house with Josiah seemed endless. She wanted to run. Aiden should be back by now. When she received a surprising message from Rosemary requesting to meet with Josiah before he left, she kicked at a stone. What did she want now?

Although the shadows reaching toward them had covered half of the labyrinth, the sun still hugged the bench. She did a mental head-slap. Of course. Kitty. She'd forgotten her grandmother, who missed nothing. Kitty had alerted the Clan. Rats.

After Lia told Josiah about the message, his reaction surprised her. Instead of dismissing it as unimportant, she caught his gaze flicking to the garage. “Forget it. You can’t sneak out. I’m not facing the music alone.”

Clan members waited in the living room, a jury of her peers. She shook herself. Time for the inquisition. Josiah, refusing a seat, leaned against the door frame, his annoyance imprinted on his face. Lia perched on an ottoman about a foot from Josiah. From her vantage point, she could see everyone and be close to the exit.

Rosemary nodded to Duncan, who addressed Josiah. “Mr. Warren, according to your calculations, the warlock will liberate the demon tomorrow night. Correct?”

“That’s right.”

“And you’ve been working with Lia for two days. We’d like to know why. What link does she have with the warlock and the demon imprisoned in the amulet?”

“Nothing, unless we find them.”

Franki clasped Lia’s shoulder. “What are you doing to my daughter?”

Josiah’s nostrils flared. “I’ve taught her a few spells to make up for her psychic loss.”

Duncan cleared his throat. “Those spells have incorporated powerful magic. I think it’s time you explained what’s going on.”

“I can’t, but her gifts are strong.”

Nick jumped up. “She’s lost her powers.”

Lia interrupted. “They’re back.”

She lifted her hand and called up a small breeze, thrilled with the pain-free magic.

Her mother hugged her as the others expressed their delight. Then Rosemary cleared her throat and turned her attention to Josiah. “While we’re all thrilled that Lia’s gifts are back, what you conjured today was different. A lot darker.”

Josiah ran his hand through his hair. "I can't tell you how, but I'm sure Lia can help us locate the warlock."

Rosemary walked over to Josiah. "I'm afraid that isn't good enough, Mr. Warren. You've kept us in the dark throughout. Now, we want transparency. If you can't give us that, please leave and stay away from Lia."

Lia detected worry before Josiah masked it with disdain. "Lia may be our only hope to stop the warlock."

As Josiah spoke, Lia's breathing deepened, and a strange inner voice rebelled at Rosemary's ultimatum. Warmth spread from the stone resting against her chest. She couldn't stop the words, "Tomorrow's the last day. What can it hurt if he comes back? What if we can figure it out?"

Rosemary's eyebrow lifted. "You have something to tell us?"

Guilt tugged at Lia's chest. She'd always respected Rosemary, impressed by her courage and leadership. Tonight, for the first time, she felt her Clan leader's disapproval. Hurt and confused, she looked toward Josiah for help. His icy features and unmoving stance gave her the answer.

Lia's shoulders sagged. A mouse with nowhere to turn—the cat beside her, and the hawk above. Afraid to blurt out the truth and unwilling to lie, Lia prepared to face the thing she dreaded—her Clan's disappointment.

Duncan's voice interrupted her internal battle. "Wait a minute. Aiden says he has a lead on the man who hurt Lia. His name is John Gruber."

Lia stopped listening to Duncan as Aiden's voice entered her head. *Hey, beautiful. I won't be back tonight. Can you live without me?*

He was such a jerk, but her smile widened. *I think I*

can make it until you get here in the morning.

He explained about the lead on her attacker and that they were starting their search. Then continued in a sultry tone, *Think of me when you're lying all alone in your bed tonight and what I want to do to you the next time we're together.*

Her insides flamed. She forgot where she was until Josiah poked her. He'd been whispering to her, and she'd missed it. *Damn!* Heat filled her face. He'd know Aiden had been in her mind.

Trying not to attract attention, she muttered, "What did you say?"

"Meet me at the hotel tomorrow morning at six a.m."

Before she could answer, he slid out of the room. Was he serious? She'd have to greet another dawn? A touch on her arm startled her. She turned to see her mother and Rosemary.

"We'd like to speak to you," Rosemary said.

She felt a telltale squiggle in her mind and reinforced her shields. Someone had tried to infiltrate her thoughts. Fury rippled through her body. A sneak-attack from one of her own? She realized that since her assault, she'd let everyone dictate her actions. She had to admit she'd been complicit in the disrespect she'd encountered in this room tonight. Enough!

She stood up, squared her shoulders, and lifted her chin. "I don't know which one of you just tried to read my mind, but I don't appreciate it. Who do you think you are? I have always been an important member of this Clan, willing to do whatever was necessary to protect our members. Since when do you question my loyalty?"

She looked around at the stunned faces. Rosemary

had the grace to back away.

Her mother, in a hesitant whisper, said, "It's not that we don't believe in you, it's that…"

"You think I don't have enough sense to recognize when I'm being used? What you think of Josiah doesn't matter, but I damn sure expect you to trust me. I'll tell you this once. What happens between Josiah and me can never be revealed. The magic you're all concerned about is part of a spell to protect me."

Before she marched out of the silent room, she said, "Open your minds. Secrecy rules our lives, from the Templar Council to other Watcher Clans. You relied on a mysterious phone number that delivered a Templar agent, yet you refuse to honor his necessity for confidence."

She took a deep breath and looked at each member of her Clan. "Know this. I've accepted a new Templar gift. If revealed, it would endanger my life."

****

Lia marched upstairs, swept into her room, and flicked her finger to slam the door. *Oh, that felt good.* She had her powers back. When she called for her phone and it flew into her hands, some of the anger left her. The sound of Annie's soft purr released the rest, and she lay down on the bed next to her cat who stretched and licked her hand. "Hello, my pretty baby," she said as she stroked the golden fur. "At least you trust me."

A while later, she picked up her cell, scrolled to the alarm and punched in four three zero then cringed as she hit the AM button. Tossing the phone onto the bedside table, she sent a silent apology to her body for the insult it would receive in the morning.

The light blue curtains fluttered as a soft breeze

caressed her face. She moved to her balcony and swirled her hand. The wind picked up, its warm currents blowing her hair back. As she watched evening transform the scene, she thanked the gods for her restored gifts. The magic that allowed her the minor act of closing a door or manipulating the air made her feel whole. With her own powers available, her new Seeker status held less fear.

She recognized the hesitant knock on the door as coming from her mother. “Come in.”

Franki had a tray of food. “You didn’t have dinner.”

The smell of roast chicken caused Lia’s stomach to grumble. “I forgot. Thank you.”

Her mother’s bracelets jingled as she stood there, worrying her hands. “I’m sorry for what happened. They shouldn’t have tried to pry into your mind. But, sweetheart, we’re worried about you.”

“I know.” Lia hugged her mother. “You can’t help me with this. When we find the warlock, I’ll call the Clan.”

“We want to help now.”

“I’m sorry, Mom. Nothing you can do.”

“If it’s that dangerous…”

“Only if the secret gets out. I’m not saying anything,” she paused and grinned, “and you know Josiah won’t open his mouth.”

“Oh, that man. I don’t like him.”

“He isn’t my favorite person either, but I need his guidance, and his motives are good.”

While they talked, Rosemary sent Lia a message apologizing for her interrogation and her attempted breach. *It was Rosemary.* Lia accepted her apology, shooed her mother out of the room, and sat down to eat.

She took a bite, enjoying the hint of lemon on the

crunchy skin, and sent a quick message to Franki. *Thanks, Mom. Delicious.*

Annie hopped off the bed, sauntered over to sit in front of Lia, and issued a plaintive meow. With a laugh, Lia broke off a piece of chicken and gave it to her.

"That's it—all you get."

While Annie concentrated on her treat, Lia thought about Aiden. She missed him, wanted to be with him, but worried about her oath. Could their relationship survive the secrecy? What if they wanted something more permanent? *Ooh!* She thought. Did they?

Lost in contemplation, the familiar sound of Annie knocking something around the floor cut into her musings. Annie's toys didn't make that sound when they hit a hard surface.

"What have you got, Annie?" The cat sometimes stole things from Lia's bureau or nightstand. If Lia didn't rescue it now, she might never see it again.

She bent down to retrieve the cat's prize. An earring. Not hers. As she turned it around in her fingers, a familiar tingling slid up her arm. Of course. The jewelry from the cabin. She'd forgotten all about it. She recalled the vision she'd had of a dark-haired young woman, her face wreathed in terror.

Lia held the gold loop in her hand. Maybe this could help them tomorrow.

Chapter Eighteen

As Aiden drove over the Newport Bridge, he paid little attention to the harsh cries of seagulls in his ears. He didn't want to leave Lia, but his men had developed a good lead on one of the warlock's flunkies. He knew Lia intended to see Josiah again today, but since tomorrow was the full moon, when the warlock would release the demon, he needed to act. He smacked the steering wheel and stretched his neck, stiff from too much stress. He hated being away from her, but if they were able to capture this bastard, he might lead them to his boss.

Aiden hadn't been back to work since his brother-in-law's death. Jaime had covered for him. Now, as he pulled into the driveway of AOC Security, his chest ached. It was his job to clean out Smitty's desk and locker—and that would not be easy. With Jaime and a few of the crew searching for the warlock's accomplice, Aiden tackled Smitty's desk. The lump in his chest expanded as he sat in the chair that still held the imprint of his friend's butt.

When the familiar scent of Smitty's aftershave ambushed him, he almost lost it. He tightened his jaw, pinched his eyes closed, and pushed away the pain. Time to get to work.

The laptop was no problem. Everyone knew the password. Aiden and Jaime had teased Smitty mercilessly over the lapse in security. His throat tightened as he typed it in. *MyMeg4ever!*

His sister's smiling face greeted him on the screen. With a growl, he jabbed at the keys and pulled up Smitty's folder. He'd have to reassign clients, but that could wait. After copying what he needed to his own hard drive, he checked the other documents. Just notes to himself and personal things. One file opened to pictures of Smitty and Meghan's wedding.

"Enough," He slammed the laptop shut.

What he needed was action and chasing down the scum who attacked Lia. A telepathic message from Jaime elicited a grim smile.

We've got the guy who hurt Lia. His name's Gruber, but he goes by Jago. We're bringing him in.

****

An hour later, Aiden joined his men in an empty ground-floor office. He glared at the suspect—a slimy son-of-a-bitch—and hoped he'd try to run. No dice. He slumped there with his left eye swollen shut and cuts on his forehead, nose, and mouth.

Jaime pulled Aiden aside. "I've worked on him, but he swears he knows nothing. He may be telling the truth. When I asked him about the fires at Lia's place, the police station, and the Newport wharf, he swore it was due to some coin belonging to the warlock. We should turn him over to the police."

Aiden sat across from their prisoner and peered into his eyes. "What do you know about the warlock? Who is he?"

Jago shook his head. "The girl, Gianna, called him Kane. Me and Tapper just called him Boss."

But Aiden wasn't listening to the declaration; he

was too busy searching through the morass of Jago's mind. "When did you meet him?"

"About a year ago."

Aiden received an image of the warlock paying Jago for something. "Where did you get the amulet?"

He snorted. "That thing's nothing but trouble."

"Where did you get it?"

Jago slid his gaze away from Aiden. "From some fancy house. He told me to take everything from the locked safe in the basement."

"Who owns this fancy house?"

He didn't know, but he gave him the address. When Aiden looked it up, he recognized the name. Why would a private collector have Templar artifacts? Furthermore, how did the warlock know about them?

After a few more questions, Aiden saw nothing important in Jago's mind. When Aiden forced him to call the cell number he had for the warlock, it went nowhere. The bastard had cut off all ties.

Satisfied, he said to Jaime, "Hand him over to local law enforcement."

He rubbed his temples. He still had to clean out Smitty's locker and bring his things to Meg. It would be a long night. He'd never make it back to Newport. After alerting Duncan to their lack of progress, he sent a suggestive message to Lia and laughed at her bold retort. If nothing new happened between now and the time he saw her tomorrow morning, he planned to whisk her away for a private interlude.

****

Lia sat on her bed, holding the earring her cat had just found in her palm. When Annie tried to swat it out of her, hand, she said, "No, honey." She scratched her pet's golden fur, then tightened her lips. "This is my toy."

For a second, she thought about trying to locate the owner, but the memory of the warlock's angry countenance changed her mind. Though mastery of her Seeker powers had strengthened since the day at the cabin, she'd also learned the dangers associated with its use. She wanted Josiah with her before she attempted future contact.

Should she call him now? If she did, he'd want her to meet him right away and open a link. Plus, the warlock might be with the woman. No. She was too tired to deal with the warlock or Josiah. She'd wait till tomorrow.

Sleep evaded her for what seemed like hours. When the alarm rang in the morning, she ripped herself out of a tortuous dream in which the ruthless warlock had maneuvered her into a deathtrap. Sitting up, heart still pounding, she shook her head to get him out of her mind. For a minute she even considered concealing the earring discovery from Josiah.

She rubbed her eyes and headed for the shower. Hot water cleansed her body and restored some of her composure. Scrubbing away the remnants of her frightening dream, she analyzed her options. Other than cowering in fear and hoping for the best, she had only one. Find the warlock and stop him.

She turned off the water and used her inherited magic to open the glass door and call for a warm towel. The return of her gifts helped restore her confidence. She was part of a Clan with the skills to defeat those who coveted their ancestors' cache or threatened the innocent.

As her self-assurance returned, the seeker stone issued a warm current through her body. Josiah had insisted she always wear it, even in the shower, although she hadn't worn it in the swimming pool. From now on, though, she'd comply with Josiah's request. The song of the ruby infused her with faith and determination.

She dressed, closed her eyes, and let her senses roam the house. Since wearing the necklace, Lia's ability to seek the signatures of those around her had increased. No one was up yet, but, just in case, she'd grab breakfast at the hotel.

With the earring tucked in her purse, she rubbed the ruby for luck and snuck out.

****

At five thirty a.m., Newport's deserted downtown resembled an off-season winter day. Very few people and sporadic traffic. Although the cars and tourists were missing, the packed hotel garage assured Lia the sightseers were there, hibernating until their next foray into the delights of the city. She chuckled as she maneuvered into her parking space. Seeing her here before noon would be a shock to the staff.

Before she could scare up something to eat, she had to stop for friends welcoming her back. After lots of hugs, she picked up a newspaper and headed to the kitchen in search of sustenance. She planned to relax, have her coffee and bagel, and read a bit before alerting Josiah.

Unfortunately, he'd had the same idea. She bumped into him on her way out of the kitchen. "Where did you get the food? There's nothing out here yet but coffee."

"All right." It was too early to put up with his overbearing attitude. "Follow me."

With breakfast in hand, they found a table. "You're here early," he said.

She glared at him. "Hmpf."

He ignored her petulance and ate his eggs. Lia refilled her coffee and tried to enjoy her breakfast, but Josiah, having wolfed down his food, sighed and tapped his fingers on the table. As she finished, he said, "Are you ready?"

She gulped down her coffee, but a flicker of nerves made the last bit of bread stick in her throat. She had to swallow a few times before nodding.

"I'm on the second floor," he said.

Mauve and gray drapes stood open in the room, and sunlight flickered onto the matching bedspread. This was their deluxe accommodation with a king size bed, kitchenette, two armchairs, and a dining set. While Lia automatically checked the hotel amenities, she smiled to see Josiah had made his bed.

He pointed to the comfortable chairs, and Lia sat down. Turning to face her, he said, "We have a lot to discuss. I'll tell you what to do when we find him. He pushed you out the last time, but I've got an idea. Maybe if we cloak you prior to the spell…"

She interrupted him. "Before we go there, I have something else we might try." She reached into her purse and pulled out the earring.

His eyes widened. "I'd forgotten about that. If we find the woman, she'll know where he is. Good job."

"It was my cat, Annie, who found it."

"Ah. The animal you tried to save the night of the attack. Interesting."

"This should be easy."

"Yes. But before we try the contact, let's discuss what you do if she leads us to him."

"Okay. What do I need to know?"

“One of the most important skills. How to kill him.”

A quick inhale made her choke. “Kill?” She hadn’t thought about that. “Couldn’t we just capture him?”

“Depends.”

She didn’t know if she could play the part of executioner. “On what?”

“If he hasn’t released the demon—maybe we can capture him. I doubt it, though. Psych yourself up to destroy the threat.”

Lia stood up and walked to the window. She looked out at Newport Harbor, her mind in flux. Impressive yachts lined the docks while smaller craft bobbed in the wakes of early morning boaters. He was asking her to commit murder.

His voice, from right behind, startled her. “When the time comes, the Seeker will take over.”

“How can you be sure?”

“The Seeker always recognizes a threat against humanity and neutralizes it. Think of the warlock as a monster masquerading as human.”

This conversation made her ill. Her trust was wearing thin. She placed her hand around the necklace and inhaled its strength.

“One troubling concern,” he said. “I’m afraid we have to go back to your house.”

She spun around. “Why?” It had been difficult enough to slip out.

“The weapon of the demon’s deliverance is there.”

She tensed, hands on hips, eyes and lips tightened. “You want to explain that?”

“Do you know where to find your family’s athame?”

“Huh?”

“You know what an athame is?”

"A ceremonial knife. So what?"

"Each Watcher family has a sacred blade infused with Templar magic to vanquish demons."

Lia flopped down on the chair. Their heritage had never interested her. What he was saying could be true. Bree would know. She shivered at the thought of her aunt giving her trouble.

"My aunt has that information, but she won't cooperate unless I give her a reason."

"Maybe we won't have to ask her."

****

Lia stood outside her home, infiltrating it with her senses. She found only one person, Bree, in her first-floor office. No sign of her father or Alex. She cast her search toward the studio above the garage and found her mother's signature. Perfect.

As they crept through the kitchen into the library, Josiah spoke in a whisper. "This seems a likely place, unless you know where your family keeps the Templar documents?"

She knew, but she'd never seen them. "In the cellar. There's a vault next to the rec room. That's where Bree always disappears."

"Okay. Let's go."

She used her enhanced sense to seek out Bree. Still in her office. Across from the library, Lia opened a door leading down to a huge entertainment area featuring ping-pong, a pool table, TV, and a well-stocked bar. A door opened into a small office. Tall filing cabinets flanked a large desk.

Lia pointed to a spot in the wooden paneling next to the corner seating area. "That's the door."

Josiah looked around. "Nice. You'd never guess it

was there."

With a bout of nervous guilt, she bit her lip and twisted a hank of hair around her finger. "I don't have any idea how to open it. I think Bree's the only one who knows."

"Not a problem. Let's sit for a minute."

She hunched her shoulders and looked all around. This was no time to relax. She hated acting like a thief in her own home. If they didn't hurry, Bree would find them. Although the rooms were sound-proofed, she whispered, "We can't do the spell down here."

"Calm down. Just grasp the stone and think of the athame."

"But I've never even seen it." She knew they didn't have to speak softly, but she was jumpy.

"Lia!" He snapped at her. "Just do as I ask."

Where did he come off being such a grouch? It wasn't his family they were invading.

She stopped twirling her hair and grasped the ruby. After a couple of calming breaths, she felt the warmth stealing through her. She smiled as she recognized the rush of magic. *Where is the Brendani athame?*

The air in the room thickened and her thoughts whirled. Seconds later, a picture developed in her mind. The sacred relic. She knew its location. Opening her eyes, she said, "It's in the vault." She shrugged. "I don't know the code."

Josiah rubbed his hands together and grinned. "With practice, you'll get that, too. Right now, though, it's my turn."

Lia held her breath as she watched him approach the door. Had she just given the secrets of her Clan to a safe cracker?

Josiah closed his eyes, spread his hands toward the vault and intoned a spell. The door opened. Lia blinked. He'd done it. Bree wouldn't like that.

He beckoned to her. "Come here."

She sidled over, keeping her eyes on Josiah. "We're looking for the knife. Nothing else."

"It's all right, Lia. I won't touch anything. You need to call for your dagger. Let it know its master is here."

When she opened her mouth and took a step back, he continued. "The Seeker and her weapon have a special bond. There is only one Seeker per generation in a family. Once the athame finds that person, it will belong to no other."

Lia investigated the small room, about six feet square, filled with her Templar heritage. Though she'd never cared about it before, she experienced an intense urge to pore through the closet contents. Flexing her hands at her sides, she pulled her concentration back to the current problem. Necklace in hand, she pictured the jeweled knife. *Athame! Come to me*.

Rustling began in the back. Lia almost choked and tried to ignore the cold rippling through her spine. A cabinet opened, and a scrolled wooden box appeared. She'd never seen it before, yet her heart knew it. The lid snapped open with a flash that hurt her eyes. She gasped and held her hand up in front of her face.

Then everything changed. Dominance and tenacity swelled within her. The hard slap as the cold weight hit her hand made her smile. She knew its heft. Her fingers wrapped around her trusted companion. *Mine!* She raised the knife in the air. It felt right.

"Now you are one," Josiah said. "The athame is yours."

Neither she nor Josiah heard the door open.

"Lia. What have you done?"

She spun around. "Aiden."

****

Lia froze. Anger flashed in Aiden's eyes. She heard Josiah swear. Her triumph faded. She dropped her arm, faced the man she loved, and prepared to lie until her voice gave out. She had to protect her secret.

Although she hated to part with it, she placed what now felt like part of her arm on the desk to begin her cover-up. "Only an athame can kill a demon. It has a special Templar magic. We came down to get it in case we find the warlock. I…It's so beautiful, I wanted to hold it."

She waited for Josiah to back her up, but he remained mute. Aiden's expression pierced her heart. Disappointment. Then his eyes blazed, their color shifting to green. "And we're back to lying. I thought we were past that unflattering trait." He nodded to Josiah before continuing. "Did you think I wouldn't notice your magic? Or maybe you think I'm mentally deficient?"

Lia kept up the farce, trying to protect her secret, but her heart bled at each one of Aiden's barbs. Even if she begged for his understanding, it wouldn't help. "You're right. I'm sorry. The magic you felt was us opening the door to release the athame. I knew the family didn't want me with Josiah anymore, so I snuck him down here to perform the spell."

Aiden's mouth curled. "You act like you're the only ones involved in this nightmare. As if your family, your Clan…me are unimportant. You think you and," he jerked his head in Josiah's direction, "can take care of the threat alone?"

"What's going on?" Bree edged around Aiden and stormed into the room. She pointed to the open vault. "Who did this?" Then she looked at the desk. "Our athame."

"It's mine." Before Bree could take possession, Lia opened her hand, and the weapon obeyed her. At Bree's gasp, Lia steeled herself. Time for some truths.

"Aiden, please close the door. What I'm about to reveal must not leave this room."

Aiden raised an eyebrow but complied.

Bree's horrified stare twisted Lia's insides. "When Josiah came here, he recognized my latent abilities. In my hands, the athame becomes more deadly. You can see it obeys me."

She brushed at her face where the hair had come loose. With the strength of her weapon's retrieval, the kerchief had flown from her head. "Believe me. When Josiah explained everything, I thought he was lying. Then I was afraid and tried to ignore it. I wanted no more responsibility, especially if it involved danger. But what could I do?" she said with one last plea. "After I learned the amulet's threat, I realized I had to accept my legacy."

She turned to Josiah. "Once he administered the Templar oath, my mind filled with information about all kinds of monsters and their vulnerabilities. However, if my skills became known or even suspected, every demonic beast trying to save their hide would seek my death. You must keep my secret. No one else can know."

Aiden gave Josiah a death glare while Bree placed a hand on her chest and whispered, "What else?"

Lia turned to Josiah, and he shrugged. "Lia is a Seeker. Each generation produces one, but only the stone," he brandished his ring, "can determine who it is.

Sadly, there may be more." He lifted his hands in surrender. "Without the ruby's touch, we can't know who."

Bree broke in. "I thought that was a myth, something to unnerve anyone working against the Templars."

Josiah shook his head. "It's to our advantage and the safety of the Seeker to deny the truth. That secrecy works against us in the search for women with this gift."

Aiden spoke. "Women?"

Josiah sighed. "Always."

Aiden glanced at Lia and then Josiah. "How can we help?"

His business-like tone hurt. She'd lost him. She'd known she would. The pressure in her chest felt like it might explode. Her hand crept to her throat. She refused to cry. "Josiah and I have to leave."

"Before we do," Josiah said, "you need to swear an oath to keep Lia's secret."

Lia watched their features go from offended to resistant. She lifted her chin. "That wasn't a request. It's a matter of life and death. Mine."

****

In less than a minute, Aiden and Bree had sworn their secrecy. Though Aiden refused to meet Lia's gaze, her aunt's stern glare at Josiah softened when she looked at Lia. "This has all been a shock. I'm not pleased with the danger he's put you in, but I'm proud of you. You've always been selfless." She looked at the ceiling. "Please God, it doesn't kill you."

"Can we leave now?" Aiden asked.

Lia's answer stuck in her throat. She nodded.

He started out, then turned back. "We discovered that the warlock lives in New York, so I'm headed back home." He directed his next words to Josiah. "Let us know if you find him. We'll head out right away."

With that, he left.

She couldn't help herself. She sent a quick message. *I'm so sorry.*

She didn't expect an answer, but she felt him in her head. *So am I. Be careful.*

"You'll need this," Bree said. She held a piece of leather in her hand; it looked soft. She smiled. "It's a sheath to hold your dagger."

As she handed it to Lia, she said, "Let us know when you find him. We'll back you up." She kissed Lia's forehead. "We better get upstairs before anyone else arrives."

Bree placed the carved box back in the vault and closed the door. The finality of that action mirrored the death of Lia's former life. And, still, she had to lie. Keeping the truth from her mother would hurt. On the positive side, her mother wouldn't live with the constant worry the truth would generate.

Chapter Nineteen

Aiden left the cellar, confused, angry, and worried. *What had Lia become? His sweet, sexy Lia.* Seeing her raise that knife like some avenging angel unsettled him. If he was honest, the sight scared him. He could concede his reaction may have been too strong. Hell, it was way off base. Since Lia had lost her powers, he'd been acting like a caveman protecting "his woman."

That type of attitude had never worked for him. It brought out the clingy reliance he despised in women. One thing he'd always liked about Lia was her spirit. Her sass. Although this new skill didn't make her different, it would make her life more difficult. He surprised himself when, in his head, he changed *her life* to *their life*.

Her voice purred into his mind. Damn! She was sorry. Standing there with his hand squeezing the porch railing, he regretted his deliberate, impersonal demeanor, aching to hold her in his arms. How could he leave her on such a cold note? He sent her a message, *Meet me on the porch, please*, then held his breath as he waited for her answer. She agreed, and he exhaled.

When she stepped out to see him, he stared for a second before blurting out, "I don't care about your powers."

She rushed into his arms, and he kissed her with a desperate hunger, born of the knowledge he might never see her again. He pulled away while he still could. She stroked his face. "If only we had more time. As soon as we have any information, I'll tell you."

He groaned and crushed her against him once more, wishing he could keep her there forever. "Be careful. I don't know what I'd do if I lost you."

She grinned and tweaked his nose. "I can take care of myself."

****

Lia watched Aiden leave and brushed her fingertips across her lips, still warm from his kiss. She'd sensed his passionate desperation. Before she could evaluate her own feelings, Josiah appeared. "You ready to go?"

She heaved a sigh of regret. "All set."

As they moved out to her car, Josiah raised one eyebrow and lifted his lips in a half smile. "When we track the earring's owner, she might lead us to the warlock."

"What if he's with her?"

He shook his head. "He won't have any idea you're in her mind."

"Good. I don't want to deal with him again."

"Unless she's a witch and feels your presence. Then she might tell him."

Damn! Did he have to deliver bad news with such relish?

His lip curled up a bit at her obvious aggravation. "Hence, the solution."

His long pause annoyed her. "Well. What is it?"

"I've found a shielding spell that should protect you although I don't think you'll need it. An object is easier to track than a photograph because the subject can't feel you."

Lia wanted to hit him. This wasn't a game. Any mistake would make her a target. She closed her eyes as he held his hands out to her and recited the incantation. When he finished, he nodded to her, signaling she should begin her tracking.

She held both the earring and her necklace while she concentrated on the owner. *Find her.* As before, the woman's face appeared. This time, Lia felt a distinct pull. She accepted the compulsion and started the car.

An image followed the tug. Almost like a global directional system, it showed right and left turns. On the Newport bridge, a map of highways floated in her mind.

Josiah kept interrupting, wanting to know if she saw where the woman lived. He had no idea how this Seeker thing worked. Annoyed, she said, "I'm being directed to drive toward Connecticut. Please be quiet. I'll let you know if anything changes."

After a while, the directions pointed to New York. "Maybe she lives with him."

He snorted. "A high-level warlock would want his privacy. You didn't feel any power emanating from the earring, so she can't be very strong if she is a witch. He wouldn't keep someone like that close to his lair. I only hope she has an idea where to find him."

Lia's gift led her to a busy neighborhood a few miles over the New York border. Outside an apartment complex, she felt a powerful pull toward one building. "This is it. I sense her inside."

Josiah rubbed his hands together, looking like he'd just received a present. "Wonderful. Can you tell which apartment?"

Each building had three floors. Lia pressed the earring against her necklace. An image of the woman and the number 101 appeared. "First floor."

"Good. Makes it easier." Before exiting the car, he paused. The nervous ripple in Lia's stomach threatened to turn into a storm. What did he want now?

"It just occurred to me you can make this much easier if you use your healing powers to calm her down when we talk to her."

"Fine."

He touched her arm. "You're sure she's alone?"

A streak of cold slid through her. She leaned back and focused her energy on the woman's apartment. Only one signature. She let out her breath. "Yes. No one else."

Josiah knocked on the door. Lia was too nervous. She hoped she wouldn't feel like this every time she used her gift. She flinched when the door opened.

A beautiful woman with dark hair and lovely brown eyes gave them a questioning stare. "Can I help you?"

Lia hadn't even considered how to explain their presence, but Josiah surprised her with a heartfelt smile. "We're working with the police on burglaries in the area. Could we speak to you for a few minutes?"

She gave a nervous look around. "I…I guess so."

Josiah in his sweet new persona asked, "Do you mind if we come in?"

The woman's tone became more self-confident as she asked to see identification. Josiah pulled something out of his wallet and handed it to her. While she looked at it, he nudged Lia.

Understanding dawned, and Lia leaned over to touch her arm, inhaling her expensive perfume. "Thank you so much for speaking to us."

Gianna's questioning glare softened. She handed the ID back to Josiah and invited them inside.

The living room reflected its owner, bold and flashy. Gianna lowered herself onto a black leather accent chair while directing them to a white leather sofa. Splashes of color adorned the walls. "What would you like to know?"

Josiah took out the warlock's photograph. "Tell us about this man. I know he's a friend, but he's very dangerous, and we're concerned about you."

"What? Who are you?"

As Lia handed the picture to Gianna, she touched her shoulder. "Please help us."

Gianna took the photo, let out a tiny noise and dropped it. "No. You don't understand. You don't know what you're dealing with. Please leave before Kane gets here."

"He's coming over?" Josiah asked.

She jumped up from her chair. "You have to leave."

"When do you expect him?" he said.

"I don't know. This afternoon sometime."

Lia stood and placed both hands on Gianna's shoulders. When she saw the calm settle in, she said, "I'm Lia. What's your name?"

The woman's shoulders sagged. "Gianna."

Lia looked at Josiah. "Better than we thought. We don't have to find him. He's coming to us."

Gianna jerked away from Lia. "No. He'll be furious."

Lia clutched Gianna's arm. "You don't have to be afraid. We'll keep you safe."

In the ensuing silence, the ding of the microwave made Lia jump.

"Sorry. I'm making lunch," Gianna said. Then she blinked and gave a heavy sigh. "Would you like something to eat?"

Josiah frowned. "Time to get ready. He could be here any time."

Gianna waved her hand. "Oh, no. He rarely gets here before four o'clock."

They followed her into a small but efficient kitchen. The smell of tomatoes and cheese from the open microwave encouraged Lia's stomach to growl. She checked the time. After eleven. *Damn!* She'd forgotten to give Aiden the address. She sent him a message with directions and information they'd gleaned from Gianna, including the warlock's probable time of arrival. *Can you get here before then?*

Aiden said he'd leave immediately and relay the message to her Clan, but he wanted her to leave Gianna's now. She refused. This was their best chance to catch Kane by surprise. They had to take it.

As Lia and Josiah discussed a plan for the warlock, Gianna cried out. She'd burned herself on the dish. Lia wrapped her hands around the injury. Gianna's yelp of pain changed to a look of wonder. "You're a witch."

Lia gave her a comforting smile. "Not exactly. Are you?"

Gianna nodded. "I'm just starting out, but Kane is a powerful warlock. He's promised to help me with my spells."

Josiah snorted. At Gianna's wild-eyed gaze, he said, "The only thing he'll teach you is the peril of trusting a warlock. If you value your life, you'll stay away from him."

A noise from behind them made Lia reach for her athame.

"It's just Brimstone," Gianna said, "coming through

his cat door."

Josiah stood up. "I need to use the restroom, then we'll get set up."

While they waited for Josiah, Gianna talked about Brim. "He appeared at my back door one day. A noisy black kitten who insisted on coming in." She grinned. "He's been here ever since."

The cat rubbed against Lia's legs and purred. She dropped to the floor to pat him. As Josiah returned, Lia sensed something wrong. Sparks of cold stung the back of her neck. Then Josiah yelled. Before Lia could react, Brimstone raked his claws down her face. The cat's attack pulled her attention away from the warlock who had entered the room. She felt a strong pulse of magic, and Josiah was down.

She grabbed for her athame, but Brimstone bit her hand. Seconds later, sulfur clogged her nose, and a spinning vibration racked her body. A numbing cold seeped through her. Her muscles cramped. She clenched her teeth against the pain, trying to stretch out her limbs and stop the torture. Then, as quickly as the agony came, it disappeared. She let out a grateful sigh, but her relief was short-lived. She understood what Kane had done.

Her muscles no longer hurt because he'd frozen them. She couldn't move. The only control she had in her body was over her breathing. She couldn't even blink. Her eyes were stuck open.

Although she couldn't see the warlock, she heard him chuckle. "Well, well, Gianna. Who are your guests?"

As Gianna pleaded for forgiveness, Lia cringed or would have if she could move. Kane sounded in good spirits, though. "Never mind, dear. Not your fault. Hello there, Brimstone. Come here, kitty. Good job. You obey better than your mistress."

Lia, a kneeling statue, stared at Gianna's feet and Josiah's still body, the agent's warning echoing in her head. "Never turn your back on them."

****

As Kane pulled up in front of Gianna's apartment, his sense of satisfaction deepened. By tonight, he would possess the powers of Agamorth. He'd want for nothing. He'd be omnipotent! And the lovely Gianna would ensure his success.

The minute he opened the car door, his pleasure dissolved. He sniffed. *Trouble*. The same psychic energy he'd sensed from his Newport enemies. *How had they found him?* He twisted his lips in a sneer and dug his nails into his palms. An ambush? Logic told him to get out, but he needed Gianna for tonight. Nothing would ruin his plans.

After he cast a spell to mask his magical essence, the sight of Brimstone suggested a plan. *Perfect.* "Here, kitty. Do me a favor." A feline purr answered.

A few minutes later, Kane cloaked himself and slipped into the house. He sniffed the air and sent out feelers from the hall for any sign of magic. Finding none, he followed the sound of voices to the kitchen, peeked in, and surveyed the situation.

Gianna and another woman sat at the center island, talking. The flapping of the cat door announced Brimstone's presence. When Gianna's guest knelt to pat him, he purred, and a man walked in.

While Kane directed Brim to scratch the woman, he took care of the man. The sound of his body slamming against the floor caused the woman to hesitate. Kane smiled. *Fool.* Her hand reached for a weapon. Too late. He froze her.

Satisfied he'd taken care of the threat, he exhaled. Time to calm Gianna, whose eyes widened in terror. Her pleas for forgiveness grated against his ears. In her panic, the foolish witch had spilled tomato sauce all over her. Hiding his disgust, he strolled over and massaged her shoulders. "Honey, you've ruined your dress. Go in and change." A flick of his fingers and a compliance spell took care of the rest.

The silky haired witch whose dusky eyes and sensuous body had distracted him from her true, worthless reality would play an integral role in his most important ritual.

Before she left, Gianna blurted out everything she knew. Kane recognized Josiah as the one who'd taken his picture in Newport. He figured that must be how they found him and gave him a kick. Didn't matter. Either the bastard was dead or would be soon. Kane shrugged and turned his interest to Lia, the blonde whose powers smelled so sweet. He walked around in front of her and bent down to her level. He recognized the face he'd seen in his vision in the pet store. Looking into her eyes, he grinned and introduced himself.

His senses reached out, expecting the comforting smell of her fear. But her reactions were off. He knew she could see and hear him. Most people would have wet themselves. Instead, in this one, deep anger overrode her apprehension.

"You're different. I like that." Rubbing the back of his fingers down her cheek, he said, "You'll be a lovely bonus for Agamorth."

****

Locked in a kneeling position, Lia stared into the warlock's cold eyes. His grin, a sadistic parody of caring, made her ill. But she wouldn't give him the satisfaction of showing her feelings. These monsters thrived on inflicting fear and pain. She ignored his touch and recalled her data about defeating a warlock.

She knew she'd have to kill him. While she reflected on the best method, he assumed an insulting imitation of compassion. "You must be so uncomfortable. I'm going to release your body, but I'm afraid it might hurt a little."

When his whispered words released her muscles, she wanted to howl. As she toppled sideways, bands of pain screamed through her body—spasms so intense, she couldn't move. She fought to conceal her mewling sounds of distress, furious when some leaked out.

"Tsk, tsk. Sounds bad. I hate to make you move, but it's time to go. Let me help you."

The agony increased as he lifted her up. A wave of embarrassment enveloped her when her legs collapsed. Kane commanded Gianna to hold up one of Lia's arms. He took the other one, and they headed out to the car.

Lia cringed as Kane fitted her seatbelt around her but sighed in gratitude as the torment decreased to a stinging pins and needles sensation. Her fingers flexed with a longing to grip her athame. Kane had seized the knife, unaware it would answer her call. She needed to wait until her strength returned, and he made a mistake.

He started the car, looked her over, and then chuckled. "I hope Brimstone's attack won't leave any scars on that pretty face." He must have noticed her wiggling fingers because he frowned. "You're getting the feeling back. Can't have you trying to attack me while I'm driving."

Although whatever he did this time didn't hurt, it immobilized her. All but her head. She looked around and discovered her voice also worked when a couple of choice swearwords spilled from her lips.

"Ah. She has spirit."

Lia wanted to tell him what she thought of him, but he'd only enjoy her anger. She kept quiet the rest of the way, memorizing the directions. Unfortunately, he'd also shut down her telepathic skills, so no messages to Aiden.

****

After the third time listening to the shock and commiserations of Smitty's clients, Aiden was ready to destroy the phone. On edge, waiting to hear from Lia, he checked his watch. Again. Over three hours since he'd held her. Before he damaged something in the office, he stalked outside. The inaction curdled his gut, and he slammed his hand against the building. Minutes later, he jumped at her voice in his head.

She gave him directions, explaining that the warlock wasn't due until later in the afternoon.

It's already 11:20, he responded. *Get out of there. Wait somewhere until we get to you. We'll be there by two thirty.*

As he spoke, he hurried inside to get Jaime.

His cousin met him in his office with Maeve in tow. Before Aiden could protest, she said, "I knew something would happen today. I want to be there."

"It's too dangerous. I've alerted Duncan. He'll meet us there."

"I think you're forgetting I can take care of myself, not to mention how important an extra healer can be."

Aiden objected, but Maeve raised her hand in front

of his face. “Stop! I’m coming. Lia may need me.”

Although he intended to protect Lia when he got there, Maeve was right. Her gift was important. He gathered a handful of weapons, wondering if they’d be any kind of help. Then they headed to the car.

With Aiden at the wheel, they ignored the posted speed limits and arrived a little after two o’clock. The burning smell of magic hit Aiden as he exited the car. He started running, kicked the door, and smashed it open. The place stank of the warlock.

He tried telepathy but got nothing, then bellowed, “Lia!”

When he heard Jaime call, “In the kitchen,” fear exploded in his chest. He ran to his cousin and saw Josiah on the floor. Aiden inspected the agent while Jaime moved off to check the other rooms. Josiah was breathing. Barely.

“Maeve!”

She was already beside him. He watched her brush back a strand of her red hair and spread her hands over Josiah, checking his chest and his head. Her expression was grave. “He’s had a hard hit of dark magic. Let me see what I can do.”

Jaime came back from his search and hung his head. “No one else.”

Aiden’s insides burned. Josiah was their only hope of rescuing Lia before it was too late. “You’ve got to save him, Maeve.”

He sent a message to Duncan, then searched the place, looking for anything to suggest where Kane had taken Lia. Address book? Letters? A calendar on the wall? Nothing. No mention of the warlock anywhere.

When Aiden questioned Maeve about Josiah, she

said, "He's better. I think I can heal him, but it will take time."

Aiden slammed his hand down on the counter. "We don't have time." A noise from the front startled him, and he spun around. He relaxed when he heard a familiar voice in his head. *We're here.* Jaime led Aiden's father and brother into the kitchen.

The Newport Clan arrived half an hour later. Templar descendants crowded the little apartment. Aiden introduced the Stuarts and Brendanis to his relatives.

By that time, Aiden's family had gone through every item in Gianna's apartment twice.

They sat and stood around the bright living room, trying to make sense of what had happened, each hyper-aware of the ever-diminishing window to stop the warlock from releasing the demon.

Though Josiah was still unconscious, Aiden and Duncan persuaded Maeve to rest. "We'll wake you in twenty minutes," Aiden said, and rubbed his hand across his face. "This waiting is driving us all crazy."

A sudden noise sent the three of them into defensive mode. Duncan laughed when a black cat swished through the room. Aiden swore. "Sorry. I'm so jumpy."

Duncan rubbed the back of his neck. "You're not alone. I just pray Lia's okay."

The cat brushed up against Maeve and meowed. "I think I will take a break. I'll get the cat some food. He's sweet."

****

The hours ticked by, adding to the mounting anxiety in the apartment. It was dark before Josiah regained consciousness. He remembered the warlock's attack, but not what happened afterward. “He got me. That’s all I know.”

The cat tapped his paw against Josiah, who gave him a quick pat. “Hello, Brimstone.”

Maeve leaned over to give Josiah a hand up, then jerked it back. Her eyes rounded as her hand went to her chest. “What was that?”

“What the hell?” Aiden said as he pulled Maeve back.

“No. It’s important,” Josiah said, excitement overcoming his shaky recovery. “Give me your hand again.”

Aiden shook his head at Maeve, but she ignored him. This time when they touched, Josiah said, “Do you feel it?”

She nodded. “But what does it mean?”

Josiah closed his eyes, pulled in a deep breath, and grinned. He looked at Aiden. “She’s like Lia.”

Aiden didn’t want to believe his aunt had such a dangerous gift, but if it were true, at least she could find Lia.

“Help me up,” Josiah said. When Aiden pulled him to his feet, he had to steady him.

“Take it easy for a while,” Maeve said.

“Never mind me. Start touching things until you feel something, any trace of Kane or either woman.”

Maeve’s eyes narrowed as she tilted her head. “What are you talking about?”

Only Josiah, Aiden, and Bree were privy to the truth. When Josiah asked for privacy, Duncan left, but Aiden remained to hear Josiah explain about the Seeker. At one point, Maeve turned to Aiden, who nodded and said, “It’s okay.” But he wished his aunt wasn’t part of this terrible legacy.

After Josiah gave Maeve his ring, she touched everything in the kitchen with no success. Aiden watched as she moved to the bedroom and Gianna's personal things. Still nothing. He dropped to the bed and put his head in his hands. He'd had so much hope. The defeat in Josiah's voice stung. "He cleansed the place before he left. What about Lia's car?"

Maeve hurried out to the vehicle, but still felt nothing. "Maybe I don't have the skill you think I have," she said.

"You do. He's just one step ahead of us. A cleansing spell obliterates all traces of a person—scrubbed away by magic. He'd be wary of someone tracking Lia. Hence the car."

Nine-thirty. Aiden's heartbeat raced as he thought about Lia. Not much time, and they had no location. Although Lia could be close by, they were helpless to find her.

Maeve sat down. "I'm sorry."

"It's not your fault," Aiden said. The others agreed. Franki came over and hugged her. And the cat also leaped up to Maeve to share his comfort with her.

"Hi, kitty. Brimstone, is it?" She ran her hands over the animal and twitched. She clutched the ring and held him close. "This is it. I sense Lia, the other woman, and—" she let go of the cat. "Evil." Her body shook as she said, "I can see him."

Chapter Twenty

The ride with Kane took less than an hour. Lia committed the main roads and a few of the side streets to memory. Enough to lead someone here when she had her telepathy back.

They stopped at a large ranch-style home in a quiet neighborhood, and Kane released the spell on Lia's legs so she could move. As he opened the front door, he spoke to Gianna, "You wanted to see my place. Well, here it is."

The modern furniture in muted tones of gray gave no clue to the personality of the owner, but, for a Seeker, the acrid scent of dark magic revealed his true nature.

"Do you like it?" he said. Though Gianna remained quiet, Kane went on in a genial tone. "The rec room is my favorite." He pointed to a door. "You go down first. I'll make sure our guest doesn't fall."

His fingers dug into Lia's shoulder as he followed her descent. A primal urge for retribution ricocheted through her body. They stepped into a comfortable family room—white walls, bright paintings, leather furniture, and a large TV. He had a state-of-the-art sound system and a well-stocked bar. The innocent space didn't fool Lia. Her nose picked up the sulfuric identity of Kane's real playroom.

He sauntered to the bar and reached for one of the fancy spigots identifying the brands of beer. "I think you'll like this one." The red handle bore the name *Satan's Brew*. When he depressed it, the wall beside them swished open.

With a welcoming grin, he gestured to the door. "Ladies."

Though he'd returned mobility to Lia's legs, her upper body remained inert. As Gianna preceded her, Lia could smell the young witch's terror. The room stank of burnt offerings and fear. Nerve ends pinged along her neck. It was a room-size cave. No windows. No furniture. A wooden table sat against one wall with shelves above, populated by varying sized jars, boxes, candles, and herbs. The jars held disgusting things suspended in fluid.

That wasn't the worst, however. What liquefied her bowels was his shiny collection. Knives, hatchets, and other vicious sharp objects. As she contemplated the use for which Kane intended them, she recognized the high-pitched sound that had been playing on the periphery of her consciousness. The squeak of rats trying to escape their metal prison. When Kane moved close to the cages and spoke to them, they went wild. Lia prayed she and Gianna wouldn't end up making the same terrified squeals. She shuddered as she peered around at her captor's laboratory.

Gianna went into a full-blown panic. "Kane! What is this place? Why are we here? I want to leave." When she turned to go, Kane made a sound of disgust. He mumbled something and flicked his fingers. She stopped.

He pushed her to the floor against the wall, then turned to Lia. No longer the gracious host, he said, "Sit next to her, and keep quiet." Then his lips flattened into a terrible smile. “Unless you’d like to be frozen again.”

Lia walked over and, because she couldn’t use her arms or hands, slid down the wall next to Gianna, who looked close to comatose. Lia tried again to send out a message to Aiden, but nothing happened. She prayed this spell would wear off soon.

As she adjusted her position, she felt something bump against her chest. Her Seeker’s necklace. She sucked in a deep breath. She could do this. It was her destiny. In the meantime, she watched as Kane whistled his way around the room, and she waited.

****

Aiden stared in uncomfortable fascination as Maeve held the cat. When she said, “I can see him,” Josiah shouted, “Close the connection!” His outcry scared Maeve and the cat clawed his aunt as he tried to escape.

Aiden reached to help, but she’d already soothed Brimstone. A still shaky Josiah shuffled over to her. “Hold the ring against the cat and picture Lia. Only Lia. The warlock can sense your connection. We don’t want him to expect us.” Maeve turned at the sound of loud voices from the other room—Aiden’s brother demanding to know what was going on and Duncan’s attempt to calm him. Then Franki’s anxious cry, “Look at the time. We’ve got to find Lia before he releases the demon.”

Josiah waved his hand in the air. “Ignore those people. Use the ring on the cat.”

Maeve nodded and tucked Josiah’s ring into Brimstone’s fur while Aiden asked everyone in the living room to be quiet. He returned in time to see his aunt snap open her eyes and gasp, “I can see her. They’re all together.”

"Calm down," Josiah said. "Just concentrate on Lia. Ignore the others. Use your power to find only Lia. Focus on her. Be firm. You're in control. Demand to locate her."

While she closed her eyes to concentrate, Aiden held his breath and checked his watch. Quarter of ten. Less than an hour to the full moon.

Moments later, Maeve leaped to her feet and said, "I have to go."

"I'll drive," Aiden said, as he hurried her to the door and told the rest of the crew to follow.

****

"What?" Aiden said to his aunt. He had trouble staying in the present. All he could think about was Lia. What that bastard was doing to her.

Maeve had to repeat the directions she'd given him. "Pay attention. We're close." His mouth went dry, and he sent her message to the other cars that were following them.

They were driving through an upscale neighborhood. Houses sat well back from the road, allowing for privacy.

"It's near," Maeve said. "Slow down."

The night sky had changed. A slight illumination appeared in the east. The tip of the rising moon. "Hurry. Are you sure this is where he brought Lia?"

She pointed to the last house. "She's in there."

He jammed on the brake and leaped out. The sharp slam of car doors echoed behind him, but he didn't wait. He hurled an energy blast at the front door that ricocheted and flung him backward. Maeve ran to him. "You fool! We're dealing with a high-end warlock. He'll have protection. All you've done is slow us down and alert him." She worked on healing Aiden while Josiah checked for a way in.

He returned moments later. "He's warded the whole house, but we can get in." Josiah held up his hand at Aiden's questions. "I need Maeve."

She hurried to meet Josiah at the front door. "I'm going to give you a spell. Take my ring," he ordered, "repeat what I say, and demand that the door open."

"I'll try."

She grasped the ring, closed her eyes, and intoned the spell. The door opened soundlessly. With a grim smile, Josiah ushered the group inside.

****

As Lia watched Kane place a table against the wall, she tried to work her fingers and hands. If she could get the feeling back in her arms, she could use her athame. She'd seen him place her knife next to his own instruments. Its jeweled hilt so close, her fingers itched to call for it.

Unable to use her gifts, she tried reasoning with him. "I don't know what your plan is, but it won't work. My people will find us. The amulet won't be enough to save you against so many."

Kane stopped what he was doing and turned with a smile. "If you're any sign of the strength of your people, I'm not impressed. You and the old man together couldn't stop me. What's a few more?"

This time it was Lia who smiled. "After your lackey attacked and injured me, I lost my powers. Otherwise, you'd be in my position. Trust me. You're better off surrendering the amulet and letting us go."

He tilted his head and gazed at her for a minute. "Agamorth will love you."

While he lit candles, Lia asked, "Agamorth? Is that the demon in the amulet?"

He didn't bother to face her. "Aren't you the clever one?"

"What makes you think you can control him?"

"That's enough talk. I'm busy."

"He's using you. Once he's back, he won't need you anymore."

Spinning around, Kane yelled, "Enough!" He leveled his arm at her. "Sleep."

****

Lia felt groggy—her senses off. A strange mantra filled her head. Alien words spoken like brief prayers. She tried to shake off the fog in her brain and forced her eyes to open. Why was she sitting on the floor? Then she remembered. The warlock. She checked to see if Gianna was awake, but she was gone.

The muted voice still droned on in brief spurts. Lia lifted her head and followed the sound. Kane. Though concealed by a black hooded cape, she knew him. He read from a book filled with tissue-like pages. Its tattered dark cover looked old and well-used. After reciting a few words, he'd look up and lift his finger.

Small background sounds captured her attention. A constant drip, drip, drip. Scrabbling rodents, and mouse-like squeaks that seemed to correspond to Kane's gesturing. Then she almost gagged as a terrible coppery scent reached her nose. Her stomach clenched, and she whipped her head around. She'd found Gianna.

Candlelight flickered against the silver framework surrounding the naked witch. Gianna was bent over. Her silky black hair hung in matted strands. As Lia watched, Gianna's eyes opened. The dying woman sent her a silent plea as she whimpered in pain. The sight of Gianna stuffed in a dog crate, hanging from the ceiling, incensed Lia. She struggled to move her hands. If she could gain control, she could stop him.

After a few minutes, she gave up and studied the warlock's actions. She realized what he was doing. For the first time in her life, she wanted to kill. Each time Kane chanted and aimed his finger at Gianna, black symbols appeared on her skin. They began on her cheeks and moved down and around her torso. But it wasn't just ink. The runic characters carved themselves into her body. Streams of blood erupted from each new entry.

Gianna was in agony. Now, though, instead of fighting the pain, she'd accepted defeat. Lia watched Gianna's hands unclench. They lay open as if she were asleep. Streams of red blotted out the symbols.

Lia, helpless to do anything, wished she could cover her ears against it all—the warlock's chant, Giana's faint moans, and the steady sound of her life force ebbing away.

Drop by drop, precious liquid flowed from the defenseless witch into a golden vessel beneath her cage. The warlock wanted every bit. She wondered why he didn't just stab her. Then she realized the magical writing was for the demon. Part of the spell to release him. When Gianna died, the demon would use her blood to live.

Lia couldn't let that happen. She tried again to move her limbs. She squeezed her eyes shut and concentrated, trying to wring out any speck of her power to help her. A tingle tickled her hands. She focused all her energy there, but it was too much. Her breathing stuttered. She had to take a break. She tried not to panic. But at this rate, Gianna would die before Lia could act.

Unable to move or use her telepathy, Lia despaired. What a fool she'd been. Josiah had told her not to turn her back on her enemy. But when she'd seen Josiah fall, her healing instinct overrode her self-preservation. She'd lost her chance. Now, here she was, bound in her own prison, watching Gianna die. She tried to extend her healing gifts, willing the young woman to hang on.

Thoughts of the demon reminded her of the amulet. She looked around and saw it on a table next to Kane, but she hardly recognized the lethal sphere.

Glowing red and swollen, its symbols stood out like 3D graphics. Her breathing hitched as she watched the demon's prison mimic the rhythm of a beating heart.

****

At the completion of Kane's vile spell, Lia sensed a gentle tug on her spirit as the fragile connection she'd clung to with the witch was severed. She bowed her head. Gianna's pain was over, her hopeful curiosity extinguished by a power-hungry warlock.

With the release of Gianna's soul, Lia felt a shift in the air like the end of a storm. She shivered as Kane picked up the throbbing amulet, held it in the air, and spouted a final triumphant exhortation. She gagged from the stink of sulfur that clogged her nose and tried to deny what was happening. But the truth played out before her. Cradling the blasphemous object in his hands, Kane murmured, "You're mine."

Lia's stomach revolted as he knelt on the floor and immersed the amulet in the blood-filled vessel. Seconds later, a bright explosion seared her eyes. She blinked against the red dots from the brilliant flash, then froze as the slimy hand of evil touched her. She watched in horror as the crimson glow faded. Gray mist rose from the bowl and encircled the crouching warlock. He stood, pulled back his hood, lifted his arms and stretched, as if awakening from a long sleep. A terrifying laugh issued from his mouth, more frightening because the lips weren't Kane's. Large and fleshy, they dominated his elongated jaw. This creature's face jutted out at angles—cheekbones sharpened, and eyebrows bulged out over red-tinted eyes. He stood at least seven feet tall.

A noise from within the house sent a surge of hope, cleansing her skin of the demon's corruption. Her Clan.

Agamorth seemed to read her thoughts and smiled. "Your friends are too late."

****

Aiden rushed past Josiah into the house, then hurried back to speak to Maeve, who was leaning into Duncan, drained from healing her nephew. "Where's Lia?"

Maeve pushed past him and pointed. "This way." She led them into the kitchen, paused, then opened a door. "Down there."

Aiden sprang in front of her. The rest of the crew followed behind him in the enclosed stairway. Confusion reigned as he entered an empty rec room. Furniture faced a large TV and there was a bar at the end. Unable to contain his fear, he snapped at Maeve. "Where? I thought you said she was here."

She threw her hand in the air. "Quiet." She held her head in her hands. "Beyond that wall."

Before Aiden could try to break it down, Lia's cousin Alex stopped him. "Wait. She's pointing at the bar."

Aiden twisted his head all around. "Who?"

"There's a spirit, a beautiful dark-haired woman. She's hovering and pointing."

"I don't have time for some stupid ghost. We'll break through the wall."

He turned, but Maeve put a restraining hand on him. "Just a minute."

He pulled his arm back from Maeve and snapped at Alex, "Hurry."

She scrambled to the spot the spirit had shown her. "Here." She reached for a red tap and yanked it down. The panel next to him opened. As a sulfurous mist spilled out, Aiden charged in.

The sight of the lifeless body inside the cage stopped him. His breathing ceased. He felt as if someone had sliced into his chest with a jagged shard of glass. His defenses crumbled. Too late.

He turned to the warlock and choked. Aiden's gut churned as he saw what looked like a living gargoyle sneering at him. Revenge spurred him forward, but as he lifted his arm to attack, the nightmare struck. Long, skeletal fingers spun in the air, and a brutal punch kicked against his shoulder, knocking him off his feet. As his head crashed against the floor, he heard her call his name.

His last thought was, *She's alive.*

****

The moment the hell-spawn that had been Kane turned its gaze on Lia, her throat went dry, and her bladder threatened release. Sharp, yellowed canines protruded from thick gray flaps that posed as lips. Words grated across long unused vocal cords. "I'll enjoy playing with you."

She sucked in her breath and felt like throwing up. Ignoring her trembling limbs, she forced out the growing fear. She was a Templar. A Seeker. She dug her nails into her palms. The stinging pain surprised her. The warlock's spell ended with his demise. She could move. She could fight. Every instinct screamed for her to call for the athame and strike, but she needed to catch the demon off-guard.

She squirmed in the silence as blood-red eyes regarded her. The whisper of the opening door felt like an explosion. Aiden charged into the room. He looked up at Gianna's crumpled body and froze, leaving himself vulnerable. Before Lia could warn him, the demon swept his bony arm like a backhand slap. The psychic force knocked Aiden onto the floor, and the Clans retaliated. Some used energy bursts. Others threw knives. They'd expected to fight a flesh and blood warlock, but Agamorth's hide ejected their blades. He was quick to dodge the missiles and send the weapons back at their owners. Aiden's brother reacted too late, and his knife sliced into his upper arm.

Lia leaped up and struck from the demon's blind side. Cyclonic spears of wind caught him by surprise. He swung around, malevolence in his glare. Fingers like wrinkled snakes flicked out, and she ducked, but not fast enough. The impact with the wall took her breath away. As she dragged herself up, she heard a roar. What she saw made her smile. Alex and Rosemary used their shields to thwart the monster's thrusts.

Moving hurt her shoulder. She clamped her mouth shut against the pain and applied enough magic for her to function. She couldn't risk tiring herself with too much healing. While she paused a moment for her strength to return, she looked for Aiden. *Where was he?* She reached out to his mind. Nothing. No answer. Her chest constricted, and she found it difficult to breathe.

Unbidden, bloody images of another fight and bodies who didn't make it assailed her. As she watched her clansmen fall, her insides buzzed like an angry swarm of bees. She didn't think she could survive losing another loved one. She had to do something. Sulfur scorched her nose as bolts of magic streamed through the room. The demon moved so fast that he was hard to hit. Direct strikes only bothered him for a few seconds before he rallied and fought back.

Someone cried out, and she saw blood spurt from Aunt Bree's leg. Then Nick clutched his side. His fingers turned red. Duncan reached out to attack, then yelled, grasped his hand, and went down. Maeve crept over to help them.

Lia ducked behind a table and resumed her offensive. A shaft of pain slid down her arm as she hurled her psychic current. When it hit its mark, the demon grabbed his shoulder. She'd stung him. *How?* All at once, she realized her pain was gone. She'd somehow sent it to Agamorth.

Time to use her athame. She called her sacred dagger to her, but Agamorth was watching. Eyes wild with fury, lips drawn back from enormous fangs, he knocked the knife from her hand and threw a powerful gust of energy that stole away her breath and shoved her backward. She slammed into the cages of rats and the table full of knives.

While she fought to inhale, the creatures screeching in her ear muted the sounds of battle. She evaluated her injuries. Beyond the bruising to her shoulders and back, razor-like stings radiated along her arms and torso. The knives. But the worst was her leg. A sharp fiery pain, then a sickening smell of blood enveloped her. As she tried to move, tiny claws reached through their metal enclosure, piercing her skull and cheek.

With a shriek, she shook them off. Praying that none had escaped their confinement, she reached down to pull the knife from her leg. Blood spurted from the wound, but she wrapped her hand around it to stop the bleeding. The copper smell that turned her stomach also attracted a couple of loose rodents. One bit the hand that clasped her leg. Without thinking, she used her Seeker's power. Opening her hand and slowly closing her fist, she dragged the breath from their lungs. Her gut clenched in horror as she scanned the lifeless bodies. The new power shocked her with its brutality.

While she struggled to heal her leg and look out for other rabid rodents, she lost track of the battle. Though the Templars hadn't hurt the demon, they'd slowed him. He was too busy to pay attention to her. Could she slip behind him now? As she prepared to move, she heard a tearing sound and saw the ceiling rip open. A Hellhound leaped out. From her Seeker initiation, she knew this one was dangerous. Scarlet eyes embedded in a massive dark, hairy shape pinpointed her Clan. Saliva oozed from a snarling mouth filled with razor-sharp teeth. A shudder seized her body. If she vanquished the demon, she'd still have to deal with this devil cur.

When it moved a few steps, issuing a deadly threat, Lia poised, ready to join the fight, but stopped. Something about the creature was off.

The enormous canine attracted half of the Clan's assault, giving Agamorth more freedom to attack. She wondered why the disgusting beast didn't charge. It moved back and forth. Missiles strafed it, but none hit. She wondered why those huge, scarlet-tipped claws made no sound on the concrete floor. Then she understood. The brute was a thought-projection. She sent a quick telepathic message to alert everyone that the dog wasn't real.

The Clans found it difficult to ignore the vicious creature. More than one pair of eyes flashed between the demon and the mirage. When the monster made no move to close in on them, they ignored it and concentrated on Agamorth.

The demon was strong, but renewed multiple attacks distorted his aim. Pieces flew out of the wall rather than his enemy. Was Agamorth tiring? She hoped so. If her Clan could keep this up, it would be easier for Lia to advance on her prey.

Amid the chaos, a popping sound and a bright flash seized her attention. She swung her gaze to the air above Agamorth and saw a creature the size of a large vulture, reddish feathers but with hands instead of claws. It had short wings ending in pointed talons, and horns protruding from the sides of its skull. This abomination circled Agamorth. Short screeching sounds issued from its pointed beak.

A Devil's Condor. With the vicious carnivore cruising above them, she had to shake off her panic. Illusions couldn't harm them. The Clan did the same. The chilling vision didn't stop their barrage against the demon.

Another burst of light. A second condor. The first one paused its circling. Lia sucked in her breath and inhaled a rank odor. A putrefying scent that came only from live animals. Before she could send out a warning, one of the pair launched itself at Nick's head. His roar alerted the others. Someone knocked it down, and Nick blasted it. The savage monster exploded in a spray of black goo. Then the other beast headed for Aiden's father. With a wild shout, he pulled a knife and plunged it into its heart, leaping away from the disgusting gunk. Most missed him, but Lia saw puffs of smoke rising from his arm. Like demon blood, it burned.

Seconds later, she heard more noises from above. Agamorth was summoning his pets to help in the fight. With the Clan's focus on killing the little devils before they reached them, Agamorth could do some damage. First Alex went down and then Aiden's cousin Jaime. As Lia watched Alex jerk backward and Jaime collapse, she felt as if her insides were being torn apart.

With their numbers diminished, her clansmen clustered together. Condors screamed and charged but smacked against an invisible barrier. Even Agamorth's strikes bounced away. Rosemary stood tall with her hands held out. She'd furnished a shield, strong enough to cover them all. In protecting her clansmen, though, she also prevented them from mounting their offense. They couldn't strike out at Agamorth.

The monster, recognizing his advantage, stopped his barrage and stepped closer to the Clan. He thrust out his chest. "Puny humans, desist. Your barrier is cracking. You've lost. Bow to the power of Agamorth. Or die!"

Lia saw the strain on Rosemary. She couldn't maintain her shield forever. The demon would win. It was only a matter of time. Lia had to do something. Her leg had stopped bleeding, but the healing had taken its toll, leaving her light-headed and weak. She searched for her athame.

A shift in the atmosphere alerted her, and she flipped her gaze to the enemy. The demon's red eyes pulsed. He raised his arms, and the cloak slid away. Her stomach twisted at the sight of gray flesh hanging from his bones. He was decomposing. He needed more blood. And this room was full of donors. When he slammed his fists down as if pounding an opponent, the air vibrated, and her ears became blocked. Rosemary fell back, and the barrier shattered. The remaining Condors burst open, spraying demonic ick over the floor. Agamorth was through playing.

She needed to strike now. Calling upon the gifts that had always been part of her, she twirled her hand. A breeze lifted her hair and then a noise like the roar of a flooded river filled her ears. She smiled as a spinning vortex sprang up around the demon. It should be enough to conceal her advance. She launched herself up, ignoring the pain in her leg. Her body ached with the need for rest, but this was her chance. Above her, the drained shell of Gianna acted as an incentive.

Before she'd taken two steps, though, Agamorth opened his mouth. His entire face seemed to stretch. She watched in horror as his lips continued to spread. He was sucking up the twisting wind. She hurried to reach him, but a loud whoosh signaled the end of the funnel. He snapped his gaze toward her, knowing she'd conjured it. The disgusting elongating maw closed and formed a smirk as his arm shot out. Lia choked against the bony fingers wrapping around her neck.

Chapter Twenty-One

Agamorth's sharp fingernails dug into Lia's flesh as the demon held her in the air. The pressure on her throat felt like it would sever her head from her body. Searing pain vied with the struggle to breathe. She had to resist the urge to kick her feet, knowing she'd strangle.

The moldy smell of death blasted from his mouth. "Cease fighting or she dies!"

Duncan gave the order to stand down. Lia's heart cried at the confusion and anger on the proud faces as they raised their hands in surrender. Most of them, unaware Lia could defeat Agamorth, would rather fight to the death than give in to a demon.

A familiar voice cried out. "Put her down."

Aiden. Her heartbeat quickened. He was alive.

The unholy fiend glared at the man she loved and then smiled. "My new toy?" He laughed and pulled her toward him. Then tipped his head forward, sniffed her, and slid his tongue along her cheek. Her stomach contracted at the stench from his mouth, and her skin felt raw from the sandpapery assault.

Aiden's brows lowered and blood rushed to his face. He vibrated with the need to destroy the demon, but his anger only seemed to entertain Agamorth, who licked his lips. "Delicious. Can't wait to ingest her powers."

Not if she could help it. He put her down and released his hold on her neck. She gave a quick healing massage to her throat.

Agamorth turned to the others and swept his hands out in an encompassing gesture. "What a feast of magic you present to me. You." He pointed to Aiden. "Come here."

When a mutinous frown telegraphed Aiden's refusal, Agamorth grabbed Lia's neck again. "You want her blood on your hands?"

She sent Aiden a message. *Play along. Keep his attention on you. I just need a minute.* Then she contacted the rest of the Clan with her scheme.

Though she could feel Aiden's rage, his features never changed. As he took a step forward, Agamorth threw Lia aside like a piece of trash to inspect his latest prize. "Oh yes," the demon said. "I detect something different here. Intriguing."

Ignoring her newest injuries, she waited until the hell-spawn reached out to Aiden, then sent one word, *Now.*

The room erupted in magic. As streams of energy pummeled the demon, Aiden moved to protect Lia. But she was no longer a pawn. She flexed her fingers and whispered in her mind, *Come to me.* The weight of the dagger in her hand burned with determination. Time to fulfill her destiny.

Agamorth must have sensed the athame's power behind him. He twisted around and sneered. "That puny knife can't hurt me."

No longer able to reach Agamorth's kill spot, Lia had to leap away from his attack. The bolt missed her body but caught the edge of her foot. When he swerved to deal with the remaining Clan members still able to fight, she had time to regroup. She'd have to hobble.

Trying to heal it would take too much of her strength. If she could reach the demon's back, she could kill him.

Aiden's voice entered her mind. *Are you okay? We'll distract him for you. Rosemary and Alex are straining to maintain a psychic wall we can duck behind between attacks.*

She had to act now. Agamorth was gathering his power to break through the barrier. Only a few feet separated them. The air vibrated with increased pressure as the demon prepared to annihilate the shield and those standing behind it. Pain shot up her leg as she limped toward her target. She squeezed her hand around the blade hilt. Before she reached him, he spun around. His rank smell made her gag. His face was deteriorating. The gray skin hung in folds below his chin. His eyes drooped, exposing black gunk beneath the bloody orbs. He intended to unleash his pent-up fury on her. She was going to die.

She blinked as a hand appeared and pulled the monster away. Aiden. Now was her chance. She sprang at her target, ignoring the pain. The sacred knife guided her to the core of his power. As she plunged the athame through the demon's leathery husk, Agamorth's scream of rage triggered a sense of satisfaction and closure.

When he turned to her in astonishment, Lia peered into his eyes to deliver her ancestor's spell. As she began, "In the name of the Poor Fellow-Soldiers of Christ—"

Agamorth cut her off with a laugh. "This is what's become of the terrible Knights Templar?"

But Lia continued. "And the Temple of Solomon, I remand you to your earthly prison."

His eyes flashed with fear as he hissed and crumpled to the ground.

Lia stretched her shoulders and flipped her hair away from her face. The athame flew back to her hand. She smiled. Both Clans saw her dominion over it. She was the Seeker!

Josiah rushed over to her, but she ignored him. Where was Aiden?

"What's happening?" someone yelled.

Black mist swirled from the body. She backed away, but it followed her.

"Will you listen to me?" Josiah yelled. As the evil mass reached for her, she remembered the red cloud that had encircled Kane before the demon possessed him. "You need to send him to his prison."

She didn't understand. *How could the demon still be alive?*

The vapor circled around her. She screeched, then shivered as the cold slime touched her skin.

A shove from Aiden knocked her aside, then Josiah pushed something into her hands. A plain wooden box, no bigger than two decks of cards. "Hold this open and recite the Templar spell. Hurry!"

The fog twisted around her again. It wanted to possess her. She flipped up the top, weaving to avoid the persistent stream. As she repeated the words of her ancestors' spell, the demonic mist ceased its aggression and churned in place. The minute she uttered the last syllable, a snake-like flow surged toward the rectangle in her hand.

She watched in fascination as glowing runes carved themselves into the wooden surface. When she snapped the lid shut, a bright flash made her look away. Then she blinked and turned to Josiah. Her voice vibrated with anger. "Why can't I kill him? His essence still lives in here. What if someone else unleashes him?"

Josiah gave her his hard stare. "Pretty full of yourself, aren't you? You think you're the savior? That you did it all?"

How could he say that? She was the Seeker, the only one who could kill the demon. Lips compressed and feet planted, she said. "I stopped him."

Josiah gave a disgusted snort. "The only reason you could get close enough to use your weapon was because your Clan distracted him. And you were so proud of your work, you almost allowed the demon entrance to your body. You were lucky today. It will take a lot of training before you can claim your title."

Lia's first thought was to give him a show of force. Thankfully, her head cleared enough to realize what he said was true. She still wanted to smack him but satisfied herself with a snarky look. She adjusted her attitude and rephrased her question. "Isn't there a permanent solution for this monster?"

"You can't kill this type of demon. That's why the Templars relegated him to the amulet. We've learned more since he was first entombed. The sacred writing surrounding his prison can only be unlocked by another Seeker. And only if she knows his name."

Not perfect, but it would do. The container no longer gave off any light. Scraping her fingers across the deep indentations, she noticed something strange and brought it up for closer inspection. No matter how much she twisted the box, she couldn't find an opening. What she held was nothing more than an interesting block of wood with strange markings.

With a smile, she tossed it in the air. "I imagine you have someplace safe to store this?"

He snatched the vessel and glared at her. "Never make the mistake of thinking you're smarter than a demon."

He turned and walked away.

He was right. What had she been thinking? She'd almost taken a victory lap around the room for crying out loud. In the middle of berating herself, her mother squeezed her in a big hug. Lia half laughed as she felt her bruises. "Ow."

"You can heal your cuts. I'm just so glad you're still my daughter."

Lia turned to help Maeve with the wounded when Aiden approached. He had a grin on his face, but his arm hung at an unnatural angle.

Cold, pin-like sensations peppered the back of her neck. "You're hurt."

He dipped his chin, his voice a grumble, "Damn demon."

She placed her hands on his arm. "Broken."

"Son of a bitch."

Lia laughed. "Good thing I'm a healer."

Before she could work her magic, he wrapped his good arm around her and gave her a very thorough kiss. "I didn't think I'd ever hold you again."

"Right back at you." Then she chuckled. "If you hadn't shoved me out of the way, you could have had a demon lover."

He squeezed her against his side. "I'll settle for a sexy healer any day. Fix my arm, please."

Chapter Twenty-Two

Kane's secret lair lay in shambles. Deep gouges scoured the walls; huge lumps of concrete created a hazardous maze across the floor. The air smelled of ozone, blood, and putrefying animal matter.

Lia ignored it all to heal Aiden. She placed her hands around his arm. "This will hurt at first. Okay?"

He gave her a quick grin and took a deep breath. "Ready when you are." She closed her eyes and pictured the bones knitting together, hating to cause him any pain. As she worked, she heaved a sigh, thanking God everyone had survived. Then she heard Nick cry out, "No!"

She whipped her head around. Nick knelt beside his father while Maeve tended to Duncan. Lia curled into herself as she sent a question to Maeve. *What's wrong?* Her friend looked over with sorrow in her eyes. *Duncan lost two fingers.*

Her chest ached. *Can't you reattach them?*

The demon blasted the fingers to pieces.

Her breath left her body as she sagged against Aiden. Cradling her face, he said, "How bad?"

Blinking back tears, she told him. Her head felt woozy. Time to stop. "I need to rest. Don't move that arm. You should have a sling."

He gave her a hug. "I'm fine. It feels great." Then his eyes slid toward Duncan. "I'll go over with you."

He kept his good arm around her. Duncan was standing now, and Lia reached up to give him a kiss. He looked dazed. She knew it was shock. A life-changing injury would do that. They'd always believed that their healer could cure anything.

Maeve's shoulders slumped. Lia touched her arm. "Take a break. You're worn out."

Maeve rubbed her eyes. Her voice cracked when she spoke. "Nick, Aiden's father, and Bree will have permanent marks from the secretions of those flying devils."

Lia took a step toward her family, ready to run over and use her own skills before she recognized the futility. When she felt Maeve's hands on her face, she remembered those nasty vermin. "I'm okay. Take care of that later."

"Shush. You've got quite a few scratches."

Lia grimaced. "Kane made Gianna's cat scratch me." Then she choked on her words as she gazed at the cage holding the remains of the naïve witch.

"What happened here?" Maeve said as she touched Lia's other cheek.

"Those damn rats got me."

"There are some deep gouges."

As heat surrounded her face, she closed her eyes, content that Maeve would take care of it.

The healing took so long, Lia worried Maeve was over-tired. She took her friend's fingers away and squeezed them. "You're exhausted. You can finish this later."

But Maeve tugged her hand back and reapplied her healing. When Lia saw worry emerge in her friend's eyes, a finger of cold teased her neck.

"There's something wrong," Maeve said. "I have to look at those rats."

Lia's hand flew to her face. Tiny bumps marred the smooth surface. But that was crazy. The marks should have healed. She touched her other cheek where Brimstone had scratched her. Nothing. No blemish. With a tired sigh, she decided to fix her scars later. She noticed the rat bite on her hand and covered it, using her own skill then jumped at Maeve's voice.

"Bad news. I think the warlock was experimenting on the rats. They're infused with black magic. Their saliva is as toxic as the Imps." She pulled Lia into a hug. "Although I healed your open wounds, I'm afraid the scars will remain."

Lia looked at her hand and found a nasty puckering against her smooth skin. She slid her fingers along her damaged face, then stared at Gianna's crumpled body, runes still defiling her flesh. Her fingers curled, aching to tighten around Kane's throat. Too late. The bastard was dead, but he'd left his mark.

She watched the men take down the cage, allowing Rosemary and Franki to take care of the rest. Franki slid Gianna out as if she were a sleeping child and placed her on a burgundy blanket someone had found. Drained of blood and covered in runes, the poor girl's skin resembled a printed body suit made from a pinched seersucker material. Rosemary bent over Gianna and gently positioned her in her shroud. When she bowed her head, Lia did the same, sending up a prayer for the woman's soul.

An arm encircled her waist, and she leaned into Aiden. He kissed her forehead. "Don't worry about the clean-up. My father is on it. I'll drive you back to your car." He held her face and kissed all around her injured cheek before his lips found hers.

Oh God. After this, we'll never be the same.

****

Maeve and Josiah joined them on the ride back to Gianna's.

In the car, Maeve surprised Lia with a question. "How did you get the athame to obey you?"

"Uh…" She was at a loss for words.

Josiah answered. "That's part of her Seeker powers."

Lia spun around in her seat, almost coming out of her seatbelt. "What are you doing? We can't reveal that."

To Lia's horror, Josiah chuckled. He held up his hand to quiet her. "You don't need to hide anything from Maeve. She, too, is a Seeker."

Lia couldn't help a quick glance at Aiden. "Aiden knows," Josiah said. "He was there when I discovered her gift."

Emotions swelled inside her. *Surprise* at finding another Seeker, *shock* that it was Maeve, and a sinking feeling. She'd lost her status as the *special* one.

A sudden thought made her smile, though. No longer did she have to face the terrifying aspects of her new reality alone. A deep sense of kinship and pride washed over her as she reached for Maeve's hand.

"I'd say congratulations, but our new gift is more than daunting. Prepare for a drastic change in your life." She flipped a hand in Josiah's direction. "Don't let him scare you. He's not as mean as he appears."

Josiah scowled and grumbled, "I don't know what you're talking about. I'm not mean."

While Maeve and Lia discussed their strange

situation, they arrived at Gianna's apartment.

A heavy lump settled in Lia's chest, and she swallowed.

Josiah marched forward and opened the door. "We must clear out any Templar presence. I don't have a cleansing spell, so that will mean wiping every surface."

"Don't worry," Lia said. "I know the spell."

Josiah's eyebrows rose, but he said nothing. Maeve asked if it was part of the Seeker knowledge.

Lia shrugged. "I guess so. When I heard Kane invoke it, something inside me remembered it. I still have a trove of information to learn by research or recall."

They stepped inside, and a black form darted at them. The cat was rubbing around the women's ankles and purring. Maeve bent down. "Brimstone. Poor baby. You're an orphan."

A gruff voice from the kitchen said, "He's a cat."

Maeve ignored Josiah and scooped Brimstone into her arms.

Josiah clapped his hands. "Come on. We don't have all night."

"What about Brimstone?" Maeve asked.

"Bring him to the pound," Josiah said.

"What!" Maeve and Lia screeched in unison.

Josiah made a sour face and marched past them.

It was almost four a.m. when they were ready to leave. Maeve met them in the living room with a huge garbage bag.

Aiden lifted it. "What have you got in here?"

Maeve cuddled Brimstone. "If she took the cat, she'd want this."

Josiah snorted.

Lia patted the cat and whispered. “You’re taking him, aren’t you?”

Maeve smiled and nodded.

“Good. He’s a special cat who needs a special mistress.”

At the door, Lia stopped to perform the cleansing spell and bowed her head. The last time she’d been here, Gianna had been so alive, excited to discover Lia’s powers. A young ambitious witch, foolish in her choice of a companion. She didn’t deserve her painful death.

Aiden tucked Lia under his arm. “Remember the lives you saved.”

Images of the young woman dying in a cage tortured her. After berating herself for turning her back on an enemy, she vowed to embrace her new power and dedicate herself to hunting down the monsters who cared nothing for the sanctity of life.

Chapter Twenty-Three

Lia stood in front of her bedroom mirror, bracing herself to face the day. The horror of two nights ago would be forever imprinted on her mind and seared into her face. Kane's legacy would follow her for the rest of her life: four ugly scars to remind her what happens when you turn your back on a monster.

Her thoughts turned to Aiden, the man who dominated her dreams and most of her waking hours. Was she still the same woman who'd inspired his passion? She fisted her hands and, with a disgusted snort, turned away.

A knock on the door distracted her. Alex entered. "Aiden and Maeve just arrived. Josiah is already digging into paperwork and muttering."

"Thanks," she said as she smoothed her tee shirt over her shorts. At least her figure hadn't changed.

Josiah's imperious voice greeted them in the crowded dining room. "Is this everything?"

She grinned when she heard Bree snap back. "Are you insinuating that we're hiding things?" Lia chuckled. Josiah had met his match in Bree.

When Aiden slipped an arm around her, she smiled. He kissed her ear and whispered, "What are you doing later?"

His lips set up delicious shivers. She smiled. *What did you have in mind?*

For an answer, he slid his hand down to cup her behind. Although she gasped with a sudden burst of desire, the sound of Josiah's complaint cooled her passion. "I'd like to know how the warlock knew about the amulet?"

"You think someone supplied information to him?" Lia asked.

He gave an emphatic nod. "Someone who knew more about the Templars than they should."

Josiah's answer set her pulse racing. *How many monsters knew their secrets?* She needed to talk to him alone. She edged over and poked his arm.

****

When Josiah followed her to the back porch, Lia tucked a lock of hair around her finger and cleared her throat. "I've changed my mind about working with another Seeker right now. I know I asked you to find someone for me, but I think I'm needed here."

He scowled at her. "Sit down."

Glad to have that off her mind, she made herself comfortable in the chair and lifted her head to savor the tangy salt air.

He leaned back and smiled. "I've already contacted a person in England who is willing to teach you."

"Well, that's great. I'm thrilled you were able to finagle something so quickly. The Kane probe should be finished in a couple of months. I'll be free to go then."

His smile dissolved. "That's not the way this works. You don't dictate when the time's convenient for you. I only know of three people who might help you, and they have lives. A bony finger jabbed in her face. "You're lucky to have anyone take the time to mentor you."

"But…"

“This is not up for discussion,” he said, glaring at her. “You go now or not at all.”

Fingers of dread played along her spine. “When do I leave?”

“Sunday. I purchased the tickets and secured safe accommodation paid for by the Council. The Seeker will contact you on Monday.”

“That’s only four days away!”

She couldn’t believe it. He’d made all the plans without consulting her. A spark of anger had her leaping to her feet. She glared at him. “That’s too soon. I need time if you want me to track down whoever stole Templar artifacts and help the Clan.”

With a disdainful snort, he brushed his hand in the air as if shooing away a fly. “They don’t need you, now. They’ve got Maeve.”

She blinked at his sudden dismissal. “But…She doesn’t understand how it works, yet.” As she spoke, she heard the desperation in her voice.

“I’ll teach her.”

She opened her mouth to speak. He stopped her and narrowed his eyes. “Just like I taught you.”

She felt her shoulders droop. Her status had changed from valued Clan member to useful tool for Josiah and the Council. In four days, she’d be in England with a woman whose expertise was killing demons.

“Enjoy what time you have left here. You’ll be too busy once you begin your lessons.”

He meant her last few days of life as Lia Ferguson, gifted healer for the Watcher Clan. Soon, she’d have a new identity as a hunter and slayer. Her gaze drifted out toward the river. “How long?”

“A few months. You’ll be back before you know it.”

He walked away leaving Lia feeling empty and alone. The path she'd chosen was one of responsibility and danger, leaving no room for love.

After Josiah left, the screen door clicked again, and the smooth cadence of Aiden's voice washed over her. "I thought we had a date. You prefer Josiah to me?"

Her pulse sped up, but her attempt at a smile failed. "I'd be happy if I never saw him again."

He touched her shoulder. "Come on. Let's talk."

****

Aiden and Lia sat on the bed in his room at the Stuarts. "Okay. Out with it," he said as he kissed the top of her head. "What did the bastard say that upset you so much?"

"I can't tell you."

"You can. Remember, I know your secret."

He was right. She'd forgotten.

"He's found a Seeker willing to mentor me."

"That's good, isn't it?"

"She's in England."

He rubbed his knuckles across her cheek. "Just a plane ride away."

As she gazed at his handsome face, the dark wave across his forehead, and the sensuous tilt of his lips, her chest tightened. There was no other way. She had to abandon him.

"I-I don't expect you to wait for me."

He wrapped his arms around her. "I want to go with you."

"I'll be gone too long."

"A few weeks is no problem."

She hung her head, then looked up and held his gaze. "Months."

"That much?"

A hint of green drifted across his blue eye. Not good. Her stomach churned. She wanted to run and hide.

"When do you have to leave?"

"Sunday."

"What?" He scowled at her. "Why so soon?"

"The Seeker in England is doing me a favor. That's when she can meet me."

A deep frown clouded his handsome face. With a heavy sigh, he said, "I thought I'd have more time." He stood and paced. "It's tough for me right now. There's this Kane investigation." He waved his hand in dismissal. "That's no problem. I can leave that to the others, but my business needs me."

Pain filled his voice, and the sorrow on his face made her want to hold him and kiss away his torment. This so-called gift had ruined their lives.

"Since Smitty's death, we've been understaffed." His voice cracked a little. "Jaime's been doing a great job while I've been here, but we need to fill that position." He frowned and dropped his gaze. "It isn't easy."

Hopelessness washed over her. She'd known this arrangement wouldn't work. Unable to watch him suffer for another minute, she went to him and stroked his shoulders, then nuzzled his neck with healing vibes. He smelled so good.

When he buried his face in her hair and massaged her back, she tried to ignore the hunger building inside her. "Don't worry about it. I'll be fine over there. You can keep me updated on the investigation and your business, and I'll tell you how tired I am."

He brushed her hair back and kissed her eyes, her

scars, and her lips. Her pulse quickened at his touch. "My sweet Lia." He let his fingers tease her skin. "I don't want to lose you for a day, let alone months. I'll work something out."

When he dipped in for a kiss, she melted in his arms, then pulled back. She had to be sure. Breathless, she managed to say, "You might not want me after I become a hardened killer."

He moved his hands through her hair and whispered against her lips, "I've seen you in action. If I hadn't been so scared, I'd have been turned on." His fingers traced the curve of her cheek and the outline of her mouth. "Nothing will change the inner beauty I've seen or the woman I've fallen in love with."

"Love?" The fist squeezing her chest vanished.

He cupped her face in his hands and covered it with gentle kisses. She sighed and relaxed against him.

"I fell for you the minute you threatened me with that gun."

Warmth filled her chest. When she tasted his lips, he growled, pulled her tight, and. captured her mouth. Heat shot through her, and she dug her nails into the hard muscles of his back. Her breathing hitched.

She shrugged out of her blouse, and he tore off his shirt. The sight of his muscled chest sent her pulse racing. The rest of their clothes fell in a heap on the floor.

Blue blazed from his eyes as he guided her to the bed. "I love you, Lia."

Her heart felt like it would burst. "I love you, too."

She gasped and cried out in pleasure as talented fingers stroked and teased her skin.

You like that, sweetheart?

Yes. Please. His powerful body aroused a raw

hunger, and she arched into him. Her breathing hitched, and her senses swam. It felt so good. She loved this man more than she could say. As his hands and lips tormented her, the aching between her thighs built into a raging flame. Her heart threatened to burst. A storm of passion swirled around them.

Moans of pleasure became frenzied cries. She couldn't hold out much longer. Then it happened. A fiery psychic explosion. A flash of lightning that merged their souls. It nearly shattered her.

As she lay there trying to breathe, she gasped, "Oh my God, Aiden."

He choked out, "Sweetheart," and crushed her to him until their pulses returned to normal. When he spoke again, it was with a grin. "I'm glad you didn't include rain."

"What?"

She looked around in shock. Aiden's hair stood tufted on his head. Pictures on the wall tilted at crazy angles. Curtains wrapped around the rod, and pillows lay scattered against the wall.

"I did this?"

He rubbed at a small, charred spot on the headboard and chuckled. "You've ruined me for any other woman."

When he wrapped his arms around her and claimed her lips once more, she ignored the chaos around them and dismissed every single doubt in her heart. Together, they could face whatever surprises life had in store for them.

A word about the author...

Margo, an award-winning author, crafts dark tales of suspense and supernatural intrigue. Her gripping novel Trace of Evil immerses readers in the haunted streets of Salem, Massachusetts, while her Watcher Clan series, beginning with The Convent House, uncovers the eerie secrets of Newport, Rhode Island. Now living in Florida with her husband Paul and their unapologetically spoiled cat, Margo draws inspiration from the shadowy, gator-infested swamps nearby.

The haunting mystery of Newport's ancient tower, rumored to have been built by the Knights Templar, sparked the creation of her Watcher Clan series.

MargoCarey.com

The Amulet is a work of fiction. Characters and various locations are products of Margo's imagination.

Thank you for purchasing
this publication of The Wild Rose Press, Inc.

For questions or more information
contact us at
info@thewildrosepress.com.

The Wild Rose Press, Inc.
www.thewildrosepress.com

www.ingramcontent.com/pod-product-compliance
Lightning Source LLC
Chambersburg PA
CBHW072108020726
47501CB00003B/757

* 9 7 8 1 5 0 9 2 6 1 5 4 3 *